BLAIR DENHOLM

Kill Shot: A Jack Lisbon Crime Thriller

Acknowledgement

Thanks to everyone who helped me put together this first book in the series *The Fighting Detective*. Special mentions go to Don Hawthorne for his eagle-eye and Big Tony for his advice on police matters. Everyone else who supports me, you're all bloody legends.

And, as always, to Sandra.

Books by Blair Denholm

The Fighting Detective Series
    Fighting Dirty (prequel – FREE on Amazon)
    Kill Shot (Book 1)
    Shot Clock (Book 2)
    Trick Shot (Book 3)

Game Changer Series
    SOLD (Book 1)
    Sold to the Devil (Book 2)

Chapter 1

The searing heat prickled, nipped and stung. Beads of moisture dribbled from his forehead, infiltrated clenched eyelids and lashes. Fluids in his aching body were heating up. Humidity crushed like a ton of lead. *Take shallow breaths; stay still to keep the core temperature down.*

Bright tropical sunlight bore through the window, combined with the ambient swelter to turn Detective Sergeant Jack Lisbon's bedroom into a torture chamber. *Remember to close the venetian blinds next time, moron. And get the air conditioner serviced.* Lying in bed now unbearable, he stood, wobbled a fraction. In his semi-delirium, he determined to take a cold shower before the Good Lord claimed him.

Lisbon tottered towards the bathroom. He rubbed his eyes softly as he went, wondered how red they'd be after last night's binge. He'd stayed more or less sober for three years with the odd gentle tumble off the wagon. Last night's call with his ex-wife had a bigger impact on him than he could have imagined. After he'd hung up the phone on Sarah, he cracked a bottle of Bundaberg Rum, intended as a gift for a colleague. He'd demolished half of it in an under an hour and headed off into the balmy night to continue the party.

At least that's how he remembered it.

Bathroom reached, he turned the cold tap on full blast, splashed water on his face and neck, over his chest and under the armpits. The shock of the cold water took his breath away. He repeated the process two times. He must have looked like a tired elephant dousing itself.

Thoughts again turned to Sarah.

Why wouldn't she let me speak to Skye?

His daughter was seven now, she needed contact with her father. Jack loved and missed her achingly. He'd turned his life around full circle. From alcoholic bent cop to paragon of virtue. Kept his ugly busted nose clean and earned rapid promotion, in a foreign country if you please.

What was the point of Sarah's bloody-minded recalcitrance? She and the kid were a million miles away from him, far from his *destructive* influence, safely tucked away in their council flat in Peckham, South London. What harm would there have been in chatting with his daughter, for heaven's sake? He was at his wit's end with the situation and had no idea how to get Sarah to see reason. Constantly contacting her on the phone or Internet could be deemed stalking if she made a complaint. The last thing he needed was trouble with the job. It took four years to settle into life in Australia, now at last he was starting to feel at home. *Don't jeopardise it, Lisbon.*

He pulled aside the mould-flecked plastic shower curtain, stepped over raised tiles into the small cubicle and reached for the cold tap. Relief would be like an orgasm.

Make that a delayed orgasm.

The mobile phone on his bedside table burst into life. The ring tone was The Clash's driving punk anthem "London Calling". A reminder of the life he left behind, his beloved job, a copper with the world famous London Metropolitan Police. He retraced his steps to the bedroom, snatched at the mobile. Sweat beaded on his brow like condensation on a bottle. 'Yeah, wot?'

'Is that how a senior officer with the Queensland Police answers the phone? How long have you been in Yorkville?' Constable Ben Wilson's poorly disguised voice was chirpy as ever. Jack usually appreciated the cheeky geniality, this morning it merely aggravated his hangover.

'Long enough to know it's you on the other end, Wilson.' Jack scratched an armpit, scrabbled in his coat jacket for nicotine lozenges. He popped one into his dry mouth and started sucking like a hungry baby. Headed back to the cool refuge of the bathroom. 'And watch the familiar tone, sunshine.'

'Sorry, sir.'

'Apology accepted. Bear with me one moment, will you?'

Headache worsening, Jack sat the phone down and spat the lozenge into a tissue. He fussed about in the bathroom drawers, flung little cardboard boxes, disposable razors and condoms about to reach their use-by date out of the way until he found what he needed. He picked up the phone, cradled it between neck and chin as he tore aspirin from its foil packaging, dropped two white disks into a glass of water.

'Go ahead, Wilson. Why the hell are you disturbing me? I'm not rostered on until this afternoon.'

A cough on the other end of the line followed by a gulping sound. 'Just so you know, sir, you're on loud speaker. Detective Constable Taylor's listening.'

'Understood. Now answer my question. What's going on?'

'A car's been found abandoned.'

'Where?'

'Connors Road, edge of the industrial estate near the mangroves. Five clicks heading west, just after the point where it turns into a gravel track.'

'An abandoned vehicle heading bush is no reason to get excited. Probably joy riders got sick of it and dumped the car when it ran out of fuel.'

'Not likely. The keys were left dangling from the ignition, engine running, radio on and no one within cooee. Also, what the caller thought might be blood stains on one of the seats. Suspicious as all get out.'

Jack took a deep breath, pinched the bridge of his nose. 'Right. Anything else?'

'No, sir. DC Taylor and I are en route to the scene. The tip off came via the hotline.'

'Has forensics been despatched?'

'No.' It was the voice of Detective Constable Claudia Taylor, sultry to match the weather. 'We haven't established a crime's been committed. Could be an innocent explanation for it.'

'Then why does it take three of us to check it out? Two's plenty for preliminary work.'

'I'm bringing Wilson along for the experience. He's been stuck on desk duty for weeks and things are a bit quiet in the old town. Besides, I think he could become a good detective later in his career.'

'Should I care?' A short uncomfortable silence after his sarcastic remark. *Make amends, Lisbon.* 'Sorry, I'm not feeling a hundred percent today. It's great the lad wants to better himself. Most laudable.'

There'd been no baffling crimes in Yorkville for a while. The chance to investigate something unusual could be an interesting diversion. Even with the annoying Constable Wilson tagging along. 'I'll get there as soon as I can.'

'Better hurry,' said Taylor above the soft crackle of the two-way. 'There's a thunderstorm forecast.'

'If a cool change comes with it, I don't care if it's a bloody cyclone.' The cruel weather in the far north enervated the body like nothing Jack had ever experienced. Three years pounding the pavement as a uniformed cop in sub-tropical Brisbane was bad enough. Then he got the promotion he'd worked like a dog for in the capital: plain clothes detective. Only trade off, it was up here in the sweltering furnace of hell. The humidity was a killer, but he was gradually acclimatising. At least the fishing was good.

'You know how to get here, sir?' said Wilson.

'Ever hear of GPS?'

'Of course. See you soon.'

The ritual morning home gym work out and run would have to wait. Lifting weights and punching the bag would have been painful anyway, so the early call out was an excuse to skip it, at least until the afternoon.

He guzzled a can of icy diet cola to accelerate the effect of the aspirin. On went a lightweight cotton suit. Locked doors. In the car. Gone.

'Nice change you joining us in the pub last night, Jack. It was a huge surprise seeing you lumber through the door half an hour from closing.' Lisbon's partner Detective Constable Claudia Taylor, crossed the road with a carboard tray containing two cups.

It was a surprise to Jack too. He didn't remember meeting colleagues at the pub. *Fuck.* 'Ah, yeah...'

'Don't worry. You didn't do anything you'd regret.'

Thank God. Reputation intact.

'You don't look anywhere near as jovial as you did last night.' She handed

Jack a coffee. 'Get this into you.'

'Are you kidding? It's too hot for coffee.' He grunted and waved it away.

'Come on. Don't be ungrateful. It'll put a spring back in your step.'

Jack took a sip, spat it straight out. 'Jesus, I understand you have to sweeten service station coffee to make it drinkable, but seriously, how much effing sugar did you put in it?' He handed her back the cup. 'I'd be a diabetic by the time I finished that.' The only spring caffeine induced in Jack was the desire to spark up a match and light a cigarette. The lozenges he consumed and the patches he wore under the suit helped; no tobacco for three weeks. He sucked in his guts, patted firming stomach muscles under his shirt. *Don't go back to your bad habits, son.*

'Whatever.' She frowned as she tossed the contents of the second cup on the grassy verge, replaced the empty cup in the tray. 'Here, you can't refuse these.' She handed him a pair of sky-blue surgical gloves and donned a pair herself.

'Who called it in?' Jack tugged on the gloves, wiped sweat from his forehead with a shirt cuff.

'A truckie heading north to fetch a load of bananas.' Constable Ben Wilson appeared from behind the abandoned vehicle. 'Called the info line.'

'Did he leave his name?'

'Yeah. Don Hawthorne. Gave us some basic info. Got his number if you want to follow up.'

Jack nodded, scuffed black leather shoes in the dirt. He looked up. Dark cumulonimbus clouds were gathering in the east, the promised storm was building nicely. They'd have to work the scene fast. 'Probably won't be needing him further. Let's have a closer look at the vehicle. You,' he pointed at Wilson. 'Check the immediate area for anything odd.'

'Such as?'

'Use your initiative, Constable. You want to be a detective, don't you?'

Wilson trudged off in a huff.

'He's keen,' said Taylor. 'Give him a chance.'

'Whatever. He was rude to me on the phone this morning.'

'I'm sure he didn't mean it.'

The statement hung in the air without comment as Jack opened the driver side door of the late model maroon Mazda 6 sedan.

The first thing to catch his eye was a dark stain on the passenger seat. 'What do you reckon?' he called over his shoulder. 'Blood?'

Taylor peered inside the car. 'Could be. Want me to get forensics down here? The whole scene looks dodgy.'

Jack shook his head. 'Spidey senses tingling, are they Taylor? No, I'd like to know who the owner is first before we run at this like a bull at a gate. Have you called in the registration and VIN number?'

'Not yet.' Jack sensed a trace of annoyance in her reply, but she could suck it up. 'I was busy getting the coffee you didn't want.'

'Do it now.' Jack had learned to give commands like they were polite requests. If you stick the Australian rising inflection on any statement you can turn it into a kind of question. 'I'll have a shoofty through the interior.'

'Can you pull the lever so I can find the VIN, please?' Taylor's tone was now brusque and businesslike.

Jack's answer was the sound of the bonnet popping.

'Thanks.' She said something else Jack didn't catch. With her head under the hood, Taylor sounded like she was underwater.

The first thing Jack examined was the dashboard, littered with receipts, dockets and assorted papers. He pressed a button to open the glove box, more papers fluttered out like falling leaves. He scanned a few but nothing grabbed his attention. It'd take hours to go through them all thoroughly; he'd leave them to the forensics team if he and Taylor decided it was worth calling them in. *What else?* On the floor, take-away wrappers, most from a famous fried chicken outlet, grease-stained white paper bags you get hot chips in. Maybe the mark on the seat was old tomato ketchup?

'Got the number, Jack.' Taylor dropped the bonnet with a thunk, walked around to the wound-down driver window and peered in over the top of a pair of designer glasses. 'Just calling in now with the rego and VIN.'

'It's a wonder the officer who took the call didn't ask the truckie for the number plate. We could have had the details before we even got here. Might have even spared us a trip.' *And I'd be lying on the couch watching classic title fights on YouTube.*

'Apparently the truck driver was already back on the road when he rang it in.' Taylor ran fine fingers through her hair. 'Didn't bother to take note of the plates. Said he didn't have time to hang around 'cos his boss was riding his arse about deadlines. He'd seen the driver door wide open and no one inside or near the vehicle, so he stopped to check no one was sick or whatever.'

'Haven't there been attacks on women in this area lately?' Jack asked.

'You're right. Maybe the truckie knew that too and it spurred him to do his civic duty.'

'Maybe.' Jack looked up from the debris. 'Or he was seeing if there was anything in the car worth stealing.'

'You're a bloody cynical bastard.'

'I grew up in South London, luv. Shaped my outlook somewhat.'

'I've got a little more faith in people. According to the call transcript, the guy discovered keys hanging from the ignition and the engine idling. Had a quick look about, saw nothing else suspicious and thought the driver had headed into the scrub to ah..., how can I put it, evacuate their bowels.'

A laugh escaped Jack's lips. 'For God's sake, Claudia. Can't you just say take a shit?'

Taylor mumbled something.

'Pardon?' A receipt lay among the junk food debris. Jack held it up and squinted to read the faded ink. A generic cash purchase, unknown vendor, not paid for by credit or debit card. Not helpful.

'I said no need to be crude.'

'You think that's crude? You should hear me when I lose money on a boxing match. I lose my fucking rag.' Jack wrinkled his nose as he came up for air. The floor of the car gave off a mouldy smell to match the rubbish.

She ignored his remark. 'Anyway, once the truckie was on the road again, he had second thoughts, wondered if the stain on the seat might be blood, and called it in. Hang on, I'm about to get the name of the vehicle's owner.'

'I'll keep digging in this mess.' Jack knew from long experience nine times out of ten a car left on the side of the road wasn't a big issue. Usually it's been nicked and the thieves scarper when the petrol runs out or they get bored. A sticker gets slapped on the windscreen and the owners are notified to come and pick it up. After a specified amount of time if no one collects, it's towed away, sold at auction if it's in good condition or crushed at the wreckers if it's unroadworthy. Something felt wrong about this car, though.

Jack grabbed the lever under the driver seat and tugged, slid the seat back and peered underneath. More rubbish. A rummage in the front and rear passenger seats and floor spaces rendered nothing but more detritus. He stepped out of the car, popped the boot. Inside, a broad blobby stain on a piece of old carpet that looked like a Rorschach test. Could be blood.

'Got a name.' Taylor ended the call. 'Terrence Bartlett.'

'Say again?' Jack's inner voice told him he'd heard that name before.

'Bartlett. Terrence Brian Bartlett.'

Yes. Jack did remember the name.

Chapter 2

The name of the MMA fighter turned elite trainer instantly rang a bell with Jack. Terry Bartlett was well known to those who followed the primal sport of bare-fisted fighting in a cage. DC Taylor had never heard of him.

'Who is he again?'

'A mixed martial arts fighter who became a trainer. Absolute star brawler in his day, so they say.'

'I thought you were more into boxing, sir.' Wilson slugged mineral water from a clear plastic bottle. 'Not cage fighting.'

'The technical term is "octagon". I appreciate all combat sports for their own unique qualities. The local MMA scene up here's small-scale, but growing. I've been meaning to get along to a fight, just haven't been able to find the time. Anyway, you're back from that search a bit quickish.' Jack shot him a narrow-eyed reprimand. 'Find anything?'

'Not a sausage, sir. The scrub's almost impenetrable once you get a few metres into it. You'd need a machete to get further. My guess is no one from the car is going to be in the vicinity, either dead or alive and hiding.' Sweat dribbled from the constable's chin, spots had formed under the armpits of his uniform shirt. Fat splotches of intermittent rain added to the collage of moisture. 'Any luck here?'

'Some suspicious stains. Come tell me what you think of this?' If he wanted to be a detective, Wilson could show what he's made of. The constable shuffled past Taylor, hopped into the driver's seat.

'If we had a field Kastle-Meyer test, I could tell you for sure.' *The bloke's no dummy, despite appearances.* 'Since we don't, I can only give you my considered opinion.'

'Based on?'

Wilson grinned through slightly gapped front teeth. 'Appearance, scent. Hang on.' He bent his head, took a sniff. 'No idea, sir. It seems to have been there a long time. Perhaps blood. My bet, tomato sauce. Look at all these—'

'Yes, we're aware of all the food wrappers.'

'I'm surprised a sporty guy would be eating so much takeaway food, going by the amount of junk in there.' Taylor scratched at a spot below her ear.

'Who says it was him that ate that garbage?' Jack felt comfortable calling his old favourite snack garbage; his holier-than-thou self was chowing down on broccoli and lean chicken these days. The diet had helped him shed five kilos in the last month. 'Yeah, might be a family member eating all this shit, a friend, one of his acolytes. Anyway, people who work out like machines can afford to eat high-calorie food and not get fat.' He jerked a thumb towards the rear of the Mazda. 'Take a look in the boot. There's another stain in there. Unless someone's been playing hide and seek with a bag of chips and a bottle of ketchup, my money's on it not being a condiment.'

The two detectives and Wilson peered over the lip of the boot as if they were staring into a well. 'Definitely not ketchup this time.' Wilson wriggled on a pair of rubber gloves, ran a finger over the dark patch. 'Dry as a bone.' He smelled it. 'Not giving off any scent.'

'You think it's blood?'

Wilson nodded. 'From my limited experience and what I've read and studied about forensics, I think the likelihood of this particular stain being blood is quite high.'

'For fuck's sake, Sergeant, speak normally. You've been watching too many episodes of CSI.'

Wilson took a step back, blushing to the roots of his light ginger hair. 'I'm, ah...just...'

'Relax, son. I'm riding your arse. We reckon it's blood too. DC Taylor.' Jack patted dust and lint from his trousers. 'Call the forensics team in. If we're right about this being blood, we need to start investigating, pronto.'

'I had a thought,' said Taylor. 'Don't MMA fighters bleed more than the average citizen? Maybe it's simply blood from after a fight, off a towel, bandages or something. Nothing sinister at all.'

Jack shook his head. 'Cut and bleeding fighters, whether from a fight or full-contact training, get patched up on the spot by specialists. They don't drive home with blood pouring out of them like stabbing victims.'

Taylor's phone rang, cutting short Jack's lesson about the life of your average fighter. 'Uh huh. Got it. Thanks.'

'What news?' Jack peeled off his rubber gloves.

'We've got Bartlett's home and work addresses.'

'Phone number?'

Taylor nodded. 'Yep. We could have found that ourselves. He's not exactly elusive. Apparently he's got his number all over the Internet, touting for business as a fight coach and gym instructor.'

Jack dialled Bartlett's mobile. No answer, straight to voice mail. He thought about hanging up, decided to leave a message. 'DS Jack Lisbon of Yorkville CIB. Please call me back as a matter of urgency.' He glanced at his watch. 10:46am. 'Right, Claudia, come with me to Bartlett's workplace. If he's not there, we'll try his house. Wilson, wait here for the boffins to arrive. Contain the scene; if anyone stops, grill them. You know what they say about perps returning to the scene of crime, right?'

'Yes, sir.' Wilson smiled broadly. 'Anything to help.'

'Take notes. We're counting on you.'

At the next roundabout, take the third exit. The Sat Nav lady spoke in an efficient, affable tone.

'Ever think of trying out for that job?' Jack flicked the indicator with a forefinger and gently turned the steering wheel in the thick traffic. Other drivers drove with due care and caution, perhaps they knew they were in the company of an unmarked police vehicle.

'What job?' Taylor screwed up her eyes.

'GPS voiceover. You've got those deep, husky tones to set men's hearts aflutter.' Jack wasn't sure if this was over-stepping the mark. Taylor's throaty chuckle told him he hadn't crossed the boundary. Her next comment confirmed it.

'Why just men's hearts? I'll have you know a few of the female constables flirt with me, too.' She did a pop diva hair flick.

Jack felt his Adam's apple bobble. 'Really?'

'Sure.'

Jack couldn't tell if she was being serious or not. 'Aren't you still going out with that Duty Sergeant from the Southern Districts station?'

'Nah. Turned out he was hooking up with all kinds of women on the side.'

'You're not a detective for nothing.' He touched the side of his misshapen nose.

She turned to Jack and smiled broadly. 'You've got that right.'

He was about to question Taylor again about her current relationship status when he was rudely interrupted. *Your destination will be on the right in 50 metres.* Taylor cheekily repeated GPS woman's words with the same intonation; in Jack's assessment, there wasn't much difference between the two.

The gym loomed large in an area where suburbia and industrial grunge melded seamlessly. Poorer folks lived here in the suburb of Thurston, one of Yorkville's working-class suburbs. Well behaved compared to areas with better employment rates, the crime stats would suggest. Go figure. Next to the blue-collar residents sprawled a hectare or two of steel hangars and sheds, take-away shops and storage facilities. Recreational sea craft, machine parts, snack foods in this street alone. Half a dozen legal brothels operated in the precinct. Jack, missing the intimacy of female companionship, had been tempted to visit them. So far he'd resisted the temptation. He'd only been in the deep north six months. *Give it time, son. You'll meet someone nice sooner or later.*

Billboards dotted the industrial landscape advertising the various businesses, most of them owned by Yorkville's well-heeled white collar elites. They lived far from the poverty, on fancy canal estates by the azure waters of the Pacific Ocean or the ritzy elevated suburb of York Hill with views to the horizon.

Nestled among all of that, a gym and fight club, The Iron Horse.

Outside, it presented as an imposing double-storey breeze block edifice. A huge sign sporting the red, black and white logo of a horse snorting fire was affixed above the entrance. Manicured tropical gardens surrounded the club, filled with decorative coconut and fan palms, fragrant hibiscus and frangipani, red and deep-pink azaleas.

The automatic glass doors whooshed open, ushering Jack and Taylor into a cool air-conditioned space, chequered brown and beige carpet tiles adorned the floor. This was a world away from DS Lisbon's old South London stomping ground. McNair's boxing club was a no-frills shit-hole. The Iron Horse was deluxe all the way. The air smelled of fresh paint; the interior renovated to within an inch of its life. A clinical-white melamine reception desk shielded a young woman, presumably hired to greet visitors, file stuff and answer the phone. Behind her, a large colour portrait of the gym's owner and manager; the name at the bottom: Carl Masiker. Say it aloud and you get "massacre", Jack realised. The man's battle-scarred mug suggested he was capable of carrying one out.

'Looking for a membership?' White-as-milk teeth shone through the girl's purple lips, puffed like a wasp had attacked her. Packed with filler, most likely. Geometrically perfect semi-circular eyebrows sat closer to her hairline than her eyes. Jack wasn't sure, but he thought the brows were tattoo jobs. A cherry red blazer revealed cleavage bookended by golden tanned breasts so fake someone who'd never seen fake breasts before could spot them a mile away. The name tag said Melinda O'Hare.

DC Taylor placed her arms on the shiny surface of the counter. For the first time Jack noticed a tattoo on her inner left forearm, a blue wren or some bird or other. 'No, Melinda' said Taylor. 'We're looking for a chap called Terry Bartlett. We understand he's employed at this club.'

'He is, yeah. But he's not here today.' She fussed about with some papers, stuffed them into a ring binder, snapped it shut. 'Sorry I'm not able to help.'

'Is the boss in?' Taylor gestured towards the portrait. 'We'd like a word with that handsome fellow.'

'I'll just check.' She picked up the phone, exchanged a few words with someone, put a hand to the mouthpiece. 'Can I say who's asking?'

'The police.' Jack said flatly.

'You're in luck.' No muscles in her Botoxed face moved. 'Follow me.'

Melinda led the two detectives down a wide hallway, water coolers spaced every fifteen metres. A soundproof glass wall ran down the right side allowing a full view of the innards of the gymnasium. Jack's eye was drawn to the frantic activity of young men, and a couple of females, training their guts out on state of the art equipment. Lifting weights, skipping, punching speed balls and laying into heavy bags. In a raised ring, a slight, well-toned Aboriginal lad in blue headgear toyed with his sparring opponent like a cat terrorising a mouse; the white fighter was unable to land any punches or kicks, all energy spent on desperate defensive moves. Jack smiled at the proficiency of the Indigenous man, fists a blur as he pummelled his victim. He'd have to find out the man's name and get some betting money ready. The kid looked unbeatable.

Inside, the manager's office reeked of money, power and influence. The gym owner stood and extended a hand the size and colour of a large rump steak, first to Taylor then to Jack. He towered over both detectives, perhaps six foot five inches. 'Carl Masiker, how can I help you?'

The flash of a badge usually elicited a look of surprise or fear. Masiker didn't flinch when Jack showed his ID. 'Detectives Jack Lisbon and Claudia Taylor. Nice place you've got here.'

All three sat in upholstered office chairs Jack guessed cost as much as all the furniture in his own rented house. A large dark timber desk separated the law enforcers from the civilian.

'We like it. I guess you're here about the incident the other night?'

'Why do you think that?' Nothing better than receiving information from punters without having to ask.

Masiker shrugged broad shoulders that filled out a lime green polo shirt. The man smelled of expensive cologne. 'Makes sense. A casual member got kicked out for being inappropriate with one of our female members. He got so wild a couple of uniformed cops rocked up to make sure the bloke didn't do any damage. I'm not interested in taking the matter any further. All under control.'

Jack coughed into a fist. 'Actually, no.' He'd not heard about the matter. 'We're interested in speaking with one of your employees. Terry Bartlett.'

'Absolutely. Would you like a coffee?'

After the morning's disgusting servo effort, Jack agreed. If it stimulated the urge to smoke, he'd suck another nicotine lozenge. Taylor declined. Masiker buzzed Melinda, placed the order: one coffee for him, one for the copper.

'Yes,' Masiker said, walking to a side cabinet and returning with sachets of sugar and stevia. 'Terry, or Tezza as we like to call him. I haven't seen him for a few days.'

'How many days?'

Masiker placed a finger to his lightly stubbled, square jaw. 'I'd say maybe a week. I'd have to consult my diary to be certain. May I ask why you're here? I would have expected a phone call first.'

Melinda brought the coffee. Jack regretted his decision to imbibe. Weak and cold. Even three sugars couldn't improve it.

Taylor sat forward in her seat. 'That's not the way we do things. Often if you give someone the heads up, they do a runner or hide evidence.'

'A runner? Evidence?' Masiker's eyebrows elevated, furrowing a scarred brow. 'Am I suspected of something?' His voice grew louder, gruffer. 'What the fuck's going on?'

'We found your employee's car abandoned, engine running, keys in the ignition. No Terry. Looks suspicious and we're naturally worried about his welfare.'

'Have you tried his home?'

'Not yet. We tried ringing, no answer. We're going to his place after we've finished talking to you. It's a workday, so here seemed the logical place to start.'

Taylor fixed her unflinching gaze on Masiker. 'What can you tell us about him? Family, friends, colleagues, things like that.'

'He's had a bit of a rough trot in his personal life.' The gym owner took a dainty sip from his mug, winced slightly as he tasted the brew. 'Lives alone after his wife left and took three-quarters of his money. His son won't speak to him. I will say this about Terry, though. He works damn hard to attract and retain clients. His only fault, if you can call it a fault, is sometimes he gets depressed. He took the split from his wife pretty hard.'

'Did he?' said Taylor.

'Yeah,' Masiker sighed. 'It gets him down, you can tell by his demeanour. It was just over a year ago. I don't think he'll get over it for a long while yet.'

'Are you aware of any substance abuse, drinking?' Jack pondered the possibility of Bartlett getting into trouble with illicit drug suppliers, bikie gangs or triads, which may have led to him being harshly dealt with out on Connors Road. 'He could be trying to dull his senses to deal with the loss.' *Something you're familiar with, old son*, Jack thought to himself.

Masiker shook his head. 'No chance. He's squeaky clean, a health nut.'

'Doesn't touch steroids, human growth hormone?' Taylor ventured. 'I hear those things are rife in the gyms around Yorkville. All the bodybuilders are into it.'

Masiker's soft crow's feet crinkled, eyes narrowed. 'Aren't you listening to me? What did I just say? He's clean. As is everybody who trains here.'

'Really?' said Jack. 'Even that bloke who caused a ruckus that you chucked out?'

A deep breath from Masiker. 'Fair go, not every act of violence is linked to drugs, is it?'

Jack nodded. 'True.' He paused for a couple of seconds, turned his head to the people training in the expansive gym space. 'Still, HGH use is on the rise, innit? Out of control.'

'Not here it isn't!'

'I'm sure you're right.' Jack pursed his lips and gave a tiny nod. 'Only it'd be a shame for rumours like that to get out.'

'What the hell are you implying?' Masiker was standing, hands flat on the desk and fingers spread wide. Taylor side-eyed her partner with a frown.

'Nothing, sunshine. Only I'd hate for that kind of, ah, speculation, to impact on your gym's reputation.'

'Why the fuck are you saying this shit? I'm answering your damn questions.'

Jack gestured for calm. 'Whoa, big man. Relax. It's just, I dunno, I think there's more about Terry you could be telling us.'

Masiker raked a hand through his close-cropped hair, greying around the temples, sat down. 'Tezza sometimes comes in to use the gym after midnight to train.'

'Does he have a key?' said Jack.

'No. We've got keyless entry via a passcode.'

'Why does he do that?' asked Taylor. 'Bloody weird. Is he an insomniac gym junkie or something?'

'None of my business.' Masiker shook his head. 'I've never asked him. My guess is he likes the peace and quiet. He's got plenty of exercise gear at home, but it's not the same thing, is it? Our setup is state of the art. As far as drugs and booze go, Tezza's more likely to find comfort in video games. He's probably at home right now. Once he told me how he can fall into a catatonic trance on his PlayStation.' Masiker's forced smile gave Jack the creeps. Taylor's just-sucked-a-lemon expression told Jack the man was having a similar effect on her. 'He's hopelessly addicted to Mortal Kombat.'

'You don't sound very worried about him,' said Jack. 'The scenario we just described with his car is bizarre to say the least, and you laugh it off. I'm surprised by your flippant attitude towards someone who works for you.'

'You see, that's a matter of semantics.'

'Meaning?' Taylor scribbled something in a notebook.

'He rents gym space off me, then I pay him a percentage of the membership fees he gets from the fighters. With the elite ones he charges his own rates. I've no idea about those arrangements.'

Jack scratched his head. 'That's an unusual way to do business. Never heard of it.'

Another thin-lipped smiled from Masiker. 'I admit it's not a standard form of operating. Not unique, though. Fighters are first and foremost attracted to the gym, its fabulous facilities. I'll give you both the grand tour later, if you have time. We've got a spa, hyperbaric chamber, lap pool. You see, we're a complete fitness centre rather than simply a weight-training and fighting gym.'

'Wouldn't people sign on with Terry because he's a successful trainer with a great track record?' said Jack. 'Hasn't he trained a couple of champions? His reputation has to be more of a magnet than a fancy-arse fitness palace.'

If Masiker was unflustered by the badge, Jack's knowledge of the local fighting scene hit the mark. The gym owner's face paled a fraction. 'Well, ah, perhaps it's a combination of both. But be under no illusion, even a top coach like Terry wouldn't get the results if his charges were carting buckets of water around his back yard and doing burpees in his lounge room.' He stabbed his finger at an invisible mid-air target. 'It's my money, my investment that brings the wannabes to Terry, not the other way around. Thanks to me he ended up with too many on his books, couldn't handle them all. He had to hire an assistant.'

'Who's that?'

'Bloke called Andy Harlow.'

'I've heard the name.' Jack wished he could smoke right now, popped a lozenge in his mouth instead.

'You should have. He does a lot of the ringside work at fights. Terry tends to play second fiddle at the bouts these days.'

'Why's that?'

'Andy's a better motivator in the heat of battle. Terry's strong suit is teaching the skills. As an ex-fighter, Terry can demonstrate technique whereas Andy comes from a different background. Psychology.'

'Give me Andy's number. I'd like to talk to him if Terry's not found in the next, let's say...' Jack flicked his wrist around, looked at his watch. '...six hours.'

'That's a bit quick isn't it?' Masiker scrolled through his mobile, turned it to Taylor who jotted the number down. 'Don't people have to be missing for a couple of days before everyone goes into panic mode?'

'This is different,' said Taylor. 'The circumstances are highly suspicious. Besides, we don't know how long he's been missing. We only found the car today, maybe he disappeared several days ago.'

'Let's just hope he's holed up in his house then.' Masiker drained the last of his coffee. 'And by the way. If you want to talk to Andy in person, you'll have to wait. He's taken his family to Sydney for a holiday.'

'OK, thanks for your time.' Jack stood, extended his hand. Masiker shook it like he was trying to prove his strength. Jack responded in kind and the two stood frozen, hands gripped together, neither wanting to give ground. Finally, Jack pulled his hand loose from Masiker's vice-like grasp. 'We'll be heading over to Bartlett's gaff now. I hope you're right about him being zoned out on a video game.'

'Me too. I'd hate to think something's happened to him.'

'Perhaps I'll take you up on that offer of a tour later.' Jack shrugged on his jacket. 'Training in the little gym at my apartment complex is for chumps.' Perhaps he could swing a special "mates" deal with Masiker if the cocky prick turned out to be innocent of any wrongdoing.

'My pleasure. Our facilities are at your disposal.' Masiker's oily grin could curdle custard. 'Have a pleasant day, officers. Drop by any time.'

Jack had to ask. 'You look like you used to be a fighter yourself once upon a time.'

'A lot of people say that. But no, my sport was rugby league. I played in the NRL back in the early 90s. Balmain Tigers. It's a tough game, not without the odd punch-up. I copped plenty but dished it out too.'

'Cool,' said Jack, trying to appear unimpressed. He had limited knowledge of rugby league, popular in Australia's eastern states but only a minor sport back home in Britain. The two detectives headed for the car, Jack turning at the doorway. 'Oh, one last thing.'

'Yes?'

'You might have A1 facilities, but one thing lets the place down.'

'Yeah, what?' Masiker challenged, chin out.

'Your coffee's shit. Good day to you.' *Always have the last word.*

The drive to Terry Bartlett's abode took twenty minutes with a short stop for a decaf at a place Jack knew for sure served a good brew. He bought a flat white for Taylor and she agreed never to buy service station slop again.

Maybe for Sergeant Wilson, she joked.

Five minutes before they arrived, the promised storm finally broke in all its glory. Fat beads of tropical rain splattered everything it struck. Lightning flashed in the leaden clouds. The rain grew heavier, developed into a translucent screen; you had to squint hard to be able to see through it. Next stage, hail like frozen peas drummed incessantly on the windscreen and chassis of the vehicle. All conversation ceased until the detectives pulled up in Bartlett's driveway. Ahead, an empty carport. Good news – Jack could save the duco from further punishment, bad news – looked like no one was at home. Jack nudged the Kia under shelter seconds before the hailstones began to increase in both speed of descent and size.

A quick mental assessment of Bartlett's digs. If he was making a lot of money from his work, it wasn't reflected in high-grade accommodation. The house the trainer lived in was modest to say the least. The joint was almost identical to all the other houses in the middle-class suburb cul-de-sac. Neat white, two-storey weatherboard Queenslander home with grey trimmed windows, looked like a couple of coats of paint had been applied recently. Clipped weed-free lawns, decorative palms, Pebblecrete driveway.

'Looks like your average house in the 'burbs.' Jack shouted over the roar of the deluge.

'How can you tell through this rain?' Taylor cupped a hand to her ear.

Jack laughed. 'X-ray vision.'

Typical of a tropical downpour, this one was over quickly. Car doors opened, the pungent odour of ozone and fresh warm earth accompanied by the clingy embrace of hot humid air filled the interior. Jack inhaled deeply, the rich smell still a wonder to an Englishman like him.

They climbed external stairs. The front door to the house was unlocked, splinters of wood lay across the threshold. Inside the house, total chaos. Furniture upended, drawers flung open, smashed crockery. But no Terry Bartlett.

Chapter 3

D
S Lisbon's desk was a shambolic mess. Files relating to half a dozen unsolved and ongoing cases in disarray. Stationery all over the place, escapee paper clips, multicoloured fluoro Post-it notes bearing phone numbers once vital, now forgotten. He'd clean it up, as soon as they'd put the Bartlett matter to bed. If he had to give an honest assessment, his workspace was too cramped, no room for a big man like him to spread out, get comfy and think straight. Sub-par for a detective in the CIB. The London Met had been more generous than the Queensland Police Service in terms of facilities, but Jack rated his new employer higher. Why? Because the QPS had taken a punt on him, promoted him, while the Met couldn't wait to see his backside going out the door never to return. Jack seethed over his former employer for months after his "resignation". Now it was all good karma to him. *Things happen for a reason.* All that hokey mystical shit suddenly made sense.

Jack swept clear a space among the papers, laid out the glossy colour photos. Technically not "crime scene" photos yet, but his gut told him they'd soon be reclassified as such.

'What do you make of it?' Taylor leaned over his shoulder. Her perfume got under his guard; sweet but not overly so, musky without being overpowering. Amazing his olfactory senses worked at all after the physical punishment his nose had been through over his lifetime.

'Not much. It's basically what we've already seen with our own eyes.'

'What about the stains in the car? What are the results?'

He opened a manila folder, pointed at the conclusions. 'Human blood from two people, both males. Nearly 70 percent of it from one person. Types O+ and A+. The most common there are. No matches in the criminal database.'

'That's a shame.' Taylor sighed, pulled up a chair uninvited. 'Have a look at this. Analysis of samples from Bartlett's house.' She dropped another thin file on his desk.

Jack compared the documents. The data was conclusive. The DNA profile of the most copious amount of blood from the boot of the car matched the DNA samples lifted from the ransacked house. In particular, from swabs taken from an electric toothbrush and strands of hair collected in the bathroom. 'The majority of the blood almost certainly comes from Terry Bartlett,' he declared. 'This is now a missing persons case.'

'You're officially calling it?'

'Yeah. The whole business stinks to high heaven. I'd love to know who the second lot of blood belongs to. It could be completely innocuous or evidence of a deadly fight, fuck knows. Anyway, I've got hold of a little something that might be useful to the investigation.'

A drawer slid open and Jack withdrew a plastic yellow pill bottle. He held it up to the light, two capsules sat in the bottom.

'Where did you get that?'

'Bartlett's bathroom. I pocketed it before forensics arrived.'

'Come on.' A look of disapproval clouded Taylor's eyes. 'That's not the procedure.'

'Don't worry, I left plenty for forensics to play with. There were half a dozen other identical ones in a little wicker basket next to his shower.' He waggled the bottle before Taylor's bugging eyes. 'Something struck me as odd about Masiker and his set up. This could come in handy later, you know, as leverage.'

'I can tell you what they are. Anabolic steroids.'

'No shit, Sherlock.'

'Uncalled for.' Taylor folded her arms across her chest. 'It's right there in the lab analysis.'

'Yeah, I saw it. Didn't I tell you I'm a speed reader?'

'You think Bartlett's mixed up in some illegal steroid business?'

Jack leaned back in his chair, interlocked fingers behind his head. 'Hard to say. Masiker was insistent the trainer's a health nut. But even health nuts cheat sometimes.'

'You sure this case isn't affecting you on a personal level?' Taylor turned a quarter way round in her seat, her angled face reminding Jack of a kindly teacher. Not for the first time he noticed a thin scar running across her left cheek that ended a centimetre under her earlobe. A decent layer of foundation did its best to cover the blemish, failing when the light struck her from a particular angle. Her hair was always pulled back in a tight bun, twisted and secured at the back of her head with a scrunchie. A different colour for each day of the week.

'What do you mean by that?' he grabbed a pen, tapped it a couple of times on his computer keyboard.

'Stealing that potential evidence. I'm not sure—'

'Listen, I've been a copper longer than you've had...hot dinners...'

'That makes no sense!' Her face twisted, it looked like she was battling an urge to burst out laughing.

'You know what I mean.' Jack berated himself for mucking up the metaphor or simile or whatever the hell it was called. 'It's instinct.' He touched the side of his nose. 'I've got a nose for this kind of thing.'

Taylor let rip with a raucous snorting guffaw that got faces turning in their direction. 'Sorry, I shouldn't...'

Jack cracked a cheeky smile. 'OK. I know my mangled schnoz is no candidate for TV adverts, but I ain't ashamed of it.'

Taylor rested a cool hand on top of his. 'And neither you should be.'

Jack glanced at her hand on top of his and she quickly retracted it. Taylor's gesture of comfort told him it might be safe to share things with her. 'I've got some demons to exorcise, Claudia. There was some bad shit I left behind in London. Stuff that I ain't proud of.'

'What?'

'I won't go into details.' *Not all at once, bit by bit.* 'Let's just say I left a trail of damage that's gonna take a long time to repair. If ever.'

She inclined her head towards the framed photo of Skye on his desk. A treasured reminder of what could have been. 'You mean her? I've often wanted to ask you about your kid. She's definitely a cutie.'

He picked up the photo, noticed a droplet of moisture in the corner of his eye reflecting off the glass. Time to end this conversation before he started blubbering. Another nicotine lozenge would calm his nerves. 'Enough of that. I'll tell you all about it after we solve this case.'

'It means that much to you?'

'Let me put it this way. Dodgy boxing trainers and cocky gym owners aren't my favourite people. If Masiker or Bartlett are involved in serious crime here, my mission will be to make them pay.'

'What if it's someone else? Surely you want to catch criminals no matter who they are?'

'Nah. Some are more deserving of punishment that others, believe me.'

Taylor chewed her bottom lip. 'A word to the wise. This is a small town, not London. Word spreads quickly, and if you get on the wrong side of people, the animosity can linger. My advice, don't let your emotions get in the way of the job.'

Thunder cracked in the distance. 'You think you're the first person to tell me that? You're not! Leave me in peace for a moment while I study these forensics reports.'

'Sorry, I...'

'No. I'm sorry.' He rubbed his palm across his face, sweaty despite the aircon keeping the interior of the office to a comfortable 19 degrees. 'I need to pull myself together. It's Skye's birthday in a couple of weeks and Sarah won't let me talk to her. Turning eight she is, and I...'

'How about I go and make some calls. Find out when Bartlett's assistant Andy Harlow's planning on getting back to Yorkville. I've already tried a couple of times. No answer and no voice mail. I'll suss him out online, maybe he's posting on social media about his holiday.'

'You do that.' He glanced at his watch. 'I'm out of here in half an hour. Check in with the Inspector, see if he's got any other jobs for us to do while we're waiting for Terry Bartlett to show up.'

'You think he will show up?'

'Yes. Maybe not alive, though.'

The oceanside pub occupied prime position on The Esplanade, Yorkville's hub of what passed for style in the casual tropical town. Jack found himself a spot at the bar, hung his jacket over the back of the stool. Busy but not packed. Another hour or two and it would be unbearable, office workers and tourists standing shoulder to shoulder, climbing over each other for drinks. Jack would be gone by then, thank God.

He rolled the base of a glass of ginger ale around on a coaster, seriously pondered whether the next one should have something stronger in it to keep the ice-cubes company. He pulled up Facebook on his phone, sent a private message to Sarah. One last try. *Please can you let me speak to Skye on her birthday. I promise to be civil. It would mean so much to me.* Ten minutes later, no reply. It was early morning back in Peckham. Sarah always logged on before work, no way she hadn't seen his message. After fifteen minutes, Jack scanned the offerings on the top shelf behind the bar. There was a likely candidate, St Agnes brandy, a popular tipple back at Big Dave's South London pub. Popular with Jack that was, no one else touched the stuff. Having placed the order, hand extended with a twenty-dollar bill, he heard the ding of an alert. Please be Sarah. His heart pounded like a trip hammer. Her message was short and to the point. *OK. Be on time and I'll be listening. One false step and I hang up.*

'Still want the brandy, mate?'

'Changed my mind.' Still on the wagon for now. 'Give us another ginger ale.'

On the wall-mounted television, a local news program was wrapping up Yorkville's events for the day. Not one for reading the newspaper or following online outlets, Jack favoured the lazy option of commercial TV. Not too cerebral, but it summed things up for the lowest common denominator, the man and woman in the street. For a cop in regional Australia, the heavy emphasis the local stations placed on gossip helped with knowing what was happening on Main Street. Jack smiled as he recollected there actually was a

Main Street in this town, home to a myriad of tourist shops and restaurants. Now on screen, a breathless reporter in a narrow tie gesticulated wildly outside a service station. The same one DC Taylor purchased the coffee from. A graphic came up. *Brazen daylight robbery.* If the story was about the servo's coffee, the journalist had nailed it. Next, an interview with Sergeant Ben Wilson, then another graphic. *Attendant held up at knife point.* The sound was off and Jack had no idea what Wilson was saying, however he appeared calm and assured, answered questions with a professional expression, nodded sagely. Last graphic. *Offender apprehended by police in nearby house.* Perhaps Wilson really was destined for higher office.

Jack palmed his keys, removed his jacket from the back of the barstool. He bid the barman good-night. The barman switched over to a sports channel, set about cleaning glasses. Footage of two heavily tattooed and bloodied MMA fighters duking it out in an auditorium stopped Jack in his tracks. Advertising signage for local businesses confirmed it was the Yorkville Convention Centre. Jack resumed his seat. He beckoned to the barman, who smiled, pleased to have a break from wiping beer glasses.

'Yes, mate. What can I get you this time?'

'Another ginger ale. And would you mind turning up the volume a tad?'

The barman pointed the remote at the screen, a series of green bars advanced left to right until the sound rose above the ambient hum. The roar of an excited crowd accompanied jerky vision of the brutal encounter. Lots of handheld camera work around the ring. Jack concentrated his full attention on the bout. A camera zoomed in on the tortured face of the fighter in red trunks. He was putting on a brave front, sneering and giving his green-trunked opponent come-on gestures. Jack could tell the man was at the end of his tether. A vicious spinning back heel kick to the head caught Red Trunks in the temple and sent him crashing to the floor. Next camera shot showed the vanquished fighter out cold, face down on the canvas, followed by the other man's hand being held aloft by the referee. Despite winning, congealed blood and a swollen eye socket on the victor's face were testimony to the defeated man's pluck. Ad break.

'Wouldn't want to get on the wrong side of that bloke.' The barman's eyes shone. 'No one seems able to beat him.'

'You a fan?' said Jack.

'I take an interest, yeah. MMA's great for its intensity. I prefer boxing, though. More scientific.'

Jack extended his hand and the bartender shook it with over-the-top alacrity. The detective clocked him for one of those uber friendly types who talk to anyone about anything. It pays to cultivate their friendship; like taxi drivers and barbers, they know a lot about what goes on in the community. This smiling hyena fit the bill perfectly. 'That's music to my ears, my son. I used to engage in the fistic arts myself.'

'Call me Dave.' The same name as his old barman back in England. This town was starting to feel more like home every day.

'Jack Lisbon.' No need for rank and serial number yet. 'Is that a recent fight?'

The barman squinted. 'Nah. Replay of an old one. That bout established those two as rising stars.'

'Who are they? The winner looks like a world beater.'

'The victor's name is Owen Kennedy. The bloke kissing the canvas is Danny Sharpe. But the fans don't feel sorry for Sharpe, they're fucking dirty on him. There's going to be a rematch and everyone will be backing Kennedy to clean him up again.'

'How come?'

The barman leaned in, shoved a bowl of complementary peanuts towards Jack. 'Sharpe's a dirty drug cheat. It still can't give him the edge to beat Kennedy, though.'

'Has it been proven he's using drugs or is it just a rumour?' A handful of peanuts disappeared into Jack's mouth.

'Sharpe failed a test a while back, but somehow the MMA Association let him off with a slap on the wrist. They oughta suspend him to teach him a lesson. Injecting HGH, he was. Rumour has it he was popping steroids, too.'

'When's the rematch?'

'Supposed to be next month as far as I'm aware. There'll be scouts flying in from the USA to watch it ringside. Big opportunities, which means incentives to do whatever it takes, if you get my meaning.'

A giggling woman in a tight top waved for a drink and took Dave away from the conversation. Jack turned his attention back to the TV. Sport was over, weather time. More storms forecast and hot, hot, hot, and it was still a month until the calendar said it was summer. Compared to a dreary English summer, spring in far north Queensland was a moist oven. Still a preferred option. Dave returned. 'Another drink, Jack?'

'No,' he tossed on his jacket. 'Gotta get my beauty sleep.'

'I'd be getting money on Kennedy now, if I were you.'

'Will do, son.'

'Shouldn't even be happening at all, this fight. You know Sharpe's trainer used to sit on the Association's board? Some people reckon that bloke's got too much influence. How else would Sharpe have escaped more severe punishment?'

'Wouldn't be a geezer called Terry Bartlett would it?'

'Yeah.' Dave's eyes lit up under a veranda of bushy brows. 'That's him. How'd you guess?'

'Call it a sixth sense. Like coppers have, know what I mean?' Jack winked and strode out the door.

Chapter 4

'You want me to go there alone?' Surely Lisbon was kidding.

'Yeah. Why not?'

DS Lisbon had asked Taylor to conduct follow-up enquiries at The Iron Horse. She wasn't keen to go without him. She didn't know why, it wasn't that she was afraid or lacked confidence operating solo. And it wasn't the interview subject. Men like Masiker, arrogant and self-aggrandising, were thick on the ground in this macho town, full of misbehaving footballers from the Yorkville Giants and swaggering soldiers from the army barracks. Taylor had met, arrested and convicted more than her fair share of them. She'd been a detective in Yorkville for five years, a local who'd risen through the ranks. But this gym and its owner set off warning signals in the back of her brain. Lisbon himself had said something was wrong, and her gut agreed with his assessment.

'It's your area, Jack.' She tucked the phone under her chin while she put on an earring. Maybe he'd see sense and agree to tag along.

'My area? Piss off. You grew up here, I'm the new boy in town. People are more likely to open up to you. Besides, you've got a more honest face.'

'I meant area of expertise. Mixed martial arts.'

'Right,' he mumbled. 'If you're worried about going there by your lonesome, take Wilson. I see he's been making a name for himself collaring villains at service stations.'

Fuck you Jack. 'Don't be ridiculous. I'm not scared!'

'I didn't say you were scared, I said "worried". Anyway, I wouldn't consider myself an expert. Just used to box a bit when I was younger. I've got no experience in Krav Maga or Jiu Jitsu or anything like that.'

'Whatever.' She put the phone down, pressed the loud speaker button, pulled her hair back and tied it with a scrunchie. Serious navy blue today. 'Exactly what do you want me to ask Masiker?'

'Get a list of Terry Bartlett's clients, if he's got one.' Jack filled her in on the conversation with Dave at the pub last night. 'I want to question them all if we can. If there's illegal substances changing hands, everyone's a suspect in this disappearance until proven otherwise.'

'You think there's a link between the little pills you swiped and what the barman told you?'

She heard Jack sigh. 'You don't need to be Sherlock Holmes to figure that out, Claudia. Professional athletes everywhere use performance enhancing products to get the edge. Combat sports are in a class of their own. There's big money tied up in it, and when there's big money, there's men behaving badly.'

His condescension was out of order. 'I'm not an idiot, Jack. I'm aware of that. No need to be a smart arse.'

'Sorry.' No contrition. She wondered if the man had some form of autism. No empathy whatsoever. 'Just do as I ask, will ya?'

'Sure. But can you tell me why you aren't coming with me? We could do the good cop, bad cop thing.'

'I want to have another shoofty over Bartlett's house. I reckon there's more there we didn't find the first time. Forensics only tested what they found on the surface. I wanna dig deeper.'

'I'm not sure that's a good–'

Click.

Masiker greeted her with a broad smile and open arms. A façade. Taylor could tell he was seething underneath; the smile and the non-reciprocated air-hug were forced.

'So nice to see you again,' said Masiker. 'I'm surprised it's so soon, though. Terry not turned up yet?'

'Unfortunately, no.' She took a seat opposite the gym owner unbidden. His raised eyebrow told her he considered the move audacious. Which made her wonder about his attitude towards her as a woman, rather than a police officer. A shame DS Lisbon wasn't there; he and Masiker were cut from the same cloth in many ways, arrogant males. 'We're not satisfied we got enough information from you yesterday.' She leaned over, pulled a yellow Spirax notepad and pen from her handbag. 'I'd like to follow up with some extra questions. Won't take long and I'll be out of your hair in a jiffy.'

Masiker gestured towards a jug of water with slices of lemon and mint leaves floating on the top. 'Help yourself. What exactly would you like to know?'

'I'd like a list of all Terry Bartlett's clients.' Taylor poured herself a glass of water. 'We'd like to interview them.'

'All of them? Why?'

'We have alarming facts to hand. Terry's now officially a missing person.'

'Fuck me dead! What facts?'

Sharing the details with Masiker might shake him up. 'DNA from large blood stains in his car match samples taken from his house. He may have met with foul play.'

'Surely they can't all be suspects?'

Taylor chuckled softly. 'No one is a suspect at this point. But if we're to find Terry, we need information, leads. Those people might be able to help us.'

'That's a bit extreme, isn't it?' His crow's feet bunched as his lips compressed in a frown. 'Most of the punters wouldn't know anything about him outside his professional capacity.'

'There's no need to get into a fluster, Mr Masiker.'

'Call me Carl.'

'We won't be harassing your customers, Mr Masiker.' She took a long sip from her glass. The ice-cold water was delicious with the added flavours. 'We are extremely worried about Mr Bartlett's welfare. Perhaps one of his clients knows him a little better than you think.'

Masiker let out a slow, steady breath, like a student in a Yoga class getting in touch with their chi. Was he relieved about something? 'I don't have an official list as such. None of my concern, really. However I can write down the names of people I know for sure work exclusively with Terry. Local celebs and whatnot.'

Taylor passed him the notebook. He scribbled a few names and returned it. The number was disappointing. Only nine. Four men and five women. Top of the list, star protégé Danny Sharpe. At least Masiker was being honest about that. 'Surely that can't be it. I thought people were falling over themselves to be trained by Bartlett.'

'They are. He's got more clients, but I've no idea who they are. Just faces in the gym. Like I said, his business is, well, his business. Literally.'

'Much appreciated.' She gave a curt nod. 'Names on their own are tiresome to chase up. It would save us a lot of time if you or your lovely assistant, Belinda wasn't it?...'

'Melinda.'

'Yes, that's it. Melinda. I'd like phone numbers and addresses to go with these names, please.'

'I'm not sure we have them on record.'

'How about she has a little look on the computer just in case, huh? If they have a full membership in addition to being Bartlett's clients, which I assume includes use of the pool and your other facilities, they must be, right?'

Masiker's eyes narrowed in frustrated displeasure; she had him where she wanted him. He didn't like smart confident women, that was plain. She'd bet her last scrunchie he had a submissive little wife who did everything for him. Or the other extreme and he was henpecked. 'I'm sure that's a breach of the Privacy Act.'

'Don't be silly. We can find them ourselves, but why waste energy on that? You want us to locate Mr Bartlett as quickly as possible, don't you?'

'Of course.' Masiker buzzed Melinda, told her to get the names. She brought in a printed A4 sheet containing the requested information.

'Excellent, we'll be contacting these people ASAP,' said Taylor. It was better than she expected. Melinda's list contained dates of birth, next of kin, all kinds of extras. So much for the Privacy Act. 'I might even tell them not to pack their gym bags if they've got a session with Bartlett booked for today. Now Mr Masiker, one other thing.'

The surprised gawp on Masiker's face was like a goldfish mid breath. 'What?'

'Danny Sharpe.'

'What about him?' Masiker jabbed his finger in the air. 'You'll notice he's at the top of that list. Nothing to hide there.'

'It's come to our attention that Mr Sharpe failed a drug test recently.'

'What of it?'

'Were you aware of what Danny was up to?'

'Fuck, I mean hell no! Only after he failed the test. I had no knowledge prior. None whatsoever.'

'If you say so.' *He's lying.* 'But the news got out, as it always does. I imagine one of your star club members trying to cheat his way to the top would be bad for business.'

'I'll admit, when he copped the fine I was worried. But I needn't have been. Didn't affect trade one iota. Might've even sparked interest. You know what they say about all publicity being good publicity.'

Taylor wrote in her notepad. *Check club's trading figures.* 'That's debatable.'

'Anyway, Danny may be a well-known member, but we've got another who's an even bigger draw card.'

This was interesting. The way Jack told it, Danny was *numero uno.* 'And who would that be?'

'Owen Kennedy. The fighter who destroyed poor Danny. More than once. We've got the best gym in the city, why wouldn't the best fighters want to train here?'

Taylor half expected an evil laugh to burst from Masiker's mouth, he seemed to revel in the idea of one man "destroying" another.

'Two fighters, who I assume are bitter rivals, training out of the same gym. Some could construe that as being fertile grounds for trouble.'

Masiker waved the question away like a cricket umpire signalling byes. 'Nonsense. Just a bit of melodrama to give Yorkville's citizens their jollies.'

'I don't believe that for one minute, Mr Masiker. Do you take me for some kind of fool?'

'No, I–'

Claudia hadn't seen Masiker this flustered. *Alpha women scare him.* 'Who was the man escorted from the premises the other night?' She already knew the answer after speaking to a couple of constables at the station. 'It wasn't just some random gym member, was it? No point lying.'

'All right, It was Tezza. He got a bit aggro and we had to have him removed.'

That's better, she thought. *Now we're getting somewhere.*

'And why was he carrying on like a pork chop? Playing too much Mortal Kombat, was he?'

'No. When Danny Sharpe's test result came back positive, Tezza dropped him as a client like a hot potato. It pained him to cut ties with the lad, but what could he do? The other night it must've all finally reached a tipping point. He was incoherent, swearing and raving, throwing equipment around. To be honest, I've never seen Tezza so agitated. Some of the bigger lads, body builder types who train after a hard day at the bank or whatever, tried to calm him down. Tezza swore at them, took a few swings and they had to back off. Tezza knows how to fight, you know? So that's why we had to call your boys in blue.'

'Why didn't you tell us this in the first place?' Taylor couldn't understand Bartlett's pious attitude towards drugs considering what was found at his place. Unless the goodies had been planted or there was another explanation for it. Protecting Danny Sharpe from more trouble perhaps.

'Look, I may have been a bit, ah...'

'A bit of a bullshitter?' Taylor raised her voice, emboldened by his previous show of weakness in the face of her strength. 'I reckon this drug scandal with Danny has rocked your business more than you care to admit.'

Masiker's hand shot up to his face. Bravado gone. 'Yeah. You're right. Maybe I was exaggerating. You've got no idea what running this business is like? I have to deal with people whose egos are bigger than bloody Jupiter. Primadonnas, and that's mainly the blokes. Then there's my wife demanding this and that.' He forced a laugh, paced back and forth behind his desk for a few moments before turning back to Taylor. 'Confidence and bluster is key in this industry, Detective Taylor. Maybe that's why I was...'

'Never mind, Mr Masiker.' She resolved not to call him by his first name no matter what. Keep a distance, stay aloof. 'Would you have kicked Danny out of the gym if Terry Bartlett didn't?'

'No. Why would I? The lad didn't commit a jailable offence or anything. Just made a mistake. It was Terry's decision, his moral code, not mine. Not the first time he's dropped a client, so I never thought much of it.'

'Do you know if Bartlett himself was on any medications?'

Masiker eyeballed her with growing distrust. 'Why are you asking that? Tezza never had any trouble like that.'

'I mean prescribed medications. For chronic pain or mental health issues.'

'Oh, right.' Masiker shuffled in his seat. 'No clue. It's possible. Tezza was a champion fighter a few years back. Not a great technician, he won most of his bouts on sheer guts and the ability to take hits and wear out his opponents. He must've copped as many kicks and punches as he landed.'

'Sounds like a hell of a tough man.'

'Yeah. In one fight he suffered a shocking shoulder dislocation. Makes me want to puke thinking about it. There's photos if you want to−'

'Ah, no thanks.'

'Perfectly understandable. The poor bugger needed radical surgery, pretty much ended his career early. In his mid-twenties he was. That's why he became a trainer. I guess the thought of missed opportunities might have caused him grief.'

'So he's had a rough trot both physically and mentally. With Danny's drug scandal, well, it could have tipped him over the edge.'

'Are you suggesting Tezza wandered off into the bush and topped himself?'

'No, I don't think so. But we have to consider all possible scenarios.'

'Did Bartlett continue any kind of relationship with Danny after the professional split?'

'What do you mean?'

'Is it possible Bartlett still wanted Danny to do well and continued training him unofficially? I think it's possible he wanted the lad to be the best he could, not miss out like Bartlett did.'

Masiker scratched his head.

'The late night training sessions.'

'What about them?'

'How often did Bartlett come in late to train?'

'One or two nights a week, I think. Not sure.'

'Did he meet with Danny those nights?'

'Now you're getting into the realms of fantasy. They split, end of story.'

Taylor knew with a pass-key entry system there should be a log of when people came and went. And something else. 'I imagine you've got security cameras on the premises. Any chance of video footage from the day of the incident?'

'Come back with a warrant. I've got the members' privacy to consider.'

'I only want the after-hours stuff.' Taylor flashed a benign smile.

'I said get a warrant. Now, if you don't mind, I've got a business to run.'

'Don't worry. I can obtain a warrant easier than you can get a parking ticket. And don't think about deleting or manipulating any footage. Our IT guys will know in an instant if it's been tampered with and you'll be right in the frame. Got it?'

'Oh, all right then.' Meek as a mouse. 'I'll copy it onto a flash drive for you. But it won't tell you much. Cameras are only mounted in the reception area and the car park.' Masiker took a USB drive from a drawer and inserted it into the digital video recorder under his TV. Two minutes later he handed the drive to Taylor. 'Everything from that evening should be on there.'

'Thanks. One last thing before I go.'

'Yes?'

'This Owen Kennedy. I'm sure my partner DS Lisbon knows all about him, but I don't. Who trains him?'

'A fellow called Vince Armbruster. He's been looking after Owen since the lad was a teenager.'

'Has he got a tragic dream-shattered past like our missing man?'

Masiker laughed. 'Vince? No, he's much older, nearly sixty. Top boxer in his day, didn't quite reach the top but it doesn't worry him. As far as training goes, he's strictly old-school. His methods seem to be working because no one can beat Owen. He and Danny have had at least five fights. It's been close a couple of times, but no cigar for Danny.'

'When does Vince train Owen?'

'Never on the same night Danny's here, that's for sure. The boys would tear each other to pieces.'

Taylor nodded. 'You got a number for this Vince?'

Masiker scrolled through his phone, gave Taylor the number. 'You know it's funny. The old bugger's nickname is Arm Buster, and he's currently laid up at the Yorkville General Hospital with a broken arm. He crashed his bike about a week ago. Broke his wrist and a leg, poor bugger. Owen's been training himself since.'

Taylor gathered her things. 'Thanks for your time, Mr Masiker. We'll be in touch if we need anything else.'

'Why? I've told you everything you could possibly want to know.'

Taylor smiled. 'Probably. But don't leave town.'

Once she'd skipped through the hours of comings and goings in the gym's foyer, Masiker's video reached its highpoint. Two constables escorted Bartlett, jumping about and remonstrating, through an empty reception area and out the front door. A second camera picked up the trainer as he got into his Mazda and drove off, tyres squealing and smoking. No other persons figured in the episode. Taylor felt disappointment draw down the corners of her mouth into a frown. She clicked the mouse to close the program as Sergeant Wilson strode to her desk, eyes ablaze.

'What is it, Ben? You look like you've seen a ghost?'

'Almost. A body's washed up in the mangroves.'

'Where?'

'About eight kilometres from where Bartlett's abandoned car was found. I've just seen an MMS photo texted in by a witness. A bloke out checking crab pots apparently.'

'Is it Bartlett?'

'Hard to say.'

'How come?'

'The crocs didn't leave much of his face.'

Chapter 5

The place was easier to break into than it should have been. A trainer of cage fighters in a world of troublemakers and tough guys should have better security. All it took was a hop onto a wheelie bin, a grip of the windowsill and a pull-up and in. A double-bolted window proved no match for a cop with Jack's experience, especially since he'd left it unlocked on his last visit.

As he clambered over the sash and into Bartlett's bedroom, Jack had one last look to make sure no one saw him enter the property. Better safe than sorry.

Clear.

The new clean lifestyle was paying dividends. Back in London a mate would have had to give Jack a boost; now his arms were strong, his body lighter. He could take on the world, like in the old days. He checked his watch. 12:30pm. He'd give it an hour, if he found nothing, back to questioning people, door knocking, phone calls, old fashioned slog. Bartlett could pop up like a daisy, recovered from temporary amnesia caused by too many punches to the head when he was a young fighter. Christ knew it used to happen to Jack. But his instincts were screaming, *this isn't right.*

A quick sweep of the upstairs rooms and cupboards revealed nothing new. The first police search was thorough in a superficial kind of way. That made perfect sense to Jack, although it might not to the average punter. *Dig deeper, son. Look where others don't think to.*

The freezer. Bags of peas. Nope, just peas, He tried all the old "favourites"

– vacuum cleaner tubes, compartments behind false bathroom tiles, wall clock, paintings, the works. There was a lined, enclosed area under the main part of the house. The forensics team, Taylor and Jack had checked it out already, but maybe they'd missed something. Bartlett would spend a lot of time down there, so worth one more sweep.

Bartlett was an orderly man. Everything in the home gym was neatly arranged, stacked, placed just so. Like an army private prepared for inspection. A classic York adjustable weight bench and press stood in the middle of the space. Everything you need to work virtually all parts of the body. Like a perverse house breaker with an exercise fetish, Jack dropped the York's back rest, slid under the barbell and gripped the textured surface of the silver steel bar. He easily lifted the light load already on the barbell, did twelve quick reps. The contraction of his pecs with each lift felt good. Sweat ran down his brow and pooled in the armpits of his light blue shirt. The temptation was too much. *Let's see how much you can pump, sunshine. Then back to the office.* He unbuttoned his shirt, folded it and placed it on the floor. A rack of black cast-iron plates sat against a wall, marked with numbers from 1.25 to 25 kg. He grabbed one of the heaviest, strained under the weight, loaded it on one side of the barbell, turned the fastener to lock it into place. He fetched the second, took a deep breath. The plate was hollow, weighed almost nothing. *Clever, Bartlett, very clever.*

Jack located a tiny mechanism on the edge of the plate. He twisted it left, nothing. Right, and it opened with a light popping sound. The plate separated into two identical halves.

Inside, dozens of unlabelled yellow pill bottles packed in tight with cotton wool.

He wasn't sure how this discovery would progress enquiries but he'd hand them over to the lab and they could run tests. Another team would come and investigate the rest of the gym, grunt work Jack wasn't keen on. This time the place would be turned upside down. He dropped the fake plate in the boot and closed it with a thunk.

Back on the main road to the CBD, a biker wearing illegal gang colours whizzed past on a gleaming Harley Davidson at least 40kms over the limit.

Lab work could wait, there were schools around here. Jack jumped on the accelerator and darted into the afternoon traffic. With one hand he slapped the portable blues and twos on the roof; cars parted to let him through. The Who's thunderous guitar intro to *Baba O'Riley* came on the radio, perfect pursuit music. He set his mouth hard and gripped the steering wheel, knuckles white. The motorcycle was getting away with ease, weaving between traffic calmers that had little effect on motorbikes. The rear-wheel-drive, turbo-six Kia Stinger, despite torque to die for and a top speed of 270 kph, couldn't keep up. The culprit disappeared to a speck between rows of lookalike town houses. The dashcam should have got the fucker's rego. Jack resolved to track him down and pay a visit.

As he felt his heartrate return to normal, *London Calling* erupted from his phone. He snatched at it. 'Yeah, wot?'

'You seriously need to find a new greeting. You sound like a cockney Neanderthal.'

'Oi! That's not politically correct.'

'Stick it, Jack. Listen, I've got an urgent update on the Bartlett matter.'

'It better be good, I'm itching to collar an irresponsible biker.'

Taylor relayed what Sergeant Wilson had just told her. 'Doesn't mean it's him.'

'That's what Wilson said. But I think it could be our missing man.'

'Why?'

'Apparently there's the remains of a Mortal Kombat tattoo on his back.'

Chapter 6

A shredded torso, the well-chewed head barely hanging on by sinew and skin, lay disembowelled, stomach down. Mangrove tree roots stuck out of the ground around it like a gnarled pencil fence. A fluorescent green-and-black birdwing butterfly landed on one of the roots, languidly brought its wings together to form one vertical plane. Exquisite natural beauty that took your breath away. The dead body did the same, but in a different way.

'I didn't know crocodiles could read.' Jack sucked noisily on a nicotine lolly, pointed at the grisly remains.

Taylor could barely look at the corpse, glanced away every few seconds. 'What do you mean by that?' She turned her attention back to the victim. Jack saw her swallow hard, heard the sound of a dry gulp blending with frog croaks, lorikeet squawks and the loud clicks of pistol shrimps on the edge of the mangrove forest. His stomach was stronger than hers, forged like steel in the blood-bathed boxing rings of his youth. He could have been a pathologist in another lifetime. Or a butcher.

'Come here, look. Don't be queasy. It's not your job to be queasy.' He beckoned with a crooked finger as he clambered down a muddy embankment. Taylor followed close behind, grabbing his trouser belt for support. One of his feet slid out from underneath him, she tugged hard on the belt to keep him from falling face first in the mire. He turned with a smile. 'Thanks. I reckon you saved me a trip to the dry cleaners.'

They ducked under blue and white police tape marking off a 3x3 metre square, the body bang in the middle of it. Half a dozen scientists in white Tyvek suits, blue gloves and massive rubber boots fussed about the scene, painstakingly searched the surrounding sludge for evidence. The going underfoot was so sticky it looked like they were working in slow motion. Body language of slouched shoulders and the lack of chatter told Jack the boffins weren't finding much. Either that or they were concentrating on not falling over and getting trapped. The muddy water reeked of the rich, earthy muskiness of tropical wetlands.

Taylor saw what Jack was talking about. Amongst the rips and shreds of saltwater crocodile bite marks she could make out a stylised black dragon in a circle and most of the letters. *Finish him.* The famous phrase from the video game Mortal Kombat.

'See.' Jack pointed. 'The crocodile's read that and thought it was an invitation to lunch.'

'Your dark humour defies belief. Have you no respect?'

'Tide's coming in.' A woman from forensics called from a few metres away. She wasn't going to tread further into the squelch than she needed to. 'You've got about ten minutes before we're going to have to move him away from there. Have a good look while you've got the opportunity.'

Jack waved his thanks, fished out his mobile and took a photo from the head and feet, left and right sides of the body. He saw a centimetre of water lapping at the edges of Bartlett's torso. Gnarled trees and roots further out from shore disappeared, bit by bit, under the oncoming flow of water. Tiny hermit crabs scurried to and fro before ducking into the mud to wait for the tide's next retreat.

'Be careful there, drop your mobile in that muck and you can say good-bye to it.' Jack warned. Taylor was copying him, taking photos on her own phone. She gripped the device like her life depended on it. The iPhone was the latest model, barely a week old. Jack could imagine the howls if it tumbled out of her grasp.

'Would you call pictures of croc bites snaps?' Jack inquired flatly.

'Seriously, you need help.' She shook her head but there was no reproach in her words. Like most police officers, Jack used the mechanism of macabre observations as a coping mechanism. A career path where mangled and decomposing humans were a regular occurrence meant sick jokes were accepted between colleagues.

The two detectives bent low and inspected the human wreckage. No lifting or touching anything, that would be left to the geeks. What appeared to be shreds of denim around the tibia of the right leg, no other clothing visible in the taped-off zone. Left tibia was missing, most likely being digested by the acid in a crocodile's stomach. Ribs, red muscles and shredded veins, ripped skin. The head was tilted to one side on the ground, face gone, the mouth a toothy grimace of horror. The last time Jack saw carnage like this was a dead motorcyclist who'd driven head-on into a brick wall at 150 kph.

'Do these remains tell you anything?' said Taylor.

'Only that he had a pair of jeans on at some point. Apart from that, nada.' Jack stood, took a deep breath of cloying rainforest air. He and Taylor disentangled themselves from the mangrove's seductive grip, approached the leading forensic scientist, Margaret Proctor. A pair of sparkly grey eyes to match the soggy ground underfoot peered out from above her white mask. Light touches of jade green eye makeup. She pulled the mask under her chin. 'You guys finished? We need to hurry, high tide's on its way.'

'Yeah. We've got our seaside holiday photos to enjoy while you lot do your stuff.' Jack longed for a cigarette. Despite his bluff, the ragged corpse had left him feeling empty. A horrible way for any life to end. 'Any early conclusions?'

She shook her head. 'The croc ate a lot of him. I'm surprised it didn't consume the entire body. Maybe something spooked it, although once they're eating usually nothing will stop 'em. Only a thorough autopsy will tell us anything. We should have detailed results back to you tomorrow, maybe even something tonight.'

'No bullet holes?' said Taylor.

'No. No neat stab wounds, not hacked with a machete either. The man could have been stabbed with something serrated but it's simply too hard to tell among all the tissue damage. Looks like he's been through a meat grinder, to tell you the truth. I can tell you a frenzied attack took place. If the man was alive or dead when that happened, I can't hazard a guess.' Proctor looked off into the distance, perhaps trying to divine wisdom from gathering storm clouds and the oncoming delta tide. 'The multiple crushed bones were most probably caused by the animal's jaws. The victim could have been murdered elsewhere, perhaps even suicided. Two things I can say with some certainty. The shreds of clothing clinging to his body tell me he wasn't out for an innocent swim, and the lack of bullets or exit wounds strongly suggests he wasn't shot. But we can only be definitive once we've gone over him in the lab.'

'Any suspicious foot prints about, signs of a struggle or the body being dragged along the mud?' said Jack. There were, of course, plenty of prints about, the police couldn't get to the body without leaving their own.

'The old fella who found the remains was pulling in some crab pots when he spotted the body.' Proctor handed Jack a piece of paper with the witness's details on it. 'So there's his shoe prints, plus his kelpie's paw prints. Marks and scratches where all kinds of native wildlife's been scurrying about. Apart from that, nothing suss. Prima facie evidence points to the crocodile finding the body elsewhere. It would have been chomping away merrily as it drifted along beside the shore until something made it stop feasting.'

'What about ID?'

'The croc?' said Proctor, deadpan.

Taylor burst out laughing despite the gravitas of the scene.

'Touché,' said Jack, suppressing a smirk. 'I like that one. Wanna work with us?'

'No thanks. I prefer not to deal with the living if at all possible. As for the victim, there were no documents on him.'

Jack nodded.

'I'm not sure any relatives would be keen on seeing him like this,' said Taylor. 'I'm thinking of when it comes to getting an official ID.'

'We might have to resort to dental records unless someone can identify him by the tattoos,' said Proctor.

'I think I can say it's most likely him.' Taylor stared at her mobile screen.

'You can?' said Jack, eyebrows arched.

'Here. I found these.' She held up her mobile for Proctor and Jack to see.

An image on Bartlett's Facebook page showed a man, back to the camera, flexing his biceps. On the wall facing him, a framed drawing of the Mortal Kombat dragon that looked remarkably like what was left of the design on the victim's back.

'It looks like Bartlett in the shot.'

'Of course it's him.' Taylor said impatiently. 'Same hair, height, build. Besides, it's his bloody Facebook page.'

'But there's no back tattoo on the guy in the photo like there is on the victim.' Jack gently tapped the mobile screen. 'When was that taken?'

'Lemme see. The post is from six months ago. Text says: *Tattoo design. What do you think?*' Then a bunch of comments from people, mostly telling him to go for it.'

'Looks like we might be able to spare Bartlett's family the grief of identifying him,' said Jack.

As they headed back to their cars through the mangrove forest, growing thinner as they went, Jack pressed Taylor about her interview with Masiker.

'He's an interesting individual, to say the least. The man's covering up something.'

Jack sniffed. 'I don't like him one bit. I've dealt with gym owners before and most of them are scum.'

'That's a big call. I'm sure lots of them are nice people.'

He offered no response other than shrugging his shoulders.

'Masiker protested like crazy when I pushed him about drug use at the club. Repeated he had no knowledge of any activity.'

'Naïve or lying.' Jack pulled a branch aside, ushered Taylor through a thicket.

'On the plus side, I got him to fork over a list of Bartlett's main clients.'

'Great work.'

She pulled aside a low-hanging branch. 'Another thing. Before I visited Masiker I checked with the constables who attended the disturbance at the Iron Horse.'

'And?'

'It wasn't some random member running amok. It was Bartlett.'

'Holy shit.'

'I made Masiker hand over the CCTV footage from that night. Unfortunately, there was nothing useful on it.'

'Any chance he altered the footage?'

'None. I was with him when he downloaded the file.'

'Damn.'

'Masiker also told me a bit about the other fighter, Owen Kennedy and his coach.'

'Trainer.'

'What?'

'Not coach, trainer. There's a subtle difference.'

'So subtle it's irrelevant to this discussion.' She shot him a sour look. 'It seems the rival...trainer...Vince Armbruster, had a nasty cycling accident and the champ's been training himself for a while.'

Jack pressed his car's beeper to unlock it. 'When athletes get to a certain level their trainers...and coaches...are mainly there for motivation rather than technical adjustments. Kennedy would know exactly what he needs to do to keep on top of his game.'

'Wanna pay them both a visit?'

'Do crocs have big teeth?'

Taylor had no time to respond to Jack's poor-taste rhetorical question. Two outside broadcast vans from the local TV stations roared up the gravel road and skidded to a stop. They parked between Taylor's Toyota Aurion XV50 and the forensics team's vehicles. Doors thunked shut as a film crew alighted from the first van. Then the second. A reporter and camera operator each from Channel 11 and 3 strode purposefully towards the detectives.

'Here comes the Fourth Estate,' said Taylor. 'How did they get wind of this so fast? Wilson told me there'd be no media release until we gave the go ahead.' She quickened her step to avoid the eager-faced woman rushing at them. Too late. The cameras were already perched on the operators' shoulders, lights indicated filming was underway.

Jack recognised Holly Maguire, news anchor and chief journalist at Channel 11. She appeared shorter in real life than on screen, not a hair out of place and makeup caked on thick. Hot on her high heels scrambled Johnno Peroni, the male counterpart to Maguire from Channel 3. The detectives knew the reporters well from previous cases. Both were professional and enthusiastic, but right now they presented a nuisance the investigation could do without.

'Can you take us to the body, Detective Lisbon?' Peroni muscled his way past Maguire. He was a former rugby league footballer who mostly reported on sports but was known to revel in hard news when a big story broke in town.

'What body?' Jack squinted. 'Where did you get that information?'

'The croc attack victim. We got a tip off from a member of the public. He said there was a body lying in the mangrove forest. What can you tell us?' Peroni thrust a microphone at Jack's face.

It could only have been the fisherman who found the body. Looking for his fifteen minutes of fame. No doubt the media would be lining him up for an interview if they hadn't already. 'This is a secured area. Only authorised personnel are allowed beyond that line.' Jack pointed at a long line of police tape strung between two black wattle trees. 'If you enter the no-go area you may be arrested for impeding an investigation.'

Taylor edged her way past the journalists, now shoulder to shoulder, each looking to score the edge, ask the most pertinent questions. Jack imagined a scribe from the Yorkville Times newspaper would be on their way too.

'Detective Taylor,' Maguire flashed an ingratiating grin. 'Perhaps you'll be more forthcoming with information about the attack.' The men working the cameras stood a metre behind, off to one side.

'Like my colleague Detective Sergeant Lisbon said, this is now a secure area. If you have any questions, please get in touch with our media liaison team. The number is—'

'Surely you can answer some simple questions,' barked Peroni. 'There've been a number of crocodile attacks in recent years. The public have a right to know what's going on.'

'Go back to the station and wait for me.' Jack whispered to Taylor. 'Call everyone on the list you got from Masiker. Our priority is Danny Sharpe. Then try and get hold of Owen Kennedy and his trainer.'

'Got it,' she whispered back.

'I'll handle these bozos until backup arrives.'

'Sure. Don't say anything stupid. Be diplomatic.'

'You oughta know me by now.'

'That's what I'm afraid of.'

The last time Jack fronted a TV interview, he blurted out sensitive information about a robbery suspect the cops were hunting. Despite Jack's blooper, the con somehow missed the memo and was apprehended within hours. A dressing down for Jack in his new post, but no long-term harm done. You couldn't blame him though. That bloody Holly Maguire could charm the pants off a monk. Not today. He'd learned his lesson.

'Please, DS Lisbon,' Maguire implored. 'Give us something. At least tell us if it's a crocodile attack or something else.'

Taylor's car disappeared behind a corner and Jack exhaled heavily. *Where was that backup?* 'What I can tell you is the following. A serious incident has occurred that requires us to keep this location off limits to everyone, media included, until further notice.'

'Come on, our viewers deserve better than stone-walling. Public safety's at stake here,' Peroni demanded.

'The public will be informed through the police media liaison office when it is ...determined...that...'

'Yes?' Peroni growled.

'I'm afraid that's all the time I can spare you.' Two marked police cars headed towards the mini media ambush, Sergeant Ben Wilson at the wheel of the first. The reporters and cameramen turned to watch their arrival. 'My colleagues will be standing guard here. Don't even think about breaching this line. Thanks, and good day to you.'

A quick debrief with Wilson and Jack was haring his way back to Yorkville Police HQ. Two clear roads later and he found himself in heavy afternoon traffic. Without warning, rain started to bucket down. Did it ever stop for more than a day or two in the far north?

A line of crawling cars formed in front of him, traffic ground to a halt. *Bugger this.* He noticed a wide bike track running down the left hand side of the lane, just enough room for the Kia if the other cars did the right thing and moved slightly to the right. He slapped the lights on the roof for the second time today. Jack praised the compliant citizens of Yorkville as every single driver made way for him. With law-abiding people like that in this town, it was a wonder there were any villains at all.

Chapter 7

Jack gripped the edge of Taylor's desk. Her work area was the epitome of order compared to his. Didn't matter his was a mess though, he could place his hands on any important file whenever he needed. Neatness wasn't important when you were once the school champion of that game where you turn over playing cards two at a time to find pairs. Memory. *Or was it called something else?* 'Any luck with the calls, Claudia?'

'Yes. And no.'

'Bad news first.' *Always the bad news first* was his lifelong motto. No logic to it, just the way it was.

'Bartlett's clients are worried. Seems he had a great rapport with them. The way two of the women raved on about Terry, I reckon they had the hots for him.'

'Did you get hold of Danny Sharpe?'

'No. Tried his number a few times, no answer.'

'Get his address?'

'Yes, it's all on the list from Masiker. Also details for Owen Kennedy and his trainer, Vince Armbruster.'

'Talk to either of them?'

'No luck with Owen, but I got hold of Vince on the phone. He's the only one who seems to be where they're meant to be in this bizarre stage play.'

'To be expected, since he's in the hospital. Did he have any idea as to Bartlett's whereabouts?'

'Armbruster claims to know nothing. Neither do any of Bartlett's clients.

No one knows where Terry Bartlett is.'

'But we do. At the morgue. Pending confirmation from the lab, that is. So, what's the good news amongst all that negativity?'

'I rang Masiker again. I remember him mentioning Bartlett had an estranged son. Turns out Terry had dreams of turning young Charlie Bartlett into a fighter like he was. The brutality of MMA frightened Charlie too much, so he took up boxing. Reluctantly. Terry pushed him hard for a couple of years, and the kid did OK as a junior. Masiker reckons it was obvious Charlie had no heart for it. The first time he stepped into the ring for a professional bout he was overcome by fear, forgot everything he'd learned. Got knocked out a minute into the fight.'

'Oh dear. Poor sod.'

'Charlie was humiliated. He gave the game away immediately.'

'What does he do now?'

'He ended up going to a vocational college. He became a barber, if you can believe it.'

'Sounds like a kid who might harbour a few grudges against his dad.'

'To put it mildly. The news is better, though. Charlie owns a barbershop downtown. You're not going to believe the name.'

'Surprise me.'

'Uppercuts.'

'Priceless. Shall we?' Jack was already half way to his desk to grab his jacket.

Chapter 8

"Uppercuts" buzzed with lively chatter, the snip-snip of scissors, the hum of hair clippers and muted commentary from a TV. It was like a pub without the alcohol and peanuts. The air was redolent of Old Spice and Brut 33. Detectives Lisbon and Taylor sat on chairs by the window, sipped coffee from takeaway cups. Two other men came in after the detectives and set up camp either end of a long leather couch. One, a gangly teenager, scrolled incessantly through his mobile, the other, middle-aged but in denial, dressed more like a teen than the teen, flipped through one magazine after another, nothing interesting enough to grab his attention for more than a few seconds. The finger licking and flicking of the pages made Jack want to slap the guy.

'Charlie can't hate his father too much. Look at the décor.' Taylor nodded at the paraphernalia adorning every spare inch of the barbershop. Boxing gloves, red and black pairs, old styles and new, hung from the walls. Posters of boxing legends Ali, Marciano, Tyson. A sculpture in the shape of a mouthguard sat on a glass cabinet, inside it stood figurines of boxers. One wall was dedicated to Australian pugilists who became world beaters, among them Aboriginal stars Lionel Rose and Hector Thompson, immigrants Joe Bugner and Kostya Tszyu. A cork board with smaller photographs of famous visitors to the salon and local sporting heroes.

'Or maybe it's just a marketing ploy.'

'That's rather cynical.' Taylor blew steam from the top of her paper cup.

'Not really. I used to go to a joint like this in South London. They cut your hair worse than the council cuts the grass but it was all about the image. Young men flocked to it.' Jack folded his arms and leaned back to get a better view of the TV mounted high on the wall. He pointed at the action on the screen. 'Know who they are?'

Taylor shook her head. 'No idea.'

'Ali versus Foreman, Zaire, 1974. Rumble in the Jungle. Inspirational stuff. Ali was the complete underdog but he sent the champ to the canvas in the eighth round.'

'And why are you telling me this exactly?'

'Dunno, just making conversation.'

'Which one of you is next?' The name tag on the apron of the figure approaching them said Sam. Over six foot tall, large build, broad shoulders, hair shorter than Jack's, almost a number one cut. The voice was deep, but neither masculine nor feminine. Jack decided to keep everything nice and neutral. He'd misgendered an assault victim recently and his ears were still ringing from the rebuke.

'We ain't here to get our haircut,' said Jack. 'We're here to speak with the owner, Charlie Bartlett.'

'And you are?'

'Police,' said Taylor.

Sam examined their badges and pointed at the middle of three barbers tending to customers covered in white sheets. 'That's Charlie. He's about halfway done with one of our regulars. It's a tricky style, could take another 30 minutes or so.'

'We'll wait.' Jack smiled affably. The overweight barber in overalls, plaited beard and hipster hairstyle wasn't what he was expecting Charlie Bartlett to look like. Taylor's wide eyes told him she thought the same thing.

'I'm going to get us another coffee.' Taylor stood, tossed her handbag across a shoulder. 'That's too long for me to be watching boring old boxing matches.'

'Boring? Are you kidding me?'

Taylor chose not to answer, the tingle of the bell above the door signalled her exit. Jack settled in to watch another all-time classic. Buster Douglas versus Mike Tyson, 1990.

Taylor returned with fresh coffees at the very moment Buster Douglas miraculously rallied and flattened Tyson in the tenth round. Another win for the underdog. Jack smiled as Tyson scrabbled around on the canvas like he was looking for his keys on the beach. Taylor handed him his flat white, no sugars. As he took a sip, he glanced up to see Charlie brushing loose hair from the young customer's jeans. The chap had been transformed into something resembling an alarmed parrot. Charlie beckoned to the detectives, led them into a small room in the back of the salon. No chairs, just grey metal shelving and boxes of styling gel, shampoo, hairspray. 'How can I be of assistance, officers?'

'We, ah,' Jack cleared his throat. 'We'd like you to tell us where your father is.'

'Excuse me?'

'He's been missing for a couple of days and we'd like you to tell us where he is.'

Sweat glistened on Charlie's brow, his jowls shook. 'Missing?'

'Yeah,' said Jack. 'If you have any idea where he might be, please tell us now.'

'I haven't spoken to my father in over a year. He cheated on my mother, the bastard. He can rot in hell as far as I'm concerned. Will that be all? I've got a business to run.'

'Just a minute. We ain't done yet.'

'Make it quick.'

'Is your dad having an affair grounds enough not to have any contact with him?' Jack tapped a fingernail on the top box of a pile of Brylcreem. 'Do people still use this stuff? I thought it went out of style in 1983.'

'Um.' Charlie was momentarily rattled by two unrelated questions fired at him at once. 'Yes, that particular product is still popular. Making a resurgence in fact. As to dad, yes, he's a fucking arsehole. Mum found out he was sleeping with a couple of women he was training. Both married and one of them younger than me!'

Taylor was bang on the money with her assessment of the female clients "having the hots" for Bartlett senior, an attractive man by most standards. The women Terry Bartlett had affairs with being married put potential jealous husbands into the mix as suspects now. On a personal level for Jack, the case of a parent estranged from their child reminded him of his own situation with Skye. He never cheated on his ex, didn't even entertain the thought, although he'd had opportunities galore. Well, a couple. Jack put that out of his mind for now, pushed another angle with Bartlett junior. 'Did your father dabble in illicit or performance enhancing drugs?'

A vehement shake of the head from Charlie. 'Never. He's clean as a whistle. He knows other trainers and fighters are gobbling them down like Tic Tacs, but he believes you either achieve success naturally or not at all.'

'Are you that naïve, son?' Jack pushed. 'If you haven't got the edge in boxing, MMA, just about any sport these days, you finish last. And you can only get there with clever use of steroids, human growth hormone, all that malarkey.'

'Not true. Look at Danny Sharpe. He's pushed Owen Kennedy to the brink a couple of times.'

'You must be having a laugh! Sharpe got caught using drugs. What sort of example is that?'

Charlie shook his head vigorously. 'It's a bloody fit-up. Dad wouldn't tolerate a drug cheat in his camp if he knew about it.'

'What else can you tell us about Danny Sharpe?'

'What do you mean?'

'We'd like to speak to the man but haven't been able to get hold of him. Perhaps you can help us out.' Taylor's voice was soothing, calming. 'Would he be likely to have a grudge against your father?

'A grudge?'

'Well, he wasn't able to train Sharpe to a level where he could defeat Kennedy,' said Jack. 'The young bloke might think your dad's not up to the job. Football coaches get the axe when their teams underperform. Maybe Danny was thinking along the lines that Terry's methods weren't getting the desired results.'

'Bullshit,' Charlie scoffed. 'Anyway, they adore each other. At least they used to when I was more involved in Dad's life. Danny has to know, deep down, it's him to blame for not being able to beat Kennedy, not my father.'

'Why do you say that?' said Jack.

'Dad's trained title winners before. People who came from nothing. He's got the skills to lift any fighter to the next level. If Danny hasn't won the title yet, that's down to him. Or maybe Owen's simply more talented, tougher. A better fighter.'

'You spoke disparagingly of your father before, now you're practically talking him up.' Jack tapped the Brylcreem box again, saw that it irritated Charlie, and tapped louder.

'Listen, Dad may be a prick, but I've gotta respect him for his principles.'

'OK, son. It's plain you still have some love left for your dad, despite what's happened. Let's go back to the drug question. Would he be taking anything for mental health problems, for example? Rumour has it he took the break up with your mother hard. Perhaps he's been popping prescription antidepressants?'

Charlie let out a deep laugh that reverberated off the walls. 'He's pulled the wool over everyone's eyes if they think he's been moping about, sad his marriage broke up. He'd hook up with any woman who smiled at him.'

Time to try another tack. 'You've got a lot of resentment against your father for another reason, don't you, mate? Humiliation in the ring, his disappointment you couldn't live up to his high expectations. I bet he never imagined you turning out like...this.' Jack stared unflinchingly at the barber, spread his hands wide as if demonstrating how fat Charlie had become. Taylor shot Jack a vicious side-eye that said he'd overstepped the mark. If she thought that was overstepping, she wouldn't like the next bit. 'I'm gonna come clean with you, son. There's a body on the slab in Yorkville morgue right now. We're pretty sure it's your father. Can you account for your movements over the last two days?'

'Hang on, you're asking me for a...a fucking alibi...for I don't know what, and you've never even introduced yourself properly.' Charlie waved his hands about in front of his face, eyes darting all over the place. 'You barge in here, throwing questions at me. What's your name, you arrogant bastard?'

'Do forgive me. I'm Detective Sergeant Jack Lisbon and this is Detective Constable Claudia Taylor, Yorkville Police. I'll repeat the question, can you account for–'

'YES! I've been flat out at the salon and for the last two nights, no, make that *five nights*, I've been at home with my partner Jeremy.'

'I see.' *Jeremy?*

'I'm always exhausted at the end of a day's work. I close up shop, maybe drop in at the supermarket, but it's straight home after that.'

'We'll be confirming that claim with your partner later.' Jack retrieved his mobile.

'What, are you going to call him now?'

'Sorry? Oh no. I wanted to show you a photo of the body we recovered by the Boustead River.'

Taylor grabbed his hand. 'No, Jack! Enough. Put it away.'

'No, no. You can't start something and then notfinish it,' Charlie's eyes were ablaze. 'Show me the damn picture. If he's dead, I wanna see it.'

'I'm not sure you're going to want to see this, Charlie.' Jack shifted into nice guy gear. 'Perhaps we'll wait for the autopsy to confirm against the dental records or the DNA.'

A beefy hand darted, snatched the phone out of the detective's grip. 'Fuck that.' Charlie's hand shook as he scrolled through the photos. 'Holy shit. What happened?' His face turned ashen. 'Jesus, I hated him but he didn't deserve that.' Tears pooled in the corners of Charlie's soft brown eyes, his plaited beard quivered.

A fist pounded on the door. 'You OK in there? I heard shouting?' called one of the other barbers. 'Your 4 o'clock appointment's here and getting impatient.'

'All under control,' reassured Taylor. 'We'll be out in a moment.'

'Is it him, Charlie?' said Jack, leaning in close and looking at the last photo over Charlie's shoulder.

'I'm not sure.' Charlie sniffed back tears, bent closer to the image.

'Look at the tattoo. See the dragon? The writing?'

Charlie handed the phone back to Jack. 'No, it's not him.' He expelled a long, relieved breath.

'Are you sure?'

'Definitely. He hates tattoos. He can take a beating but he's been scared of needles all his life. No way that's my father.'

It was Taylor's turn to show Charlie something on her phone. 'Look at this Facebook post. He's asking his followers their opinion about getting this very design. He must've changed his mind and decided to get a tatt.'

A slow shake of the head from Charlie. 'That's not even dad in the photo. He's got a big broad scar from his surgery, it runs all the way down the shoulder blade. You can see there's no scar here.'

'But it's his page,' Taylor insisted.

'Look closer,' said Charlie. 'It's a guest post by someone else. Dad just left it there without comment or deleting it. He's not a huge user of social media, he probably never even knew it was there.'

'You know who it is?' pressed Taylor. 'Do you recognise anything in the photo?'

London Calling erupted in the small room, made everyone jump. Jack let the call go to voicemail. A weird silence fell for a few moments.

'Well?' said Jack. 'Do you know who that man is?'

A tiny nod from Charlie. 'Yep.' He jabbed a forefinger at the mobile screen. 'It's Owen fucking Kennedy.'

An SMS message alert lit up the screen of Jack's phone. He didn't have to check it. Preview mode confirmed Charlie's words. He held up the mobile for Taylor to see the text. *URGENT: DNA analysis confirms body is not that of Terry Bartlett.*

Chapter 9

The antiseptic odour of the city morgue delivered Jack a kick in the guts, set off bad memories. It propelled him back to a London hospital, three and a half years ago. Two thugs beat the living shit out of him in a dark alley after he'd pissed off a particularly nasty and vindictive boxing trainer, the late and not-much-lamented Alex Gallagher. Lying in a hospital bed for weeks, Jack somehow made a full recovery from his horrific injuries. Today it was only a tiny niggle in the lower leg. Later, Jack exacted righteous and violent revenge against Gallagher. He also separated the trainer from a large sum of cash, money owed to Jack for keeping the trainer safe from the law. Back to the wall and desperate, Jack had little choice but to despatch Gallagher to meet His Maker.

At the end of that nightmare, Jack made a hasty getaway to the other end of the Earth, to a new job, a new life. Every day since the final fatal showdown with Gallagher, Jack had been looking over his shoulder. The trainer's death was marked as unsolved, but you never knew. There was always the chance a determined London Met copper could re-open the investigation. One thing in Jack's favour – Gallagher was scum and, as far as Jack knew via the grapevine, many were glad to learn he'd been bumped off.

All those memories reignited by a simple smell. Didn't matter, though. It was all about the here and now, the living people sharing the immediate space with him and the body on the slab; solving this case.

Doctor Margaret Proctor, appearing more relaxed in blue scrubs than she did dressed as a terrestrial astronaut at the crime scene, pulled back the white sheet to reveal what was left of the champion boxer. Bones and torn meat, like the carcass of a beast slaughtered in an abattoir. Jack leaned in for a closer look, Taylor's posture remained ramrod straight, eyes fluttering and nose pointed up.

'Is there anything in the database to confirm this is Owen Kennedy?' said Jack. He and Taylor agreed not to approach any family members until they were 100 percent sure they had the right person.

'Yes. There were no DNA records in the criminal justice system, so I took a print from the only finger remaining on the left hand.' Proctor carefully held up the corpse's hand by the wrist. 'As you can see, it's swollen and putrefied, but there was just enough print left to be useful. Owen Kennedy was finger-and-palm printed after being arrested for a mid-range DUI a couple of years ago.'

'He would've given blood for the drink driving arrest,' said Taylor. 'Was there DNA taken from that?'

'No, the sample was only tested for blood alcohol content, not DNA. But the fingerprint was sufficient. It's a match.' Proctor again held up the putrefied hand.

'I'm sure you don't have to demonstrate everything,' said Taylor, gaze averted towards a wall of steel-grey filing cabinets. 'We require your conclusions, we don't need to see all the gory bits.'

'How you ever progressed beyond uniformed constable baffles me, DC Taylor. You need to harden up.' Jack turned to address the pathologist, smiled as if apologising for his partner's oversensitivity. 'Please go on.'

'If you look closely at the base of the finger here.' As Proctor spoke, Jack saw Taylor gritting her teeth, angling her head for a better look. Doing her best to tough it out, bless her. 'There's an indentation, like you get from wearing a ring over a long period. See it?'

'Yes,' the detectives said together.

'It could be one of those championship rings,' said Jack. 'MMA associations around the world have been introducing them to replace belts. They're a more personal reward than a belt that gets shared around.'

'Perhaps it slipped off while he was in the water?' Claudia suggested.

'I don't think so,' replied Proctor. 'If you consider how deep the indentation is among all that swelling, I'd say the likelihood of the ring falling off is low.'

'I agree,' said Jack, straightening up. 'Someone forcibly removed it. Those bad boys can be worth a couple of grand or more. Anything else?'

'Apart from the missing fingers, the body is remarkably intact, considering. You'd think there'd be even less of him after a crocodile attack, wouldn't you?' Proctor's tangential remark hung in the air like a thought balloon in a cartoon until Jack caught it, turned it over in his mind, and formulated the only response he could think of.

'Yeah, you would 'n all.'

Taylor said nothing.

'But like you mentioned before,' Jack continued. 'Maybe the animal got spooked by something while it was chowing down on the dearly departed and did a runner or a slither or whatever it is crocs do.'

'It's interesting with crocodiles, you know.' The pathologist droned with haughty authority, lecturing the ignorant in subjects esoteric. 'For what amounts to prehistoric monsters with brains smaller than the average house cat, crocodiles, including the saltwater species *Crocodylus porosus*, can behave in the most unexpected ways.' As the woman spoke, Jack was reminded of a quiz show host famous for savaging dopey contestants unable to answer simple questions. The eyeroll he copped from Taylor told him the coroner was giving her the shits. On the other hand, now Proctor had started, he had to know.

'Unexpected how?'

'I'm glad you asked.' She adjusted her glasses on the bridge of her nose. 'There was a case in the Northern Territory a few years back. A local psychic, can you believe it, told the police she thought a crocodile was guarding the dead body of an unfortunate tourist, protecting the cadaver from other crocodiles. Perhaps to eat it later, perhaps for some other purpose we can only guess at.'

'Yes, very interesting.' Taylor snuck a glance at her watch. 'Perhaps we can get to the matter in hand.'

'Oh, do forgive me.' The big woman gave a dainty titter that didn't match her Amazon proportions. 'I'm fascinated by the role animals can play in pathology work. Shark and dog bites are another area that –'

'Please,' Jack interrupted, gestured with his head towards the body. 'Tell us what killed him.' It took all his will to choke off the words *"for fuck's sake"*.

'Yes, of course. The body has sustained enormous damage. He was a professional athlete, is that correct?'

The detectives nodded together. 'Mixed martial arts,' said Jack.

'First, there's no involvement of firearms, as I assessed at the crime scene. No evidence of hacking with a sharp implement or stabbing with a non-serrated blade. I cannot rule out the use of a serrated knife or even a saw.'

'Right, right.' Jack tapped his foot underneath the gurney. 'We don't wanna know what didn't kill him.'

Proctor cleared her throat loudly, like she was about to let loose with a reprimand, however maintained her cool. 'Please be patient. I'm getting to that. So, there are many pre-existing injuries from his sporting activities. However, it's easy to see old scarring and healed broken bones, dental posts where he's had teeth knocked out. There's been massive amounts of tissue torn and bones crushed by the crocodile, the skull too. However, if you see this hollow here.' She pointed with a scalpel at the very top of what was left of Kennedy's cranium. 'The even round indentation is evidence of blunt force trauma. I also found bruising on the brain itself. All of this preceded any mauling by the crocodile. The blow to the head is a possible cause of death, and I'd place the timing somewhere between two days and a week ago, erring towards the latter taking into account decomposition.'

'That's a big window.' Jack pulled at a loose thread on his shirtsleeve. 'Can't you narrow it down?'

'Sorry.' A headshake from Proctor. 'Once they've been in the water, determining an accurate time of death is difficult. With changes to salt content, PH and water temperatures, it can be a guessing game.'

The detectives exchanged a knowing look. 'So someone's coshed him,' said Jack. 'Would death have been quick?'

'Impossible to say. However, you'll note I said possible cause, not likely. Look here.' Proctor pointed at a narrow pinkish line on the victim's neck. 'I found tiny blue flecks of soft plastic embedded in the flesh of Owen Kennedy's neck, all the way around the throat.'

'What kind of plastic?' asked Taylor.

'HDPR, or high-density polyethylene.'

'What's that when it's at home?' said Jack.

'Among other things, it's used to make various kinds of shopping bags.' Proctor blinked rapidly.

'Put over his head.' Jack mused aloud.

'Exactly,' said Proctor. 'Meaning the cause of death could also be suffocation inside a plastic bag prior to or after being bashed on the head with a blunt instrument. Absence of water in the remaining right lung tells me he was dead before ending up in the water.'

'Preferable to being fed alive to the crocs, I guess,' said Taylor. 'What can you tell us about blood and toxicology?'

'I've compared the man's blood with that of the smaller sample from Terry Bartlett's vehicle. It belongs to the man lying here before us. As for illegal substances, the guy was clean. No anabolic steroids, no HGH.'

Jack scratched his cheek, prickly stubble poking through in the late afternoon. 'Kennedy was likely transported in the boot of Bartlett's car and then dumped somewhere with a plastic bag over his head. We'd better get ready for a briefing with the rest of the team, Claudia. And it's time for a media release. Run it by Inspector Batista. We can't keep this shtum for much longer. Maguire and Peroni have left a ton of messages on my phone, demanding a statement.'

'Mine, too.' Taylor pursed her lips. 'They're bloody persistent.'

'Looks like a missing person's gone from a dead person to a...murder person, ah, victim.'

Taylor shook her head. 'Dear oh dear, what a way with words you have, DS Lisbon. I'm surprised you haven't been made head of the PR department with language skills like that.' Jack smiled; the Detective Constable pointing out his ineloquence was apt revenge for him taunting her about her weak stomach.

'Finding Terry Bartlett is even more urgent. He's now a suspect *and* a potential second victim.'

'I agree. The only problem is, how?'

DC Taylor typed the final full stop on her draft press release. She made sure to include the appeal Jack suggested – bring in the public. She hit send and the email message was gone to the press officer for circulation to the media, with copies to Jack and Inspector Batista. She reread the case notes for fifteen minutes and was about to head for home when an alert beeped and a small envelope appeared in the bottom left of her computer screen. *Come and see me please.* Batista.

'Good work on the press release. Hopefully some members of the public will come forward with something.'

'Thank you, sir.' Taylor scanned Batista's desk, somewhere between Jack's chaos and her orderliness. Middle of the road, like the Inspector himself. Rumour had it he got his job by patiently waiting his turn and not making waves, never actively sought promotion. By nature he was a relaxed, hands-off boss, and she liked it that way.

'Have you and DS Lisbon got this thing covered?'

'I think so, sir.'

'I've been reviewing the material you've gathered, the lab reports. Lots of ground to be covered, maybe too much for you and Lisbon on your own. If you need extra resources, let me know.' The boss's old swivel chair creaked as he leaned forward. 'This is the biggest case to hit our town in a long time. People are going to be worried, looking to us to solve the crime fast. I mean, if a trained professional fighter can't defend himself, how's the average citizen going to feel? Women walking alone at night?'

Taylor nodded. 'I agree entirely.' She handed Batista a list of clients from The Iron Horse. 'If Sergeant Wilson and the other uniforms could get on the phone and talk to these people, that'd save me and Jack a ton of legwork.' She smiled hopefully.

The Inspector scanned the list. 'Consider it done.'

'It's not all Bartlett's clients. The press release might flush out a few more. One of them might know something. Our priority is locating Terry

Bartlett, it's his blood in the abandoned vehicle after all. He could've killed his protégé's nemesis, got himself injured and done a runner.'

'Either that or he's another victim yet to be found. What about the assistant trainer, what's his name again?'

'Andy Harlow.'

'Yeah. Could he be involved?'

'Maybe. We can't get hold of him. Carl Masiker says he doesn't know where in Sydney Harlow took his family. We've checked social media, all the usual stuff. Nada.'

'You think Masiker's telling the truth?'

She shrugged. 'Not sure.'

The Inspector absently tugged on his shirt cuffs. 'And that leaves Danny Sharpe, the dead man's main opponent in the ring. Frustrated by continued defeats, in a bad head space with the drug infringement and dropped by his trainer. He's the key.'

'Jack's on his way to Sharpe's apartment right now, sir. He's not responded to any calls, so fingers crossed the DS can catch him at home.'

'Indeed.'

'May I leave now sir?' Taylor glanced at the clock on the wall behind Batista. 'It's already past the end of my shift.'

'I need you to do one more thing before you go.'

'Yes?' A sigh. She had a hot date tonight, with reality TV, chardonnay and a large packet of potato chips.

'I've just received an email news alert from Channel 3. Come have a look at this.' The Inspector pointed at his computer screen.

'Holy shit. It's a response to my media release. That was quick.'

The Channel 3 website banner headline proclaimed: *Cops claim of homicide a total croc!* Underneath the headline was a blurry photo of Owen Kennedy's body lying in the mangrove forest before the police had arrived. Below that, a staged outdoor photo of a deeply tanned middle-aged man in cargo shorts and a blue singlet sitting in a rocking chair on a veranda. Beside him, his grey-muzzled kelpie and an empty crab pot. The man, Bruce Walker, claimed he saw the crocodile attack the man on the river bank. *I seen the poor bloke, heard him screamin' for help, so I chucked a big rock and the croc swam away. If only I'd got there earlier, I might have saved him. I'll be having nightmares about this for the rest of me days.'*

'He's taken the photo on his phone, sir. Sold it to the highest bidder. He's living in cloud cuckoo land, though. The pathologist said Kennedy had been dead for at least two days, maybe a week.'

'Ring that moron and tell him to pull his head in, no more interviews, or we'll have him for...I dunno, obstruction of justice.'

'Yes, sir.'

'Let's see what the other pricks have posted.' The Inspector toggled around the media outlets' websites and respective Facebook pages. Channel 11 was yet to respond, the Yorkville Times simply reposted Taylor's press release without comment. 'All clear'.

'There's going to be a shitload of fallout from the croc story,' said Taylor.

'Exactly. Call the media officer and set up a press conference for tomorrow morning. Ask them to post denials of Channel 3's irresponsible reporting. You, me and Lisbon will front the jackals tomorrow. Get a good night's sleep.'

'Yes, sir.'

Chapter 10

The song faded to silence. Jack knew his own voice was rubbish, but it never stopped him screaming his lungs out in accompaniment to a rock anthem. He grabbed a plastic bottle of cold water from the console, chugged some down to sooth a throat sore after mangling Led Zeppelin's "Black Dog". Other drivers in the late afternoon traffic stared at him with twisted faces as he head-banged along to the tune, but he didn't care. His car, his space, his rules. The six-gong radio news alert focused Jack's attention. A breathlessly dramatic male announcer read the police statement.

Now to breaking news. Yorkville CIB have confirmed the body of missing sporting identity Owen Kennedy was recovered from mangroves near the mouth of the Boustead River two days ago. Mr Kennedy was a champion welterweight mixed martial arts exponent. Crocodile attack has been ruled out as a cause of death and the police are treating the matter as a homicide. Anyone with information that may assist with investigations is urged to contact the Yorkville Police Station. More details will be made available as they come to hand. In other news...

Thank God they didn't come at the story from the crocodile angle. He had to hand it to the local radio station, they played by the rules most of the time. TV and newspapers were another matter.

His phone buzzed. Inspector Joe Batista. Finally getting involved in the case. Jack hit the button on his mounted phone to talk hands-free.

'Sir?'

'Did you hear the news?'

'Yes. Short and to the point.'

'Our hand was forced. Channel 3 posted some bullshit about a croc mauling so we had to issue an urgent press release to clarify.'

'Wait till tomorrow when the papers come out.' Jack observed more thunderclouds as he idled at a set of lights. 'Grisly murder is almost equal to a croc attack to the scandal sheets. We'll need to outsource to a call centre when Joe and Jane Public start bombarding us with wacky leads.'

'Nice one, Jack.' His boss at Yorkville CIB was a pleasure to work under compared to the despot Keogh at the London Met. Mainly because he laughed at all of Jack's quips, sometimes when they weren't meant to be funny. 'DC Taylor tells me you're on the way to Danny Sharpe's place. I can't stress the urgency of getting him to co-operate.'

'I'm pulling up outside his apartment complex now.'

'Keep me updated. If there's anything I can do to help, yell out.'

'Will do, sir.'

'If he says he heard Owen Kennedy was killed in a crocodile attack, make sure you disabuse him of the idea.'

'What do you mean?'

'Holly Maguire's been up to her tricks again.'

Jack rubbed a palm across his brow before rapping three times on Danny Sharpe's front door. The man lived in a complex of villa units slightly out of Jack's price bracket, but not by much. Which begged the question: how does a journeyman brawler like Sharpe, who's fighting in a regional league with low purses, afford it? He had to be supplementing his income somehow. As far as Jack knew, Sharpe had no daytime job, his total focus was MMA. In the UFC, the big time, fighters earned a small base salary, here it was only what you could earn by winning fights or sponsorship. Danny hadn't won too many recently and sponsors wouldn't touch a drug cheat with a barge pole.

Lumbering footsteps, a stifled yawn. 'Who is it?'

'Detective Sergeant Jack Lisbon, Yorkville CIB. Let me in please, Danny.'

The door opened slowly, as far as the safety chain would allow. Droopy eyes stared at Jack from the gloom inside. 'Show me your ID.' The voice was tired, almost timid.

Jack raised his badge, turned side on so Sharpe couldn't miss the .40 calibre Glock 22 sitting on his hip.

'Follow me.' Sharpe slapped at a hallway light switch, led the way. He walked with a weary gait, in silence. Board shorts and a white singlet highlighted broad shoulders and a narrow waist which formed the classic V-shaped body. The occupant possessed thick arms and well-muscled legs that could kick down a steel door. Strong enough to be a champion, apparently not smart enough. Perhaps the drugs had addled his brain.

The apartment was tastefully furnished: ivory white walls, broad marble tiles on the floor resembling blue-vein cheese, muted beige lounge suite, scatter cushions in light pastel green with a bamboo pattern. In the sparsely equipped kitchen, Sharpe gestured for Jack to take a seat. 'What's this to do with? I was having a nap.' The scratch under the armpit and the yawn looked like bad acting. The aroma of recently made hot chocolate told Jack the man was lying.

A huge TV dominated the far wall of the living area. The fact it was on was more proof of Sharpe's untruthfulness. An ad announced the early edition 5:00pm news was starting soon on Channel 3. 'Have you been listening to the news on the radio today, seen any social media updates in the last hour?' Jack asked.

'Nuh. Been sleeping. Dead tired after working out for three hours solid. Why, what's happened?'

Leave Owen Kennedy up your sleeve for now. 'Who've you been training with the last week? Terry Bartlett?'

A confused look passed across Sharpe's misaligned face, nostrils flared. Jack wondered what sort of methods Bartlett had been teaching his charge. How to block punches with his face? Sharpe looked older than his 29 years, closer to 40. Scars ran riot across his forehead and chin, cauliflower ears a rugby forward would be proud of stuck out almost at right angles to his box-shaped head. His bulbous nose would've been broken and reset many times. Despite his record as perpetual contender, there was something fearsome about him. Perhaps the fact he could take so many punches and kicks and keep going. It was a strange fact of life in the fighting world: supreme technicians like Ali who were so good at not getting hit looked a lot less scary than the human punching bags.

'What do you mean? I haven't seen Tezza for a while, as it happens.'

'Why not?'

'Carl told me Tezza's been lying low for a bit.'

'Is that so?'

'Yeah. So I've been training meself. Tezza cut me, but he'll have me back once he's had time to think. I was fitted up!'

Jack ignored Sharpe's protestations of innocence. 'Has Terry ever "laid low", as you put it, before?'

'Ah, not sure.'

'Funny thing is, Danny. We can't find your ex-trainer for love nor money. Carl knows nothing, Bartlett's son Charlie knows nothing and you, his former favourite fighter, know nothing. Something doesn't feel right about this, sunshine.' Jack tapped a forefinger on the table top.

If Danny had aspirations to be a poker player, Jack thought, he could forget about it. Fear, confusion, perhaps a trace of guilt, bunched his face muscles together like he was bracing for a right cross.

'What are you trying to say? I don't get it.' Words tumbled out. 'Isn't a man entitled to take a break from everything now and again? Tezza's worked non-stop for years. Perhaps he just hit the wall, decided to have a rest.'

Jack helped himself to a green grape from a crystal bowl. 'Yes, he's entitled to do whatever he wants. Free country. Only problem is, he's a creature of habit. For him to go AWOL without telling anyone, well, that's hard for me to believe.'

'Believe what you want. I don't know nothing about it.'

Another grape down the gullet. 'Have you been worried about him?'

'Yeah.' The response was too eager. 'Of course. We're like that.' Sharpe crossed gnarled middle finger over crooked forefinger. 'Least we used to be.'

'So if we check phone records, we'll see you've tried to call him to see what's up, yeah?'

'I'm not a big phone user. If you check you'll see I hardly make any calls.

Once a month to me mum down in Brisbane, if that.' Sharpe stood, shoved his chair back under the table. 'Now, if you're finished, I'd like to go for a run.'

In his peripheral vision, Jack noticed a bright graphic pop up on the TV screen. 'Wait a second. You're going to want to see this.' This will shake the bastard up. 'Where's your remote control?'

Sharpe nodded at a coffee table covered in men's health magazines, DVDs of UFC highlight packages, and a chunky universal remote. Jack picked it up, boosted the sound almost to cinema volume.

'This'll save me some explaining, although I may have to clarify.'

What followed on the screen was a laughably corny and factually inaccurate interview between Holly Maguire and the sell-out opportunist, Bruce Walker. As it progressed, Jack watched Sharpe's expression shift more often than his ex-wife changed her mind. When the image of the mangled body flashed for a moment on the screen, Sharpe flinched, then seemed to make a conscious effort to look calm. The story came to an end. *Police will be giving a press conference tomorrow with further details. Next up...* When Jack looked away from the TV and back to Sharpe, the man sat slumped in a chair, face buried in his hands.

'This is...fuck...I can't believe it.' Sharpe spoke behind his hands.

'Isn't it awful. Fancy the champ being murdered like that.'

'Hang on. They said it was a crocodile attack. The witness...'

'He's telling porkies, Danny. Owen Kennedy was murdered, as you'll learn if you check other news sources that tell the truth. Plus, I'm telling you. And I'm the one running the investigation, so there's that.'

'Oh my God! Who could have killed him? This is fucking terrible!' The shock was contrived, Jack felt it in his gut.

'But you gotta admit, the croc version's more interesting to the viewers, right?'

'If you say so.' Sharpe laid his hands flat on the table, his eyes darted about like a cocaine addict who can't remember where the stash is.

Now was the time to mention what Jack observed within the first minute of meeting Sharpe.

'Danny, I notice you're wearing a chunky bit of bling there.' Jack gestured with his head.

The hands slid away slowly, disappeared under the table. Sharpe's eyes bulged like a cornered possum with hyperthyroidism. 'What?'

'I've been doing a bit of research. The ring. Where'd you get it?'

'Huh?'

'Maybe it's me, but it looks exactly like one the late Owen Kennedy won for knocking you the fuck out when you unsuccessfully challenged him for the title last year.'

'It's a replica. I...'

Jack was on his feet in a flash, cable tie handcuffs at the ready. 'Stand up and put your hands behind your back, please.'

'Excuse me?'

'You heard me.'

Sharpe leapt to his feet, shaped up with fists bunched. 'You know I could knock you out cold!' Spit flew from his lips.

Jack grabbed the Glock from his belt, pointed it directly at Sharpe's top lip. 'Don't push me, dickhead. Drop to your knees and slowly lie face down on the floor. That's a good boy. Now put your hands behind your back.' Jack slipped the gun back in its holster. The soft click of the plastic cuffs snapping shut sounded sweet to Jack's ears. This was the most fun he'd had since transferring to Yorkville.

'What's happening?' Hauled back to his feet, Sharpe now looked like a frightened little boy in an overgrown body.

'I'm arresting you on suspicion of the murder of Owen Kennedy, you have the right to...stand still dammit.' Sharpe wriggled hard, momentarily loosened himself from Jack's behind-the-back grip.

'Let me go,' Sharpe cried. 'I'm fucking innocent.' The suspect dipped his right shoulder and drove hard into Jack's side. The DS stumbled for a second, regained his footing, karate chopped Sharpe in the throat.

'Sorry, sunshine.' Jack leaned over the writhing and gagging figure on the floor. 'Behave yourself and I won't have to do that again. Let's go.'

Chapter 11

In the stark-white interview room, Jack sat directly opposite the suspect. Steel table and chairs, one door with a small square window at eye level. Taylor took up position in a corner, legs crossed and a spiral notebook perched on her lap. Danny Sharpe's laboured breathing blended with the relentless ticking of the wall clock. The man was more out of puff than he'd be at the end of a ten-round fight. Then again, being arrested does mess with a person's vital signs. The red face and sweat pouring off Sharpe told Jack the detainee's blood pressure and body temperature would be abnormal too. Perfect for a grilling.

Jack pressed a button on the desk that activated a camera recording the interview. 'Tuesday, November 3. Yorkville CIB, Detective Sergeant Jack Lisbon and Detective Constable Claudia Taylor in attendance with Danny Sharpe, time 19:45. The suspect is being questioned in relation to the murder of Owen Kennedy.' He recited more standard palaver, then asked the suspect to confirm he'd been read his rights.

'Not properly.' Sharpe's burly arms were folded across his chest, head angled back. 'As it happens, I was subjected to police brutality and I'd like to make an official complaint.'

'Don't make me laugh. DC Taylor, does Mr Sharpe here, a professional cage fighter, look like he's capable of defending himself against me, a middle aged man who spends most of his day behind a desk?'

'Is this a trick question?' Taylor arched an eyebrow. 'Of course he does.'

'He pulled a gun on me.' Sharpe snarled.

'Did I shoot you?'

'Huh?'

'I'll repeat the question for the benefit of the recording.'

'What?'

'Oh dear, I think you've taken too many knocks to the head, sunshine. I said, did I shoot you? DC Taylor, does the suspect appear to have been shot?'

'I'm no expert, but I'd say no.'

'He hit me in the throat while I was handcuffed.'

'DC Taylor, do you see any marks on Mr Sharpe's neck, apart from some tattoos of questionable artistic merit? Is he experiencing breathing or speech problems?'

'Not that I can see or hear.'

'Do you want me to call you a doctor? If you want to make a complaint about your arrest, be my guest.' Jack knew the tap on the throat he gave Sharpe would have no lasting effects, no bruising.

'No, but I want a lawyer. I ain't answering any more questions until I get one.'

'What's your lawyer's name?' Jack pulled out his mobile. 'I'll give them a call now.'

'I haven't got one. Youse have to give me one. It's my right.'

Jack laughed. 'Sunshine, it's not that simple. You have to qualify financially for legal aide. By the looks of your comfortable flat, you'd be ineligible. What kind of car do you drive?'

'A BMW.'

'Yeah, no legal aid for you.'

'It's 10 years old, not a new one. What's that got to do with it anyway?'

'Limited resources. Only poor folk get free legal representation. You can call a lawyer from the yellow pages if you like, but it's a Forrest Gump proposition, you never know what you're gonna get. You might pay a packet to a mouthpiece and still go to prison. In my opinion, that's the likely outcome anyway.'

'Shit, shit, shit. Tezza usually handles all this stuff for me.' Sharpe's distress reminded Jack of a road accident victim about to go into shock. 'What am I gonna do?'

'Your best option is to answer our questions honestly,' said Taylor, jotting something down. 'If you're innocent and you tell us the truth, why do you need a lawyer?'

'To make sure youse don't pull any tricks. I don't trust either of you fuckers.'

'Language, Danny, please.' Jack rubbed a hand through his bristly hair. Sharpe wasn't going to put his hand up for the murder without some fancy detective footwork. Jack sometimes yearned for the good old days when there were no cameras, when you could work over a villain's stomach with a sledge hammer and a pillow until they confessed. A bit of physical persuasion saved hours of useless investigations. These days, sadly, the bad guys had more rights than the victims. 'And that's another wrinkle in the story, innit? A question we'd all like the answer to. Where the hell is Terry Bartlett?'

'No idea, mate. I've told you all I'm going to say. Gimme the bloody phone book.'

Jack buzzed the duty Sergeant and requested a physical copy of the Yellow Pages. Sharpe's flushed face got redder and redder as he spent ten minutes ringing law firms, every call going to voicemail. He hung up on all of them, garnished with a side order of profanity, dialled the next number. Finally, he got through to a live person. Sharpe had the volume of his mobile up and the entire conversation was loud enough for Jack and Taylor to earwig without straining. The firm, fortunately, had a chirpy female lawyer working back late after business hours. Sharpe said he was desperate and could afford their fee. He'd only need their services once because the cops would soon figure out they'd got the wrong man. Unfortunately, the woman on the other end of the phone wasn't a specialist criminal lawyer and none of her colleagues could assist after hours. The best Sharpe could hope for was for someone to attend an interview with him in the morning. The police would have to let Sharpe go soon because they couldn't detain people for prolonged periods without charging them.

'So, your lot will help me?' Sharpe's voice as he barked into the phone had more hope in it than a cancer patient asking about their scan results. 'Great. I'll call you as soon as I find out the interview time.' He placed the phone in his pocket, stood with his hand extended. 'Right, take me home officers and I'll be back in the morning.'

'This is murder we're talking about, Mr Sharpe, not jay walking,' said Taylor, looking up from her notebook. 'No, I'm afraid you'll have to spend the night in the cells here at the station.'

'But you haven't charged me with anything.' Tiny tears welled in the corners of the tough fighter's eyes. 'You don't have the right to keep me here without evidence. The lady from the lawyers said you can only hold me for eight hours, and I've already been here for...' He glanced up at the clock. 'Jesus, over four.'

'We already applied to the magistrate to have that period extended and, lucky for us and not so much for you, the request has been granted.' Jack grinned broadly. 'You'll be enjoying a lock-up breakfast. Got any dietary requirements, Danny? Vegan, perhaps?'

'Fuck you! The lawyer I just spoke to said...'

'I don't give a monkey's what the lawyer said,' Jack growled. 'I have legitimate concerns you're gonna do a runner in that 10-year-old BMW of yours. I'm terminating the interview now at...21:16 hours. We'll resume tomorrow morning.' Jack switched off the camera. 'I want you to do one more thing for me before the nice uniformed officer takes you to your cell.'

'What?'

'Hand over the ring.'

Jack called into Dave's bar after the interview with Sharpe. He didn't know why, it was like the car turned into the entrance all by itself. As soon as he stepped into the airconditioned comfort of the lounge bar, the urge to drink hit strong. He made his way to the exact seat he'd occupied last time, eyed the top shelf bottles. He could start off gently, just half a nip. Maybe that would be enough. If he progressed to a second, that would be his limit. A muddled head on the resumption of questioning Danny Sharpe tomorrow would be a bad idea. He beckoned to Dave as the barman finished serving cocktails to a yuppie couple. They wore elegant clothes you'd expect to see at the ballet or opera, not a Yorkville bar on a Tuesday night.

'Good to see you back again, Jack.' Dave winked.

'Likewise.'

'Must have been my sparkling company, hey?'

'Yeah, that's it.' Jack placed his phone and wallet on the bar.

'I knew it.' Another wink. 'What can I get you?'

'Bundy rum and a coke.'

'In the same glass? That's the way most people ask for it.'

'Nah. Keep 'em separated, as The Offspring said.'

'Sorry?'

Surely the song wasn't that old. 'Never mind, sunshine.' Jack gave a weak smile.

Dave returned with both beverages, placed them with exaggerated reverence on coasters. 'Want to watch the sports channel? I remember you enjoying the fights last time you were here. There's a ripper from the archives tonight.'

'Sure, why not.' Jack sipped the coke slowly, watched kaleidoscopic colours dance in the ice cubes. Not MMA this time, tonight it was boxing. A replay of the 2017 WBO welterweight title fight when Australia's Jeff Horn defeated reigning world champ Filipino Manny Pacquiao. A close bout with pundits divided over who should have been declared the winner. Either way, it was a great day for three reasons. The local boy stole the crown from the champ, he did it on home soil in Brisbane, and Jack was at the match in a seat with a prime view of the action. Try as he might, Jack was unable to conjure the excitement of the live match and drove home with one 10 oz coke under his belt and a Bundy Rum on melting ice left on the bar.

It had been a long day. No work out apart from a friendly tussle with a murder suspect. Although he played it cool with Sharpe, the encounter got Jack's adrenalin pumping. If it hadn't been for the Glock, no doubt he'd be eating through a straw for the next couple of weeks. Still, a solo workout was in order.

No weights, just a run.

At 22:55, he strapped on a jogging headlamp and hit the deserted streets.

Still humid after the recent rainfalls, slick puddles glistened on black asphalt under the filtered streetlights. Cane toads croaked their grumpy, endless chorus as he found his groove, slipped into a rhythmical pattern. No buds in the ears, no music to accompany the run tonight. Only the sounds of nature, even if that was an imported pest no one could get rid of. *A bit like me.* Jack smiled at the comparison. A life of hard knocks and setbacks wouldn't kill him. He'd toughen up and survive, as the hunted and persecuted cane toad had done. Flourished despite all efforts to eradicate it.

Another two blocks and he turned for the return leg. The familiar rabid barking of a protective German shepherd let him know home was around the corner. Up the elevator. Stretches on the small balcony. Wipe down. Shower. Couch. TV.

Nearly midnight, tired as a dog, sleep was an unfulfilled wish.

The plan was to reinterview Sharpe tomorrow as soon as the suspect's brief arrived. It'd be after the legally allowed holding time, and Sharpe's new lawyer could make waves if they were on the ball. He grabbed his mobile, speed dialled Taylor. He expected her not to answer at this hour, and if she did, she'd probably be mightily pissed off. She picked up, but her voice was surprisingly calm, almost soothing.

'What is it Jack? I was in the middle of a nice dream.'

'Was I in it?'

'I said a *nice* dream.'

'Ha ha.'

'So, do you have a good reason for disturbing me after midnight?'

'This thing with Sharpe in the lockup. It's got me worried. If the lawyer he's contacted doesn't get there nice and early, we'll be in breach of holding him in custody too long.'

'So we let him go.'

'Are you serious?'

'Absolutely. We drive him home in cuffs, take the cuffs off, make him a cuppa, then rearrest him.'

'On what grounds?'

'Stealing Kennedy's ring.'

'You're a genius, Claudia.'

'I know. But something tells me you might have had the same idea.'

'Maybe.'

'Maybe nothing. Good night, Jack.'

Chapter 12

Jack pulled up a plastic chair next to Batista, looking resplendent in his dress uniform. Taylor sat on the other side, all business and sporting a yellow scrunchie. She'd told Jack the significance of the colour but he'd since forgotten. Before them sat Yorkville's finest media representatives. Holly Maguire was first to speak after the Inspector made the introductions.

'Inspector Batista, what progress have you made in the investigation into the murder of Owen Kennedy. The public are looking for answers but getting nothing from the police.'

'If I may, sir?' Jack shot Batista an arched eyebrow. The boss nodded. 'Thanks for your question, Holly. I'm pleased to say we have someone in custody who is assisting us with our enquiries. I'd also like to add that all crocodiles have been eliminated as suspects.'

Uproarious laughter and clapping bounced off the walls of the small media room. No doubt Maguire's channel would edit that bit out. The rival channel certainly would not.

'Is it Danny Sharpe?' snapped Johnno Peroni before a red-faced Maguire could recover from the jibe.

'Yes. However at this stage he is not officially charged with murder.' Jack chose not to add Sharpe would be charged with theft and interfering with a corpse. He hated press conferences and couldn't wait for the show to be over.

More questions about potential suspects and motives were lobbed at them and fielded by Batista, who fudged and deflected with great skill.

A young reporter from the Yorkville Times asked the last question. 'Have you made any headway into the disappearance of Terry Bartlett?'

The Inspector touched Taylor on the wrist and squeezed softly. 'Yes,' said Taylor flatly.

'Can you elaborate on that?'

'No. However, we would like anyone with information to get in touch with us as a matter of urgency.'

'So you haven't made any headway?'

Batista coughed into his fist and tapped the microphone. 'I'm afraid that will be all for today, ladies and gentlemen. As and when more facts come to light we'll let you know via press release. When charges are brought for murder, we'll call another press conference.'

On the smoking landing after the media had packed up and gone, Jack and Batista agreed the briefing had gone better than expected. They particularly looked forward to tuning into Channel 11's news bulletin to savour Maguire's humiliation.

DC Taylor was waiting for Jack in the interview room. She wasn't alone. Seated opposite her was Danny Sharpe, still in his singlet, shorts and flip-flops and smelling like he could do with a long shower. Next to him sat a jittery bespectacled female in a navy blue pants suit. The eleventh-hour brief's attire reminded Jack of Hillary Clinton in the 1990s. She even resembled the ex First Lady in younger years, except her tousled hair tended more towards ginger than blonde. Her highly mobile features hinted the young woman was low on experience and high on enthusiasm.

Taylor made some adjustments to the camera facing the interviewee and his off-the-rack representative. Jack made preliminary remarks regarding the continuation of Sharpe's questioning, introduced himself and DC Taylor, indicated for the lawyer to do the same.

'My name is Denise Hutchison, of Chapman, Kinberg and Associates. I've been engaged to represent Mr Sharpe. I'm not going to mince my words, officers. I demand you release him immediately.'

'Do you now?' Jack rolled up his shirt sleeves as leaned forward in his seat.

'I certainly do. According to the record of yesterday's interview, Mr Sharpe was arrested at his home and has been held in custody for more than 13 hours. He tells me you used violence against him, which I shall be bringing up at a later stage if he decides to pursue the matter after you release him. Even considering the magistrate's extension, you have abused your authority, as well as Mr Sharpe. I insist–'

'Which is it?' said Jack, leaning back in his chair, hands interlocked behind his head.

'Pardon?'

'Has he been held in custody for that time, or are you including the time from arrest until now?'

'What's the difference?'

'You see, I arrested him more than 13 hours ago, that's true. But he's been here, *held in custody in a cell*, for less than 12 hours.'

'That's pointless semantics. I'm pretty sure the definition means from the moment of arrest and includes time in transit and so on.' The lawyer didn't look the officers in the eye, kept scrawling on a legal pad.

'*Pretty sure?* Geez, Danny. If this is the type of legal representation you're banking your freedom on, I wish you the best of luck, mate.' Jack twirled a pencil in his hand. 'But let's play it your way, Ms Hutchinson.' Jack stood, gestured towards the door. 'Danny, you're free to go.'

'Really?' Sharpe exchanged a look with the lawyer.

'Sure. Only we're going to follow you home and re-arrest you when you get there.' Jack paused, inviting the question he knew must follow.

'Youse never charged me with murder like you was threatening. You're full of shit. What ya gonna arrest me for?'

Jack placed the championship ring on the table with a flourish. 'For theft, numb nuts. This little sucker's got Owen Kennedy's DNA all over it. You're not gonna be such a tough guy in prison. There are bigger and badder men than you inside. Some of them would love to get to know you, try their luck, if you get my drift.'

'I'm not scared of no one. Anyway, possession is nine tenths of the law,' Sharpe said hopefully.

'Not when the stolen object's got the other man's fucking name etched into it!' Jack threw his hands up in the air. 'You're done, son. Bang to rights. You really are a dumb fuck.'

A look of horror passed over the lawyer's face. She turned to Sharpe. 'You didn't mention this to me'.

He shrugged. 'That's not what they brought me in for.'

'There's really no arguing this one, Danny.' Taylor grabbed at her scrunchie. 'You'll likely be held on remand until the matter goes to court.'

'What, for allegedly stealing a bloody ring?' said Hutchinson.

'I'm going to tell the DPP we believe your client lifted the ring from a dead body,' said Jack. 'So that's at least interference with a corpse, and high suspicion of involvement in the murder of Owen Kennedy. Plus motive to get rid of his number one rival, the only thing between him and the title.'

'You've got to be kidding!' Hutchinson slapped a hand on the table, any residual timidity gone. 'You arrest my client on suspicion of murder with zero evidence, can't charge him for it, so you downgrade it to theft of a bit of novelty man-jewellery.' She picked up the ring, analysed it from a few angles, put it down again dismissively. 'That's the strategy is it? Descending order of seriousness. What next? Illegal parking?'

Taylor spun a piece of paper around. 'Look at this. Estimated value of the ring. Read it out loud.'

'Please, don't turn this into a circus.' Hutchinson looked at Taylor while resting a hand on Sharpe's wrist. 'Don't pay attention to this nonsense. You'll be out of here soon.'

'How much?' said Sharpe as the lawyer glared at him. 'What's it worth?'

'Between $4500 and $5000.' Jack whispered for extra gravitas. 'That's a conservative estimate based on its composition. The fact it belongs to an MMA champion – or should I say belonged to – would make it even more valuable. Once the investigation into Owen Kennedy's death is concluded, it'll be returned to the deceased's next of kin in Western Australia.'

'You can't prove I stole it. Owen gave it to me as a present.'

The peel of laughter from Jack's wide-open mouth made Taylor shrink into her body. 'You're in the wrong profession, Danny. Comedy's your calling, sunshine. The only lasting gift Kennedy gave you was the unnatural angle your nose is pointing at.'

'Whatever.' Neither Danny nor his mouthpiece found any humour in Jack's observation. Taylor smiled impishly. 'Anyway, I'm saying nothin' more to you bastards.'

Jack shuffled papers like a news anchor. 'Is that your final word?'

The suspect nodded twice.

'Now,' said Hutchinson. 'Either charge my client with theft or let him go. It's clear he doesn't want to answer any more questions.'

'Not a smart idea to call my bluff, Ms Hutchinson. Daniel Lloyd Sharpe, you are hereby charged with stealing Owen Kennedy's championship ring.' Jack made sure to read the man his rights comma perfect. No mistakes, no room for comeback later. 'Interview concluded at 10:43.' He buzzed an intercom. 'Could someone come and take this clown to his cell?'

'Don't worry.' Hutchinson placed a hand on Sharpe's shoulder. Perhaps Jack was imagining it, but he thought he detected a dreamy lust in her eyes as she touched the brawler's muscled flesh. He'd heard of those nerdy types with a hidden wild side. Jack had to admit to himself that he found her dead attractive. In other circumstances he himself might even muster the courage to ask her on a date. 'I'll make sure we get you out of here.' She leaned in and whispered something to Sharpe, whose face brightened a fraction. She stood, tucked a briefcase under her arm. 'I know when a person's innocent. This is going to blow up in your faces, big time, detectives.'

'I'll give you and your client some time now to get started on a defense.' Jack stood, threw on his jacket. 'We'll arrange for your transfer to Yorkville jail pending trial.'

Sharpe said nothing; the thought of going to a real prison seemed to have removed his power of speech. Hutchinson wrote something on a legal pad and said without emotion, 'Sure.'

A uniformed officer knocked, entered the room, escorted Sharpe away with Hutchinson hot on the detainee's heels. Such was her haste she almost tripped up on the back of his flip-flops.

'What did you make of the interrogation?' Inspector Batista exhaled a plume of smoke. He and Jack stood on a small square landing overlooking the back parking lot, the station's traditional spot for a quiet chat and a cigarette.

Jack shuffled closer to the boss. Batista puffed hard and Jack was keen to get some of the second-hand smoke into his nostrils. Sucking lozenges was a poor alternative to the real thing but Jack would make no compromises on his quitting journey. Not in front of the boss, anyway. 'The lawyer was a surprise package. Came over all demure and uncertain then fired up when we got serious about the stealing charge.'

'You got that right.' As with all major interviews, the Inspector had watched the show through the one-way mirror. 'You still think Sharpe's the killer?'

'I don't know, sir. He's certainly looking good for it. He's got a solid motive and I'm positive he took the ring from the body. How else did he get it?'

'Maybe Kennedy gave it to him, like Sharpe claimed.'

'No fucking way.' Jack scuffed his shoe. 'He's implicated, I'm just not sure how. I've cobbled together the framework of a case and passed the matter on to the Director of Public Prosecutions. We'll get the coroner to tell them the ring had to have been stolen. Meantime, we can dig harder to nail Sharpe for the murder.'

Batista pulled out his smokes, pointed the open packet at Jack who frowned at it. 'Sorry, I forgot you were giving up.'

'I've given up, sir.' As if to prove it, he stuffed a piece of nicotine gum in his mouth, starting chewing with exaggerated relish.

'Might explain your tetchiness.'

'Sorry?'

'You seem a bit out of sorts, lately.'

'No more than usual, boss, you know me. The grumpy English git.'

Batista chuckled. 'Yeah, that's you. Not sure I agree with your self-assessment, though. You were a bit out of line in there, particularly with the lawyer present.'

'Come off it, sir. Normal policing tactics. Make 'em uncomfortable so they reveal key information.'

'Listen.' Batista flicked ash into an empty coffee can. 'I'm aware you left the London Met in, shall we say, unusual circumstances.'

'Now, hang on a second. I resigned of my own free will.'

Batista waved his protest away. 'Don't bullshit me, Jack. I know you were asked to leave. I don't know all the details, and to be honest, I don't want to know. But you've acquitted yourself with distinction in Australia. Everyone remembers the bank robbery you foiled in Brisbane a couple of years ago.'

'Thanks, boss.' Jack looked away, felt his face blush. Yes, he'd single-handedly taken on two violent villains, killing one in the process. He was off duty and unarmed, so they made him out to be a hero. He even got a medal from the Queen. What nobody knew was the reason he was in the bank in the first place. Changing dirty money. He turned back to Batista. 'Any other copper would have done the same.'

'No they wouldn't. I know plenty who would've run a mile or frozen without a weapon on them. Be that as it may,' he tapped more ash into the can. 'it still can't excuse the language you used in the interview just now. Especially with his brief sitting there. You might think I'm a dinosaur, but I don't like profanity in front of women. Especially when they're fucking lawyers.' He smiled gently at his own joke. 'All this stuff's recorded, you can't be as cavalier as we were in the old days. As tempting as it is, you can't call people dumb fucks, even if they are.'

'Got it.' Jack stared at a patrol car nosing into the lot. Two uniformed constables inside were laughing their heads off. A handcuffed woman in dressing gown and curlers sitting in the back seat was not.

'Have you?'

'Yeah. No more calling villains dumb fucks.'

The Clash interrupted the conversation. Taylor.

Jack pressed the green button 'Hang on, Claudia. I'm putting you on loudspeaker. The Inspector's here.'

'You're not going to believe this.'

'What?'

'Andy Harlow's rocked up and he's mad as hell.'

Chapter 13

'What's all the ruckus?' Jack strode into the station's reception area, Batista half a step behind. The duty sergeant stood a metre behind the counter, probably trying to avoid a shower of spit.

'I demand to talk Danny!' Harlow, red faced, was yelling at Taylor, who stared back at him blankly. 'You have to release him. He's done nothing to deserve this, you fascists!'

Taylor flashed a look of frustration at the two cops. 'I've tried reasoning with him. I told him Sharpe's been charged with a serious offence, but he won't shut up.'

'And I won't stop until Danny's been freed. With a damn written apology.'

'My colleague is right, Mr Harlow. There's no point carrying on like this,' said Jack. 'He's hired himself a defense lawyer, so you may as well butt out. Let the legal process take its course.'

'Fuck that! He's fragile. If he stays locked up any longer he'll be mentally scarred for life.'

Batista took a step forward with a conciliatory smile, held out his hand. Harlow, eyes fluttering as the giant cop loomed before him, shook it reflexively.

'I'm Inspector Joe Batista. Please, come into my office. Detectives Lisbon and Taylor will accompany us. Hopefully we can put your mind at ease.' If ever there was a Wikipedia entry for "good cop", Batista's performance right now could score an entry as the perfect example. There was something hypnotic and calming about Batista's modulated baritone. When he needed to defuse a situation, a word or two was often enough. Jack envied the ability. His own typical response to aggression was to meet it with even more aggression. Often it worked, many times it failed.

As he and Taylor trailed Batista and Harlow into the Inspector's office, Jack made a quick assessment of the accused's second-string trainer. Late forties, 5'9" to 5'10" tall, 90 to 100 kg. A barrel stomach and perky man boobs under a mauve polo shirt spotted with sweat marks. Pink shaved head a pre-emptive strike against male pattern baldness. Too much cologne. On the end of powerful arms hung bunches of thick sausagey fingers. He walked on shiny R.M. Williams boots, legs apart, probably chafed thighs inside his too-small khaki chinos. Jack guessed Harlow was a bully at heart whose life-long mission was to make life miserable for anyone who stood in his way. He might've been a decent brawler in his younger days; even now the tree-trunk arms looked like they could do some serious damage to a face. Jack could imagine the thrill Harlow got every time the boy in his corner beat the crap out of an opponent. Bullying by proxy.

Batista closed the door gently, beckoned for Harlow to take a seat behind a wide teak desk. Jack and Taylor stood either side of Harlow, gave him no more than a metre of breathing space. The Inspector smiled again, but their guest was having none of it this time.

'Let's hurry up and get this farce over with,' Harlow barked. 'My client has anxiety issues, he'll go into meltdown imprisoned here.'

'As the Inspector told you,' said Taylor. 'Mr Sharpe has secured legal assistance – an excellent advocate, by the way. Rest assured we are treating him well. However he's about to be transferred to prison. As the duty sergeant must have told you, he's been charged with stealing while we continue our investigations into the murder of Owen Kennedy. We strongly suspect him for that, too.'

'He never killed no one. He couldn't.'

'Don't make me laugh, Mr...what was is again?' Jack squinted as if trying hard to remember the man's name.

'Harlow.' The man twisted in his seat and sneered at Jack. 'Andrew Harlow, but everyone calls me Andy.'

I'm sure that's not all they call you, Jack wanted to say but held his tongue. 'How did you know we were holding him?'

'He called me.' Harlow waved his mobile phone. 'You aren't too clever for a big-shot detective, are you?'

Jack folded his arms across his chest. 'Well, isn't that amazing. We've been calling your phone number for a while now. No answer. You hiding something, Andy?'

'What, ah, no. I never answer private numbers. Too many scammers out there.'

'We're not an effing call centre selling solar panels. Our number always shows. We've left several messages asking that you contact us urgently,' said Taylor.

'I'm not the one being investigated, here. I have no obligation to do anything you tell me.'

'No, that's right.' Batista played with a couple of paperclips, looped them and made a little chain. 'But avoiding us doesn't look good. We start to think you've got something to hide. Not only is your lad now charged with theft, your colleague Terry Bartlett's gone AWOL.'

'For heaven's sake. I've been on holiday in Sydney with the wife and kids, getting away from it all. We only flew back last night. Then I get this call this morning from Danny, tells me not only is Tezza missing, but the cops have arrested him and one of 'em even assaulted him. Would that be you?' Harlow glared at Jack.

'No one assaulted him. People imagine all kinds of stuff in stressful situations. Not a bruise on him. I'll tell you what, how about I take you in to see him? As far as I'm aware, his lawyer's still there. I'll leave the three of you to formulate your next move. You'd better come up with a good plan, otherwise Danny's going to prison for a long stretch.'

Harlow grunted something.

'I'll give you an hour,' said Jack. 'Then we can talk about Terry Bartlett.'

Before Harlow could respond, an orange light flashed on Batista's desk phone quickly followed by a loud ring.

'Hello?' Batista snatched at the phone. 'Sure. Just one second, the detectives working the case are here with me. Should I put you on loudspeaker? No?' A pause. He jotted a few words on a piece of paper. 'OK, thanks very much.' He looked up, lips tight in a flat line. 'Bad news.'

'What?'

'We've been told to let Sharpe go.'

'By whom?'

'The DPP. I'm afraid they've overturned your referral, DS Lisbon.'

'What the fuck! It's a bit early for them to be poking their head up, innit?' Jack's crows feet compressed tight.

'I'm not sure how, but that lawyer, what's her name...?'

'Denise Hutchinson,' said Taylor.

'She's got some clout,' Batista sighed. 'Apparently, with no legitimate owner of the ring–'

'He's fucking dead!' Jack slammed a fist on the table, rattling the chief's monogrammed coffee mug.

'If you'll let me finish. They tell me if there's no one pressing charges, we can't proceed. I should have seen this coming.'

Taylor shook her head. 'We all should have, but it's an unusual case. I can't blame Jack for trying.'

'Well I can.' Harlow was already on his feet. 'Take me to Danny. Now!'

Chapter 14

'I can't believe our number one suspect in a murder investigation walked away like that.' Jack slammed the Inspector's door behind him.

'Where's DC Taylor? I wanted her to hear this,' said Batista.

'She drew the short straw.' Meaning Jack had left the unwanted job to her. 'She's dealing with the paperwork for Sharpe's discharge.'

'Fine, you can pass the message on. I just got an email back from our legal team. It seems the DPP *could* follow through against Sharpe if they wanted to. Technically, they don't require there to be a distressed victim to proceed with a prosecution.' Batista remained seated, untangling the paper-clip chain he'd made earlier.

'Is that so?' Jack was sure steam was coming out of his own ears.

'They have the discretion to do so, yes.'

'Then why don't they? Who's the person in charge I need to talk to?'

'Just let it rest, will you.' Batista couldn't hide the mild annoyance in his voice. 'Maybe it's not Sharpe after all and the gods are sending us a message. Look harder for the killer.'

'We're doing all we can, sir.'

'Glad to hear it. There've been more salacious stories in the media, saying we're incompetent. Once they get wind of our "wrongful" arrest and detention of Sharpe, they'll have a fucking field day.'

'Yes, sir.'

'We need to put this thing to bed. I don't want the State Commissioner of Police giving *me* a bollocking due to *your* overzealousness, do you understand me?'

'Is that even a word?'

'Of course it is.'

Jack closed one eye contemplatively. 'One thing strikes me as odd. If Sharpe's the real owner of the ring, like he claims, why hasn't he demanded we return it to him, huh? Silent admission of the bastard's guilt, if you ask me.'

'I'm not asking you.' Batista unbent a paperclip into a straight line, wiggled it until it broke in half.

'How about we get a warrant to search Sharpe's apartment?' Jack wiped a palm across his three o'clock shadow. 'I'm sure there's something there to tie him to everything.'

'His clever lawyer will be onto us for harassment.'

'Let her try. He remains a legitimate suspect in Kennedy's murder.'

'Very well. Call the magistrate and get a warrant. Make sure you cover all bases. Put in the application we're looking for forensic digital evidence likely to prove...I dunno, use your fertile imagination, Lisbon.'

'Yes, sir.' Jack popped a Nicorette in his mouth. He wasn't hopeful of finding conclusive evidence at Sharpe's flat, but a search was always a good place to start. Then a flash of inspiration. 'I'll say we're confident we'll uncover illicit drugs.' He failed to mention to Batista he still had the little yellow bottle he swiped from Terry Bartlett's place.

'Thanks for leaving me with that lot.' Taylor pouted, hands on hips

'Hmm?' Jack's eyes were rivetted to the text on his monitor. Filling out the warrant application required total concentration. So much ridiculous detail required. Make a mistake and the thing could get rejected. It was valuable time wasted he could be using more productively. Like putting more pressure on a bunch of people who were telling lies. People like Carl Masiker.

'I said thanks for making me deal with Sharpe and his mate. What a dodgy pair they are.'

The final full stop. 'Sorry? Oh yes. I apologise. Batista wanted me urgently, so–'

'Don't bullshit, Jack. You wriggled out of it nicely, you worm.'

'Why thank you,' he smiled. 'What a lovely compliment.' He hit the print button, asked Taylor to fetch him the form off the printer for him to sign. He then handed it straight back to her. 'Tell Wilson to run this over to the magistrate's office.'

'Can't I do that? I'm dying to get out of the office for a spell.'

'Sorry, no. I've got another job for you.'

'What?'

'Look here first.' He nodded at his computer screen. On it, a syndicated story proclaiming the bungling Yorkville Police had wrongfully arrested a local sporting legend on a trumped-up charge.

Taylor tut-tutted, pointed halfway down the screen and read aloud: '*Danny Sharpe's assistant trainer Andy Harlow intends to sue Yorkville Detective Sergeant Jack Lisbon for wrongful arrest and assault while restrained in handcuffs.* Holy shit. It's damage control time.'

'Exactly. Get a press release out there immediately denying all wrong-doing on our part.'

'Onto it.'

* * *

His arms felt heavy, legs leaden, he fought for each breath. His rib cage rose and fell more than a piano accordion at an Italian wedding as he sucked in the big ones. For the last fifteen minutes he'd been throwing combinations at the heavy bag, dancing around like Ali with itchy feet. Two seconds or less between punches, a fast, high-impact session.

Time for a spell.

Jack placed a small towel on the plastic seat; signs everywhere warned patrons the gym had high sanitary standards and if you wanted to continue using the facilities, you damn well better follow the rules. He flopped into the seat, spread his legs wide and tilted his head back, focused on the slowly spinning blades of the giant ceiling fans. Georgie McGrath's was the best no-frills garage in Yorkville. Plenty of free weights and machines, bare concrete floor, bags to punch to your heart's content, frayed leather skipping ropes that had done more rotations than the London Eye Ferris wheel. Sweat dripped from every pore and a prickly heat tore through his body. It felt like his blood was nearing the point where liquid turns to steam. The place had air conditioning, but the owner must be scrimping on power, because it barely made a difference. Jack cared little, though. Working out here was the equivalent of getting a free sauna.

He stood, re-strapped his hands, winding the long strips on with care. No twists or lumps, nice and flat. Next, the white tape that combined with the cloth wraps to keep his fists aligned to deliver maximum wallop. Finally, the trusty black 16 oz Everlast gloves.

Jack took up position arm's length from the heavy bag, spread his centre of gravity to achieve perfect balance. He took a deep breath and led out with a crunching left jab. That was Danny Sharpe's head. The warrant had been approved but the search turned up nothing. Sharpe was home and the man was ropeable but still sensible enough to keep his hands by his sides. Jack had been about to place the pill bottle in Sharpe's toilet cistern and magically "find" it when a pang of consciousness made him stop. He'd solve this case, but not that way.

A right cross that made the bag thwack drew admiring glances from other patrons. That was for the media in general, smug bitch Holly Maguire in particular. Making him out to be incompetent, someone who bashes suspects. He'd show her.

The bag had some momentum up, swung in a pendulous ellipse. He ducked to the right of the incoming bag, slipped an imaginary head punch. He transferred body weight forward and down, launched a thunderous combination of body rips into the guts of all the lying bastards who'd been through the doors of the station in the last couple of days. Covering up, hiding the truth. *Crack, crack, crack.* A flurry of right and left hooks, dedicated to the miserable miscreants he'd killed to make the world a better place. A vicious left to the gut of the late Alex Gallagher. In tight to the bag again, body rips to the armed robber he'd garrotted to death in a bank's computer room.

Jack threw deafening hammer strikes in time to his breathing, in and out like a busted compression hose. A matador finishing off the wounded bull. *Rip, rip, smack.*

The bag creaked on its chain, swung far to the left, nudged a fellow gym goer tapping away in the forest of heavy bags. Jack saw it hit the smaller, older man and knock him off balance. He waved an apology and the other guy accepted with a quick, timorous head nod. What was the man to do? Jack was in one of those moods where he could hammer nails into concrete with his own eyeball. Getting into an argument with him now would be suicidal.

One final onslaught, a combination of fifteen choreographed punches. The only thing he was grateful to Gallagher for, that attention to detail and technique. Exhausted now, Jack stepped back, chest heaving, legs and arms rubber. He felt the burn of a dozen eyes on him, envious of Jack's stamina, speed and power.

A litre of water down the throat in four gulps. Gloves off. Wraps off. Stretches. Shower.

Ten minutes from home his mobile lit up, unknown number. 'Yeah?'

Heavy breathing on the other end.

'Who is it? Stop wasting my time.'

'It's me, Andy Harlow.' The voice retained a modicum of its previous arrogance, but had gained an element of phoney bonhomie.

'What can I do you for, Mr Harlow?'

'There's something I want to tell you.' Jack now detected something else in the man's voice. Alcohol. Time to press. People with a skinful of booze were freer with their words. *In vino veritas* was a cliché but Jack knew it to be true. He'd been guilty of speaking his mind on subjects that were best left in the drawer, with disastrous results.

'Want to meet up for a drink?' It wasn't professional to question a witness under the influence, but what the hell. The investigation was stuck in quicksand and going under, so Jack ploughed on. 'My treat.'

'I'd love to, Detective Lisbon, but I'm about to turn in. It's been a long day. Calming down a prize fighter like Danny isn't easy. You blokes put an innocent man through hell.'

'So, what is it you want to talk about?' He gritted his teeth, dimmed the high beam for an oncoming car.

'Basically, to tell you the woman from the TV twisted my words. Half of what I said was left out and...anyway...she was right out of order.'

'Was she? I'm in a mind to take you and the media outlets to court for spreading lies about me.'

'Come on, Detective Lisbon. We both know Danny wasn't making up how you whacked him in the throat.'

'I won't dignify that with an answer, Mr Harlow. Lucky for you I ain't the litigious type.'

'Whassat mean?'

'Means I won't sue you for slandering my good name. Is that all you rang me for at this late hour?'

'Yeah, what else did you think? I was going to confess to something?' The sarcastic laugh that followed sent a chill down Jack's spine. Harlow knew more than he cared to admit.

'Of course not. I thought you might know something about Terry.'

'I wish I did.'

'Listen.' *Play to his vanity.* 'How about you come down to the station and help us with our enquiries. Perhaps there's a detail you think is unimportant but could help us find him. You'd know Terry better than most people we've spoken to. Even better than Danny.'

'That's true.'

'We've spoken to Carl Masiker, but, to be honest, he's proven to be worse than useless.'

'Not wrong there.' Jack heard the popping sound of a can being opened. 'Masiker's a fuckwit.'

'That's bit harsh, innit?'

'Nuh. The bloke's a fool. He couldn't organise a shit fight in a sewerage pit. Masiker inherited the money to buy that gym. He's nothing but a washed-up footballer. If it weren't for people like me bringing in the punters, he'd go under.'

One more block and Jack was turning into his cul-de-sac street. 'I don't doubt it. So you'll come into the station tomorrow for a chat?'

'Love to, mate, but I'm real busy. I've gotta train Danny extra hard now.'

'Really? He'd be a shoo-in for the title now Kennedy's dead, wouldn't he?'

'You'd think so, wouldn't ya? But his headspace is a rubbish tip at the moment. Can't seem to focus on anything. He might've hated Owen in the ring, but his death has rattled him. Not to mention Terry going AWOL. So, no, he's no certainty. There's another bloke primed to step up. Young Aboriginal fighter.'

Jack recalled the flashing fists, the thunderclap smack as the lad's gloves connected with his poor sparring partner's body. 'I think I saw him doing his stuff at The Iron Horse.'

'Yep.' The glug of more alcohol disappearing down Harlow's neck. 'That woulda been Jeremy Clifford.'

Charlie Bartlett said his partner's name was Jeremy. Could it possibly be him? Surely not. 'Is he...ah...you know, a...'

Harlow burst out laughing. 'So you've heard? Yeah, he's gay. Not many come out in this caper. But it's worked out well for Jeremy. All that bullying in his life has turned him into an absolute beast in the ring.'

'Is it true he's partnered with–'

'Charlie Bartlett? Yep. It's true.'

'Who trains him?'

'No one at this point. But I'm sure Vince Armbruster would give him a go.'

Wheels spun in Jack's head. Could this be a possible motive? Get Owen out of the way so Jeremy could have a crack at the title. From what Jack remembered, the kid looked like he could knock Danny – or anyone – into next year. Jack flicked on the indicator to make the last turn. 'When can you make it to–'

Too late.

Harlow had hung up.

Chapter 15

The prawns seemed to stare at Jack with their beady black eyes. Dead eyes, like Owen Kennedy's. He averted his gaze from his meal, stared out to sea for a moment, watched the trawlers docking. Deckhands scurried about the long wooden pier, secured lines to bollards, carted ice-packed foam boxes from vessels to refrigerated trucks. The restaurant deck was crowded with animated diners. Thank God for the water mister and the sailcloth providing shade because the sun was baking everything without mercy under a cloudless sky.

Taylor had made the booking at the last minute, but the obliging owner always made sure Yorkville's finest got seats with the best views of the Pacific Ocean. Jack readdressed his lunch, picked at the prawns with a fork. He pushed them all to one side, harpooned a piece of avocado instead. He absently shovelled it into his mouth and swallowed with barely a chew.

'You on one of those fad diets again, Jack?'

'Huh?'

'You paid top dollar for the satay garlic prawns, and all you've eaten is a couple of lettuce leaves, half a tomato and a piece of avocado.'

'It's these bloody crustaceans looking at me, I can't stand it.' Jack raised his glass of mineral water, downed half and smacked his lips. 'Think I'll order a rump steak instead.'

Taylor grabbed a shrimp from his plate, deftly separated the head from the body, squeezed the pink meat out. 'See? No critters' eyes to deal with. Want me to peel the rest of them for you?'

'Why not. And while you're at it, can you peel some layers of crap from the case? I'm buggered if I know what to make of it all.'

Taylor took a bite of schnitzel and rested her cutlery. 'I know what you mean. Just when Sharpe looked good for the Kennedy murder, Andy comes into the frame looking suss as hell.'

'He does.' Jack nodded. 'Something's not right with him at all. His lack of concern about Terry Bartlett, then him calling me out of the blue, drunk, to apologise for giving an interview. I think he might've been taunting me in a roundabout way.'

'Did you call Holly Maguire to complain?'

'I gave her a piece of my mind but it was water off a duck's back to her.' Jack polished off the mineral water, pointed at his empty glass as a waiter strolled past. 'That woman's got half the town too scared to go near the water's edge with the crocodile beat-up. Social media's buzzing with talk of police brutality focused on yours truly. Honest, Claudia, I barely tapped him.'

Taylor's eyes blazed. 'You what? Jack, you swore you never touched him.'

'The tiny little pat on the neck I gave him wouldn't have hurt a sparrow. The guy's an MMA fighter, for heaven's sake. Anyway, Batista's got my back, so I'm not fazed.'

Taylor took a sip of shimmering honey-gold chardonnay. 'I agree, it's bizarre Harlow isn't more worried about Bartlett. Masiker told me they had a strong bond, been working together for years.'

'Yeah, well, me and my ex fit those criteria, and I'm sure she would've had me murdered if she'd been given the chance and immunity from prosecution.'

A squawking seagull alighted on the railing beside Jack's head, Taylor shooed it away with a linen napkin.

'Have you spoken further with Armbruster?' Jack smiled as a pony-tailed waiter with hideous black ear tunnels brought him another drink. He took the opportunity to order a steak, rare, with steamed broccoli. An athlete's meal. 'The old bloke must be upset.'

'He's beyond devastated. I was able to visit him in the hospital. I could barely get a coherent word out of him. He did manage to tell me Kennedy's parents are overwhelmed with grief.'

Jack shook his head slowly. 'I can definitely confirm that. That was the worst phone call I've had to make since I moved up here to Yorkville.'

'Yeah. That's never fun. When's the funeral?'

'Next Monday. Forensics reckon they've got all they can from the body, so there's no objections about putting Kennedy to rest ASAP. He's going to be sent over to Perth Friday night.'

'What about the ring?'

'It's going with him in a separate container.'

They fell silent for a while, finished their meals and ordered coffees.

'You know,' said Taylor, stirring sugar. 'Terry's disappearance is starting to look more and more like foul play.'

'Agreed. Let's give it one more big push.'

'What are you thinking?'

'It's close to a week now, and no leads. Radio silence from all the people most likely to know where Bartlett is. The second sweep of his house found shitloads of drugs in the hollowed out weights, but there's no way of figuring out their origin. I'll talk Batista into securing more resources. From Brisbane if we have to.'

'What are you going to ask him for?' She chewed an after-dinner mint, screwed up the stubborn foil wrapper which refused to stay folded.

'Another land search. Remember where we found Kennedy? Eight kilometres from the abandoned car. If the cases are linked, and there's no bloody way they aren't, we need to cover at least that radius. Helicopters, cadaver dogs, whatever we can muster.'

'Jack. You realise this isn't the English countryside, right? Much of that terrain is impenetrable rainforest.'

'We have to try. I'm going to put in an official request with the Inspector. Apart from further annoying people we've already annoyed the shit out of, I'm not sure what else we can do.'

Chapter 16

Jack flicked on his PC, typed the password. Skye's birthday and his shoe size. Not the most original or secure, but he was yet to be hacked. In his inbox sat an email from Nathan at digital forensics addressed to him, cc to Taylor and the Inspector. A reply to his urgent request for another analysis of all the papers found in Bartlett's car. The subject line set his heart racing.

Subject: Matching phone number found

Hi Jack,

One of the scraps of paper you provided contained a smudged handwritten mobile phone number. We were sure it ended in 3, but one of our team suggested the digit could in fact be an 8. We ran the alternate number through the database and found it was registered to an Evan Zane. Please find a summary of his record attached. Hope this helps the inquiry.

Evan Zane's rap sheet boiled down to the following. Born in Melbourne, currently residing at 49 Tallis Street in the outlying Yorkville suburb of Lockyer. 38 years old, six prior convictions for using and dealing illegal substances, including cannabis, cocaine, methamphetamine, anabolic steroids and human growth hormone. Two priors for receiving stolen goods, one for break and enter. Total incarceration time of four years, seven months. Last convicted in 2015. Twice had restraining orders imposed, now lapsed. The accompanying recent photo showed a rat-faced man with a greasy jet-black mullet.

Jack longed for a timid, co-operative witness, but something told him Zane wasn't going to be fit the bill. In his mug shot, the little toe-rag radiated arrogance and defiance.

'Oi, Claudia,' Jack called a shade too loudly to Taylor, rivetted to her computer monitor only two desks away. 'Grab your shit. We're going for a wee drive.'

On the surface, the North Queensland suburb of Lockyer looked nothing like London's borough of Dagenham. Low set wooden houses instead of grimy tower blocks, gum trees instead of concrete. But at their core, they shared the same desperation and neglect.

There was no sign of outside air conditioning units at any of the addresses on Tallis Street. The residents were either making do with electric fans or leaving windows open and hoping for the best. At the peak of this stinking hot summer, that would be a forlorn hope. Drug or alcohol-induced sleep would get many through the most humid and cloying and mosquito-infested of summer nights.

The properties in Tallis Street were so rundown it was hard to credit people lived in them. The rents were dirt cheap for the majority of houses, mostly government owned. A handful of tidier private dwellings would have charged higher rents, but not by much. Some residents had struck the jackpot; they got to live in abandoned digs, the most uninhabitable of the lot, rent free.

Jack took a deep breath and pounded on the door of number 49 Tallis Street. Paint was peeling off it in strips, cracks crazed the cobwebbed square of translucent glass at the top of the door. No answer after a long thirty seconds in the boiling heat. He pressed his ear to the warm pane. Silence inside. Peered through the keyhole. No movement.

'Check around the back, Claudia.' He nodded towards the side of the house. 'And be careful. This neighbourhood doesn't look too safe. Christ knows what lowlifes are lurking inside this shithole.'

'Relax, Jack. I can handle myself.' Taylor shook her head dismissively and trotted down the short flight of rotting wooden stairs. Jack watched her tread carefully in the unkempt grass before she disappeared around the southwest corner of the nondescript weatherboarder. He remembered snakes were active this time of year and felt a pang of guilt for sending her into the backyard jungle. Then again, the human vermin in the area were probably more dangerous to a person's health than the wildlife.

He gave three full-blooded fist pounds. Again no response. He cupped a hand to the keyhole and listened hard, not easy to do with a hundred species of insects making a racket in the surrounding bush. Was that the low hum of a radio or television set? A couple of kicks to the bottom of the door sent flakes of paint and lumps of putty flying. At last, the sound of shuffling footsteps. A thin wreck of a man who could have been anywhere between 25 and 45 stared at Jack, pupils the size of pinheads. Evan Zane.

'What the fuck.' The man scratched an armpit and yawned. 'You know what time it is, bro?'

'I ain't here to synchronise my watch with you, mate. Are you Evan Zane?'

'Who wants to know?'

'Yorkville Police CID. I'm Detective Sergeant Jack Lisbon.' He flashed his creds and gave the usual accidental-on-purpose glimpse of Glock. 'The woman standing right behind you is Detective Constable Claudia Taylor.'

Zane turned slowly, a blank expression on his pasty face, totally unsurprised someone had traversed the length of the house unchecked. He extended a hand to Taylor. She flinched when she clocked the smears of dirt on his palms and the filth under his nails. 'Not often a pretty copper sheila pays me a visit,' he wheezed through a smile that was more gap than tooth. 'Don't wanna shake me hand? Fine, suit yourself, you stuck-up bitch.'

'Watch your tongue, Zane, or I'll give you a slap. I'd ask if we could come in, but my colleague's making a face like she stepped in dogshit. I take it the joint's not too hygienic?'

'It's disgusting,' said Taylor. 'I was dodging all kinds of crap in there. Rotten food, dirty nappies, general filth. Would you mind?' Taylor gestured with her head for Zane to get the hell out of her way. He obliged with a shrug and a sidestep.

'I don't care what youse think. This is my house and I'll live the way I like.'

'And that's your prerogative.' Jack waited to see if the word registered with

Zane.

'Damn straight it's my prerogative.' Smarter than your average Yorkville junkie. 'Tell me what the hell you want and you can be on your way.'

'Put on a clean set of clothes, if you have any.' Taylor said, now next to Jack on the non-toxic side of the threshold. 'Better still, have a shower. We'll wait for you. Then you're going to accompany me and DS Lisbon to the station to answer some questions.'

'And if I tell youse to get fucked?'

'Oh, that's an easy one.' Jack pulled his handcuffs from his belt and dangled them under Zane's quivering nose. 'We arrest you for obstructing justice.'

'What?'

'You heard me. We found your mobile phone number on a scrap of paper you left in Terry Bartlett's abandoned car. We have reason to believe you can help us find a missing person. Your call.'

'I've never been in his car. This is bullshit.' Zane sniffed and rubbed his forearm along his septum.

'Not bullshit, mate. It's true. Either be a good responsible citizen for a change, or risk another stretch in prison. What's it to be?' said Jack.

'Oh Mary, mother of God. Give me five minutes and I'll be with you.' Zane's voice shook and his hands trembled. Jack's wish for a co-operative witness looked like it might be coming true.

Meek as a lamb, Evan Zane sat with his hands clasped together as if in silent prayer. There was less dirt under his cracked nails than before, but only a high-pressure cleaner would get the rest of it out. His cheeks had a just-scrubbed pink glow. He wore a cleanish pair of camo shorts and a button-up checked collared shirt that had more wrinkles than Jack's old Portuguese grandad. *He's trying, the poor sod, but it just ain't working*, thought Jack.

'Let's not muck about, hey, Evan?' Jack wanted this to be over quickly. The aromas coming from the man's body made both detectives wince. Whenever Zane turned slightly in his chair, a waft of stink reached their nostrils. Despite Zane's intentions to mask his BO, the deodorant product he'd applied perversely enhanced it.

'Yes, sir.'

'I appreciate the fact that you've not made a fuss about coming to the station.'

'You're welcome.' Zane blinked a couple of times.

Jack grabbed the underside of his chair and shuffled forward a few centimetres. Taylor sat in the corner of the interrogation room, legs crossed and a large notepad on her lap. Batista observed from behind the mirror.

'We're recording this conversation, but it's purely for protocol, okay? I assure you it's merely unofficial enquiries at this stage. You're not in any trouble. Do you understand?'

He nodded twice. 'Uh huh.'

'What do you know about the death of Owen Kennedy?'

Zane's eyes darted about. 'Nothing. Just what I seen on the telly 'n that.'

'I find that hard to believe.'

'What would I have to do with someone like him?'

'Owen was murdered, his rival trainer is Terry Bartlett, and your phone number was found in Bartlett's car. You don't have to be Einstein to see the link here, do you?'

'Well.' Zane scratched his knee with vigour. 'Maybe he just found the piece of paper.'

'No dice, champ,' said Jack. 'Not even a jury composed of certified idiots would believe that. You've got priors for dealing in substances that Bartlett's fighter copped a fine for taking. You've been selling to them, haven't you?'

'Them?'

'MMA fighters. Danny Sharpe. Maybe to others, weightlifters and bodybuilders. Why don't you admit it?'

'I ain't admitting nothin'.'

'Listen, Evan. If you can help us find Bartlett, we may decide not to proceed against you.'

'Proceed against me? I thought you said this was a friendly chat. Now you're making threats. I'd like to go now, if you don't mind.'

'Not so fast, Evan.' Taylor was now standing next to Jack, dropped a ziplock bag containing a white substance on the table. She turned on her mobile, showed Zane half a dozen photos she'd taken inside his house. Among the items was a bong full of brown water, two meth pipes and what looked like roaches in an seashell ashtray. 'Quite a collection, there, Evan. Did you have a party at your place last night?'

Zane frowned and pulled his head into his chest.

'Although we're investigating the murder of Owen Kennedy, at this point our focus is on finding Terry Bartlett,' said Jack. 'The living get priority over the dead. If we don't find him soon...we may even be too late.'

'How long's he been missin'?'

'Over a week.' Jack's pulse jumped, Zane was showing interest. 'And no one has any idea where he is or they don't want to tell us.'

'Right, right,' Zane said pensively. 'Yeah, youse have got reason to be worried I guess.'

'I'm going to be honest with you, Evan. We've seen your rap sheet, and it makes for interesting reading. Now we've got loads of physical evidence you're up to your old tricks. This is your one and only opportunity to save your arse from a custodial sentence.'

Jack could picture the wheels turning in Zane's head. To cooperate or not. He was almost on board, it wouldn't take much to tip him over the edge.

'What's with all the dirty nappies at your place?' said Taylor. 'You got a kid living with you?' said Taylor.

Jack smiled approvingly at his partner. This could be the clincher.

'Yeah, as it happens. Her mum's on parole and I offered to put them up 'cos no one else would take 'em in.'

'Are you the father?'

'Vicki tells me I am.' A hint of fatherly pride flashed in Zane's eyes.

'How old is the little girl?'

'Just over a year.'

'It wouldn't be nice for her dad to get locked up, now would it?' said Jack. 'Mum'd be out on the streets again, sleeping rough in the park. Soon after that her parole gets revoked and then she's in jail with baby snatched away by the Department of Child Safety. Adopted out to who knows what kind of people. Be an absolute tragedy for the kid.'

'Okay, okay! I'll co-operate.'

'Good lad.' Jack opened a dark blue manila folder, extracted a handful of large glossy photographs. The ones of potential suspects were lifted from online sources, added to the mix were mugshots of five random crims from the Yorkville CIB files. Like a card dealer at a casino, he flung them towards Zane one at a time.

'Cast your eyes over that lot. Tell us if you recognise any of them.'

Zane studied each photograph, uncertainty in his eyes, as if choosing the wrong one would see him sent to the execution chamber.

'I-I-I'm not sure I recognise any of these guys.'

'Not sure?' said Taylor.

Zane rocked back and forth, his whole face seemed to be break dancing at a hundred miles an hour.

'N-n-no.'

Jesus, he's having withdrawal from something, thought Jack.

'Come on, dammit!' Jack slammed his fist on the table.

'You don't understand.' The shock of Jack's fist slam sobered Zane. At least for now. 'I mix with some rough people. If I dob, I could end up in the billabong with the crocs.'

'Billabongs are home to freshwater crocodiles,' said Taylor. 'They're not known as maneaters. Jack here's the one you've got to worry about.'

'Whatever you reckon,' said Zane in a monotone. 'I'm putting my neck out for a bloke I don't even know.'

'Okay, Claudia. Read him his rights and arrest him.'

'Wait, wait, wait. I recognise this guy here.' Zane pointed at a photo in the middle of the pack.

'What's his name?'

'Andy something.'

'Last name.' Taylor demanded.

Zane scratched his head. 'Dunno, lemme think. Barlow...no, Harlow.'

'And why do you recognise him?'

'You promise not to arrest me for the...stuff at my place?'

'I promise.'

'I sold him some HGH and steroids.'

'How much?'

'Shitloads.'

'Ever sell to Danny Sharpe or Terry Bartlett?'

'Never had nothing to do with either of those guys. Were they in the photos you just showed me?'

Jack nodded.

'Then I woulda pointed to 'em wouldn't I?'

'I guess you would have.' Zane again proved he was no fool.

'When did you last sell to Andy Harlow?'

'End of October.'

'Just before Terry Bartlett disappeared,' said Taylor. 'Bit of a coincidence, don't you think?'

'So what?' Zane said, desperation back in his voice. 'No c-c-connection to me whatsoever. Youse are on a fishing trip.'

'It's called a fishing expedition, you muppet.' Jack tugged his lower lip, let Zane stew for a while. After thirty seconds Jack broke the silence with a blunt question. 'When did you last take a ride in Bartlett's car?'

'I've never been in his bloody car. Couldn't even tell you what kind it is.'

'It's a Mazda 6. This one.' Jack flipped over a photo of the abandoned vehicle *in situ*. 'Recognise it?'

'I never seen it in me life. I swear.'

'Then how do you explain the fact this was on the floor of Bartlett's car?' The note with Zane's phone number floated onto the table like an autumn leaf.

Zane shook his head. 'No idea.'

'Is that your handwriting? Take a close look. We can always get the calligraphy experts to analyse it.'

'Yeah, s'mine, I guess. Don't remember writing it, though. Me memory's not what it used to be. Listen, I'm not sure I can give youse much more. I identified Harlow. Can I go now?'

'Sure. But we'll be watching you,' Jack pointed a forefinger at Zane. 'I suggest you get a proper job, Evan. I'm not happy with drugs circulating in my community.'

'But you said–'

'Never mind what I said.' Jack buzzed the duty desk. 'Someone come and collect Mr Zane. He needs a ride home.'

Chapter 17

'He might be telling the truth.' Batista stared at his computer screen. 'He's a pathetic crook, but he's never told serious lies to the police. Says here in the file.'

'Don't believe everything you read, sir. Especially reports written by detectives.' Jack pulled on his elastic metal watch band.

'Not in this station, right Claudia?' Batista gave her a wink. 'Only facts in our reports.'

Taylor rolled her eyes. 'Sure.'

'Do we all agree it's highly probable Harlow was riding in Bartlett's car and it was him that dropped the paper with the phone number?' said Jack.

'That would seem to be the logical conclusion,' said Batista. 'We'd better get Harlow back in to explain himself.'

'How about we search his house,' said Taylor. 'We've got a witness telling us he sold drugs to him, the same drugs that Sharpe got banned for.'

'Let's not be too hasty.' Jack poured himself a glass of water from a carafe. 'We don't want to spook him. Besides, Zane's record may say he doesn't tell porkies, but it's a convicted drug dealer's word against Harlow's. As far as I'm aware, Harlow's clean. Not sure we'd get a warrant based on any statement from Zane.'

'Maybe Bartlett was involved in some kind of distribution role,' postulated Taylor. 'Perhaps his vehement opposition to drugs is a smokescreen?'

'I see where you're coming from,' said Jack. 'Yes, he had a proven drug cheat in his camp, and yes, we found a heap of illicit substances at Bartlett's house. But I believe his son's assessment.'

'Really? It seemed like they hated each other. At least Charlie hates his dad.'

'I'm not sure about that. I reckon Charlie's got some deep affection for his old man, despite what he did to Mrs Bartlett.'

'So how come Bartlett's number one client got caught?'

'Like Charlie said, it's a fit-up.'

'Who would do that? Owen Kennedy or his coach?'

'Trainer.'

'For heaven's sake, Jack! Does it matter?'

'No, sorry. I can be a pedantic git at times.'

'Ya think?'

'Sorry.'

'Anyway, Armbruster told me Owen enjoyed the fact Sharpe could never beat him, liked having him as the perpetual contender. My feeling from chatting with Vince Armbruster was the old trainer's a cleanskin.'

'That'd be a relative term in the fight game, Claudia. None of them are 100 percent clean.'

Batista reached into his pile of paperclips, stirred them around before selecting the next one to play with. 'What next?'

The three of them decided it wouldn't hurt to go back and trawl through Bartlett's list of clients, paying special attention to the fighters, see if there was any more information to be squeezed out of them. After a couple of hours on the phone, Jack and Taylor reported back to Batista.

'I spoke to one, a female by the name of Natasha Riordan,' said Jack. 'She's a twenty-year old lightweight fighter who's rising up the ranks. Works as a barista at a downtown coffee shop. She reckons Bartlett took her from zero to hero in the space of a year. He's taught her so well she's confident of winning every fight she takes part in.'

'Does she always win?'

'I checked her records. Since moving from another trainer to Bartlett her record is four and oh.'

'That's not many fights.' Taylor chewed the end of a pen.

'This isn't Vegas. There isn't a full card of bouts at the local casino every Friday night. One every few months if you're lucky. Bottom line, she denied using drugs herself and any knowledge of drugs or HGH being taken by any of the other fighters in Bartlett's camp.

'Did she have the hots for him like some of the other women?' said Batista.

'I didn't ask. What do you take me for, boss?'

'Why not?' said Taylor. 'It's a legitimate question. Bartlett's son said his dad was sleeping with a younger woman. Maybe it was her?'

Jack shook his head. 'I've got you there. This one's a lesbian.'

'Did she tell you that?'

'No. A woman answered the phone and when I asked to speak to Riordan she called out "Honey, there's a man on the phone for you." I kind of inferred it. How did you get on?'

'I got hold of two men, one a fighter,' said Taylor. 'The other is a rich businessman who pays Bartlett handsomely to be his personal trainer. The fighter, Adam Dorsey, echoed what your Riordan said. He's yet to have a professional fight, but he's been doing OK in the amateurs. Lost more than he's won but he's starting to square the ledger. Like Riordan, he credits Bartlett for his improvement. He claims to be a grinder, not gifted like some, and Bartlett rings every ounce of potential out of him. He knows, or claims to know, nothing about illegal substances in Bartlett's squad. He said Bartlett was forever threatening to boot people from the program for even the slightest indiscretion. He also reckons the business with Danny's disqualification had to have been a fit-up otherwise he never would've parted ways with Sharpe.'

'What about the businessman?'

'Archie Thaiday, owns a car dealership downtown.'

'I've seen the ads on TV,' said Jack.

'Yep, that's him. I gotta say he's a bit on the chubby side. Must be getting stuck into the pies after his workouts with Bartlett.'

'Those are old commercials. Thaiday said he's got new ones in the pipeline, all thanks to Bartlett's training. He claims he's now free of diabetes. As you can imagine, he owes a debt of gratitude to Bartlett.'

'He sure does,' said Batista.

'And get this,' Taylor continued. 'He offered to post a reward for information leading to his discovery.'

'How much?'

'Up to $100,000.'

Batista whistled. 'Jesus, that's a lot of money.'

'Yeah, but like I said, he credits Bartlett for saving his life. If we don't find the trainer within the next few days, Thaiday's going public with the announcement about the reward.'

'Jesus Christ, we better find him soon. A civilian offering a reward like that makes us look bad.' Batista leaned back in his seat. 'So, that's the client list pretty much exhausted. I'll get Wilson and some of the others to keep trying the numbers that didn't answer, drop by their addresses if need be.'

'We can't wait two more days for this reward to flush out information,' said Jack. 'Every day, every hour that passes, the higher the chances Terry Bartlett's dead.'

'Going back to Claudia's suggestion to search Harlow's place.' Batista's eyes were riveted to a fat Huntsman spider crawling along the outside of his office window. 'I agree with Jack that it's wiser not to do that. However, there's nothing–'

Jack was already on his feet. 'There's nothing to stop us paying him a visit, right?'

'You read my mind, detective. Both of you get over there now and see if he's home. Push Harlow as hard as you can.'

'Perfect,' said Jack. 'I'm just in the mood for some cage rattling.'

'Just don't punch him in the throat.'

'Inspector, would I ever?'

Chapter 18

'You reckon if Evan Zane sold more illicit gear he'd be able to afford a joint like this one?' Jack yanked on the handbrake and killed the engine.

'It'd have to be a hell of a lot more.' Taylor glanced appreciatively at Andy and Louise Harlow's palatial two-story marble façade mansion, one of only four homes on Inglis Avenue. 'I know one thing for sure. You and I will never afford it on cops' wages.'

'You got that right,' Jack agreed.

'Unless we upgrade to a rich spouse like Harlow's managed to land himself.'

Jack laughed. 'You're right again, DC Taylor.'

Back at the station, a cursory investigation into Mrs Harlow – in other words a Google search – was all that was required to learn the basics about her. The female half of the Harlow partnership, not Andy, was the one bringing in the big dollars via a beauty product company she'd been operating for more than ten years. A quick dig via the taxation system provided some general metadata on her business. Her empire, Lou-Har Pty Ltd, was run remotely: production, warehousing and distribution were all taken care of in Vietnam, while she looked after marketing and sales from Yorkville. The luxurious house bore testament to Louise's business acumen; located in the salubrious suburb of Meninga, in Jack's estimation the joint would fetch $4 million even in a poor real estate market.

Car parked beside the perfectly manicured couch grass nature strip. Clunk, clunk. Out of the comfort of the airconditioned car into oppressive humidity that sat on your head and shoulders like a microwaved wet blanket. A buzz on the intercom was answered by a laconic female. 'Yes?'

'Is Mr Andrew Harlow at home?' said Taylor.

'Who wants to know?'

'I'm sure you can guess, Mrs Harlow.' Jack leaned close to the speaker.

'No idea.'

'Yorkville Police.' Jack again.

'As it happens, he's not here.'

'Oh, that's a shame. Perhaps *you* could spare us five minutes of your time. I'm sure you wouldn't mind–'

'It's OK, Detective Lisbon.' Andy Harlow's voice interrupted. 'Louise's rather protective of me. Please, come in.'

The detectives exchanged a puzzled look before the whisper-quiet automatic gates swung open.

'*She's* protective of *him*?' Jack was incredulous. 'The bloke could wrestle a water buffalo to the ground.'

'I think it's more a motherly type of protection.' Taylor smiled.

'Oh, right.' Jack glanced up at the ubiquitous storm clouds. 'Shall we go back and get the car?'

'Don't be ridiculous, it's only 30 metres to the front door.'

'But it's hot. And what if it's raining when we're leaving?'

'Then we run. You're on a keep-fit campaign, aren't you?'

Jack failed to come up with an answer to that piece of logic. The front yard area was indeed modest, in size if not in its horticultural splendour, the bulk of the huge property was in the rear: Google Earth had shown an almost Olympic sized pool and a couple of acres of private rain forest. The beauty business must be booming.

An efficient maid who Jack guessed was from the Philippines served rich, flavoursome coffee. The best Jack had tasted in weeks. Maybe he should visit Harlow every day. Jack and Taylor sat on a feather-soft caramel leather lounge, Harlow and his wife opposite. The bear of a man contrasted starkly with the elfin Louise. She may have been anorexic thin, but there were traces of a former robust beauty lurking under that taut skin. Both husband and wife wore forced expressions that tried to be welcoming but didn't quite pull it off. Jack sensed they wouldn't be terribly upset if he and Taylor downed their coffees, asked their questions and buggered off as fast as possible.

'To what do we owe the pleasure?' Louise held her fine china cup with her pinkie extended. She crossed one leg over the other tightly. Her grimace made you think she was busting for the toilet, but Jack guessed plastic surgery and Botox were the reasons for her bizarre facial expression. 'We've never had a visit from the constabulary before, have we Andrew?'

'Not that I recall.'

'It's about your husband's missing colleague. I'm sure you're aware Mr Bartlett disappeared around a week ago.'

'I'm sure he'll turn up.' She tossed her shoulder length blonde hair one way then the other.

'Why do you say that?' asked Taylor, pen poised above her notebook. 'How well do you know him?'

'I hardly know him at all. My husband's...hobby...is of little interest to me.' Jack noted Andy flinch at the word hobby. 'However Terry Bartlett's reputation as a cheating womaniser is well known. I'm sure he's shacked up with some bimbo or other and will resurface when he feels like it.'

Jack shook his head. 'I'm afraid I have to disagree with your assessment, Mrs Harlow. The press has been giving lots of oxygen to this story. I'm sure Terry Bartlett would be aware of all the worry his disappearance has caused many people. Even his estranged son is concerned.'

'Bullshit. Charlie hates his dad.'

'I though you said your husband's...career... held little interest.' Taylor took a sip of coffee, smacked her lips. 'Perhaps you overstated things.'

'I didn't say *no* interest, did I?' The terse woman was one of those literal people you can never pin down, Jack reflected. 'Do listen. I know all about that philanderer's home-wrecking ways. Not at all like my loyal Andrew.' She rested her hand on the top of her husband's.

'I'm sure you've also heard of the death of Owen Kennedy,' said Jack. 'What can you tell us about him?'

'Now hang on a minute.' Andy Harlow rubbed a palm across his brow, beading sweat despite the air conditioning working perfectly. 'You said you came here to talk to me, not my wife.'

'She's free to leave the room,' Taylor said flatly. 'No one is compelling her to stay.'

'The absolute impertinence! Speaking about me in the third person like I'm not even here. This is my house and I'll sit where I like.'

'Indeed it is your house, Mrs Harlow,' said Jack. 'A lovely home it is, too. So lovely, in fact, I'm tempted to apply for a warrant to search it. We have reason to–'

'Wait, wait, wait,' Andy Harlow spluttered. 'How about I come down to the station. My wife's being completely honest when she says she's ignorant of my working life. She's only repeating gossip she hears from me when I get, you know, a bit down, a bit angry with the world. You know how it is.'

'No I don't,' said Jack. 'I'm single. Now, do you want a lift with us or can you make your own way to the station?'

* * *

'How about you end this charade, Andy. Come clean and tell me exactly what the fuck's going on.' Jack tapped a biro on the table.

'I've told you everything I know. Which is nothing.'

Jack took a deep breath, stood abruptly and paced back and forth behind his chair. Andy radiated calmness, belied only by sweat stains spreading under his armpits and across his chest. Mandarin polo shirt today to match fawn slacks, stylish for an overweight brute.

Time to rattle the cage. 'Everything you've told me is a lie, isn't it, sunshine? I don't believe a word you say.'

'Why not? Listen, I was on holiday in Sydney when Terry went missing. You can check if you like. Owen was probably murdered while we where there, too.'

'Where exactly were you?'

'I was with Louise and the kids.'

'Not who, where!'

'At my wife's sister's place in Manly. She's got a lovely bungalow near the beach. The swimming's better down there. No Irukandji jellyfish and no bloody crocs.'

'Yeah, I heard the sharks ate them all.'

Harlow grinned and nodded. 'Good one, Detective Lisbon. You're a funny bastard.'

Jack ignored the compliment. 'Can the sister corroborate that you were all there?'

'Of course.' Harlow held out his hands, palms open. 'Ring her. Wendy Thompson's her name. She'll confirm we stayed there from the end of October until we flew back two nights ago.'

With the imprecise time established for Owen Kennedy's death, any alibi was going to be useful for Harlow.

'Write the number down.' Jack tapped his fingernail on a Post-it note.

'There. Happy?'

Taylor entered the interrogation room bearing coffee that smelled like burnt toast compared to the ambrosia served up at the Harlows'.

'I'll swap you one cup of mangrove sludge for a phone number.' Jack handed Taylor the yellow sticky note. 'Ring this woman and ask who her last visitors were.' She gave him a polystyrene cup and scurried out of the room without saying a word.

'Why did you go to Sydney?' Jack turned his attention back to Harlow. 'Seems a huge coincidence you being away right when Owen Kennedy gets himself killed and your partner goes walkabout.'

Harlow shrugged. 'What can I say? That's exactly what it is, a coincidence. We went there as a family to get away from stress.'

'Stress?'

'Yeah. I'm under constant pressure from the fighters, especially Danny. He's a big tough man but he's got some mental issues. He needs a lot of psychological care.'

'I'm not surprised. Having your main rival knocked off and getting caught cheating with drugs will bugger up a man's mind.'

'He never had nothing to do with Owen's death.'

'Yeah? With Owen gone, Danny would be the champ by default, wouldn't he?'

'Ha ha! Not for long. Jeremy Clifford's waiting in the wings. Danny's probably more worried about fighting Jeremy than Owen.'

'Even though he could never defeat Owen?'

'He was getting closer every fight. Next bout and Danny would've beaten him, no worries.'

'Not everyone agrees with that.'

'I can assure you, Danny would rather have fought Owen any day of the week. To be honest, even though Jeremy's got no proper trainer yet, he has enough natural talent to beat anyone. He's just waiting his turn. For that reason alone, Danny would be stupid to kill Owen before he had a chance to lift his crown.'

Lifted his ring, though. Harlow had a point Jack couldn't easily argue. He'd seen Clifford sparring; the kid was destined for greatness.

'That doesn't get Danny off the hook as far as the drugs are concerned.'

'Piss off detective. He was framed, everyone knows it. Danny's never taken drugs in his life. He's clean.'

'The test said otherwise.'

'I don't trust the people who run the testing. They could tell you anything; how are you supposed to know what's true and what's not?'

'Welcome to my world.' Jack stretched his arms wide and yawned. They needed to pump more air into this little room. 'The fact he got off with a small fine's the bit I don't understand. These days cheating athletes are generally made examples of, turned into pariahs. But Danny gets, what was it, a two grand fine and no suspension?'

'Yeah. And that tells me the testing body hasn't got a fucking clue. If they were sure he was positive, he would've been banned for years. Maybe life.'

'What about the fact Terry Bartlett used to sit on the Association's board? Maybe that led to Danny getting a light punishment, if you could even call it that.'

Harlow leaned back, crossed his arms. 'You'd have to ask Terry that.'

Smart-arse. Maybe another approach would help crack this nut. Jack was sorely tempted to punch the man square in the mouth but he knew Batista was watching the entire show behind the glass. 'Hang on a minute, will you Andy. I've just gotta have a slash.'

'Don't be long. I've booked a fancy restaurant for me and Louise tonight.'

Jack thought she'd be the cheapest of cheap dates: a small green salad and a glass of water would be enough to fill her up. 'Be right back.'

* * *

'Oi, where's Lisbon? He said he'd be coming back.'

'He's been called away. Something's come up that could crack this case wide open.' It hadn't, but that's what Jack told her to say.

A scintilla of fear flashed across Harlow's eyes. Was he thinking the police had found evidence to incriminate him? If so, he wasn't saying. 'You look a bit worried, Mr Harlow. Something you want to tell me?'

'Ah, no. Why should there be?'

'No reason. Anyway, perhaps you'll be more forthcoming with a female asking you questions. DS Lisbon can be quite intimidating. He used to be a boxer back in the day.'

'That might explain why he assaulted Danny. I won't be letting that one go easily.'

'Come on, Mr Harlow. We both know that kind of allegation won't wash.'

The interviewee scowled but said nothing.

'I'd hazard a guess Louise runs a pretty tight ship, keeps you in line, am I right?'

The fear on Harlow's face was replaced by tightening lines of confusion. 'What the hell are you talking about?'

'We understand it's your wife who provides for your, how shall I put it, luxurious lifestyle.'

'Louise has a successful business, it's true. But I pull my weight, too.'

'Fifty-fifty, is it?'

'Listen, I've just about had enough of your innuendo. If you're implying I consider myself less of a man because my wife makes more money than I do, you're sadly mistaken. I'm a firm believer in equal rights. If Louise is the main breadwinner, big deal.'

Taylor coughed into her fist, then scribbled a meaningless doodle on a notepad. 'I didn't mean to offend. Just a few more questions and we'll be done.'

'Good.'

'We rang your sister-in-law and she confirms your story.'

'For fuck's sake! It's not a story, it's the truth. If you want copies of my airline bookings, credit card statement, you can have the bloody lot.'

'Again, I apologise.'

'Accepted, but only because you aren't rude like that bastard Lisbon.' Harlow glanced at his watch. 'I really have to be going soon.'

'A couple more background questions that might help us get into Terry's mindset. You know him better than just about anyone. Do you think he would go underground like your wife suggested? Perhaps he snuck off somewhere with a woman, to get away from it all, like you did with your family.'

'I guess.'

Dammit, he was going all tight-lipped.

'What about your own personal relationship with Bartlett.'

'Professional on all levels. I trust him and he trusts me. We supplement each other: he teaches the skills, I look after the motivation.'

'So you aren't friends?'

'Yeah, I guess you could say we are. We don't hang together outside of work, but at work we're mates, for sure.'

'What about his romantic affairs?'

'His business.'

'Is there a woman he could be secretly staying with?'

'I have no idea.'

'Last question. Do you know of anyone who would want to cause harm to Owen Kennedy or Terry Bartlett?'

'No. Both men were respected and well liked in the MMA fraternity. Who they mixed with outside of that is none of my business. I could only speculate a jealous husband might want to take out their anger on Terry, but that's it.'

'Did Owen have a girlfriend?'

'Hey, that's another question.'

'Can you answer it please? Then you can go.'

'He did, yeah. A sweetheart back in Perth. I heard he was making arrangements for her to join him in Yorkville in time for Christmas. Absolute tragedy for all concerned.'

Taylor failed to detect an iota of sincerity in Harlow's words. 'Thanks for your time, Mr Harlow. And since you so kindly offered, we would like copies of your travel bookings and credit card statements.'

Before he could reply, the door flew open, the handle banging on the wall.

'Please remain seated, Mr Harlow,' said Jack. 'You aren't going anywhere.'

Chapter 19

Whathat's the hell's going on?' Harlow screwed up his eyes. 'Your partner said we were done.'

'Sorry, sunshine.' Jack offered his best consolation smile. 'Not yet. There's one more thing I want to discuss with you, if you don't mind.'

'No.' Harlow's growl set Jack's teeth on edge. 'I'm gonna be late for a dinner date with my wife.' A twitch pulsated in the man's left eye.

'Don't stress. If you're straight with us, you'll make your dinner date with time to spare.'

'All right, get on with it then.' A squeak crept into Harlow's usually deep voice.

'I'm not going to beat around the bush, Andy. I've discovered your little secret.' Jack took off his jacket and hung it over the spine of his chair, which he spun around and sat on backwards.

Harlow's cheeks glowed red. 'I have no secrets. I'm an open book.'

'I may've overstated that a tad.' Jack sighed through puffed cheeks. 'Let's call it a problem then.'

'I have no idea what you're talking about.' Harlow stood, hands on the table. 'Enough is enough.'

Jack nodded at Taylor who moved to block the door. Symbolic, but the message was clear. 'I'll decide when this discussion is over, not you, understood? You leave now without answering some important questions, and I'll make damned sure what I've found out becomes public knowledge.

There's a certain TV reporter who'd love to get her grubby little hands on the information I've stumbled on. A weekend feature in the *Yorkville Times* would soon follow, I'm guessing. Embarrassing for you, Mrs Harlow, probably your kids.'

A shadow of horrified understanding passed across Harlow's face. He resumed his seat slowly, let out a deep breath.

'You can probably guess where I'm heading with this.' Jack coughed into a fist, opened a manila folder and scanned a couple of A4 sheets. 'While you were so kindly answering DC Taylor's questions, I took the liberty of delving into your wife's business affairs.'

'You have no right to –'

'Uh-uh.' Jack waggled his forefinger like Beyoncé in the "Single Ladies" video. 'I have every right. You're a person of interest in a murder investigation *and* a missing person enquiry. I have every...fucking...right...to look into whatever I want. Do you understand?'

'A person of interest? Don't be ridiculous.'

'Indeed you are. Of immense interest.'

Harlow shrugged. 'How can I be? First it's Danny, now me. You're clutching at straws.'

'We prefer to call it being thorough. Surely you, a fine upstanding member of the sporting community, would expect us to investigate properly. You should be grateful we're doing all we can to find your partner and solve a murder. The problem I have with you, Andy, is how you're acting all suspicious, your body language is all wrong, son. And that's why I know you've got something to hide.'

'If you were serious, you would've charged me officially with...something.'

'We're serious, all right.' Jack glanced at Taylor. 'Wanna know what I found out, Claudia?'

'I'm dying to hear it. Whatever it is has got Mr Harlow in a terrible fluster.'

'What I learned is that Lou-Har Pty Ltd is slipping further and further into the red and is currently on the verge of bankruptcy. The company's been haemorrhaging cash for months. The only thing saving it is intricate corporate structuring. I'm predicting soon her whole empire will come crashing down.'

'Fascinating,' said Taylor, shaking her head. 'And she seemed so...proper.'

Harlow's expression reminded Jack of a smouldering volcano, lava bubbling away underneath waiting to erupt. 'That's a total exaggeration, Detective Lisbon. Times are tough for all businesses these days. Hers is no different.'

'Maybe so. But it seems your wife's troubles are more than economic. I found an intriguing story in the online foreign press. I'm surprised it hasn't generated much interest here...yet.'

'What's any of this got to do with me?'

'Bear with me, Mr Harlow, I'm getting to it. Anyway, turns out a vigilant NGO based in Hanoi caught wind that Louise's company operates a number of sweatshops, the employees work in conditions not fit for animals. It's slavery, if I may use a layperson's language.'

'Bullshit. My wife is a model employer; she offers those people – who own nothing in this world – a chance to escape poverty. That article is a lie. Louise absolutely respects human rights.'

'Her own, maybe,' Jack scoffed. 'One of the so-called factories was forced to close down; your benevolent wife was ordered to pay a shitload of money in compensation. Probably some dirty bribes as well.'

'I'll ignore that last statement. It's beneath you, Detective. Bottom line, Louise paid what the Vietnamese government asked her to.' Harlow wriggled in his seat for a moment. 'There was a misunderstanding when she applied for some permit or other. In business, you gotta delegate. Sometimes the people under you do the wrong thing, and that's exactly what happened in this situation. She's working hard to get everything back on track again, including her reputation. A bureaucrat over there lied to Louise about licensing requirements, she didn't know about the abuses.'

'Here, look at this, Claudia.' Jack beckoned with a forefinger. 'Does she look unaware in this picture?' Jack dropped the image from the Internet in the middle of the table. In it, a smiling Louise Harlow in the company of half a dozen grey-suited functionaries inspected miserable-looking workers, some who appeared to be children, sitting behind sewing machines in a cramped space, just a few square metres.

Taylor bent her head close to the picture, shook her head slowly. 'I'd say she was aware of the conditions, all right. Not of the camera, though.'

'Correct,' said Jack. 'The photo was taken covertly by a disgruntled worker. A brave woman who did the right thing.'

'Listen, this is getting boring,' said Harlow. 'And it's irrelevant.'

'I find it extremely interesting. I'm curious as to how you're able to maintain the luxury. A champagne lifestyle on a beer budget, I believe the Australian saying is.'

'We've got savings,' Harlow said in a quiet monotone.

'Not enough for the recent purchase of a holiday home in Manly, where your sister-in-law now resides. To me, that's fucking inexplicable.'

'Louise's financial affairs and investments are handled by an accounting firm down in Brisbane. I know nothing of those details.'

'I reckon, and it's only a hunch mind, that you, Mr Harlow, are contributing more than you'd have us believe. I reckon you're selling drugs to keep your missus in the lifestyle she's grown accustomed to.'

'Ha! Don't make me laugh. You've got a loose concept of reality, sunshine.'

Jack remained silent, fixed Harlow with an unflinching gaze, daring him to speak next. It worked. 'I'm done with you pricks.' Harlow slapped an open palm on the table. 'This is harassment. I'm not talking to you again without legal representation. I can't believe I trusted you enough not to insist on it this time.'

'We forgot to ask him the most important question, Jack.' Taylor nodded at her partner apologetically like a goof who'd forgotten something totally obvious. 'Just before you go, Mr Harlow. We'd like to clarify one more thing.' She carefully placed three glossy colour photos of Evan Zane before Harlow. 'Do you know this man?'

Jack noticed a flicker of recognition in the corner of Harlow's eye as he studied the photos. The trainer looked at the images of Zane intently for about 30 seconds before shaking his head. 'Never seen him before in my life.'

'You're lying,' said Jack. 'Remember my offer: you tell us the truth or I pass your wife's story over to the media. They'll have a field day.'

Flickering eyelids, clenching and unclenching fists told Jack the man was trying to make a difficult decision, was Jack bluffing or should he come clean.

'Fuck you.'

'OK, Mr Harlow,' said Jack. 'You're free to go. We'll be in touch.'

Chapter 20

'He's been doing everything by the book,' Jack spat.

'What book's is that?' asked Taylor, stirring a takeaway chai latte with a wooden stick.

'The Book of Sneaky Lying Arseholes.'

'Haven't read that one,' she laughed. 'Is it any good?'

'No. It's terrible.' Jack turned the key in the ignition and the Kia's engine hummed to life. 'Tailing this guy is a complete waste of bloody time.'

'Shouldn't we persist for a couple more hours at least? Batista said—'

'Never mind what Batista said. Harlow's been doing nothing out of the ordinary.' Jack consulted his laptop and recited aloud the latest update. 'Constables Ben Wilson and Kylie Smith watched the suspect from after he left the station Friday evening to Saturday lunchtime when another two undercover officers took over. Apart from an uneventful dinner date with his wife, they observed no strange behaviour by Harlow.'

'How do they know what he got up to at the restaurant? Maybe he was meeting with drug dealers inside, buyers, who knows?'

'Nope. Wilson and Smith had a word with the manager who squeezed them in. An extra table was brought in; the officers observed the Harlows from a far corner. Apparently, Andy didn't talk to anyone except his wife and the restaurant staff and didn't appear to touch his phone. He only went to the toilet once and Wilson followed him in. Stood next to him at the urinal while he relieved himself.'

'Creepy.'

'You gotta do what you gotta do.'

Taylor took a slug of takeaway tea. 'Yeah, but watching a suspect take a leak...geez.'

'Those two constables enjoyed a slap-up three-course meal at the Queensland Police Service's expense. I wouldn't be complaining if I was them.'

'I guess not.'

Jack looked back to his laptop. 'Another pair of officers staked out Harlow's mansion on Sunday. He didn't leave there until 8:30am this morning and no other persons entered or left the premises while it was under observation.'

'It's a sprawling property. Was someone watching the back?'

Jack shrugged. 'I don't know. That's dense rainforest, but I get what you're saying. I guess it's impossible to cover every base unless we deploy effing drones, and they aren't exactly inconspicuous.'

'So people could have come and gone unnoticed.'

'Yes, but my gut tells me it's unlikely.' Jack flicked the indicator to turn left at the city hospital, its sandstone façade bleached almost white by the tropical sun. 'The officers followed him here to the Iron Horse where we took over at 9:00am and have been sitting and twiddling our thumbs for...what time is it now?...one o'clock in the afternoon with only one short break ... for you mind, not me... when you walked to that coffee van over there and got us a drink. So no, we won't persist for another couple of hours. I'm pretty sure Harlow's either clocked us tailing him or he's simply being extra careful.'

'What are we going to do?' said Taylor as the car eased onto the main highway. 'Go to the press with the story on Louise Harlow?'

'No. I never planned to do that. That'd be plain vindictive on my part. It wouldn't help us and would definitely fuck up the lives of their innocent offspring.'

'You reckon any children of theirs would be innocents?'

'Until proven guilty, yes.'

'You're a softy when it comes to kids, aren't you DS Lisbon?'

Jack blushed and smiled, felt a warm glow in the pit of his stomach. He had no idea why, but he liked it when Taylor addressed him by his title. 'Don't be ridiculous. I just believe in avoiding collateral damage when it comes to justice.'

Jack noted the fuel indicator was nudging empty, pulled into a service station. He filled the tank, paid and returned with two chocolate bars, a copy of the daily rag and a scowl. He tossed the paper onto Taylor's lap. 'Here, check this out.'

'How did you get time to read it?'

'I haven't. Just saw the disgraceful headline.' He pointed at it: YORKVILLE COPS CLUELESS. 'Now, read me the story.'

'*It seems Yorkville Police are no closer to solving the murder of champion MMA fighter Owen Kennedy or the disappearance of respected trainer Terry Bartlett. With both cases now a week old, the police have been strangely quiet about developments. Our confidential sources tell us the CIB are making little progress with either matter. To move things along, local identity and car dealership owner Archie Thaiday has offered a reward of $100,000 for any information that helps to locate Mr Bartlett. 'I've got little faith in the police,' said Mr Thaiday. 'Their enquiries seem to be at a standstill. All we've had is one train-wreck of a press conference at which the lead detective delighted in telling an off-colour crocodile joke, and then no updates for a week. Perhaps my offer of cash will spur the public to come forward with information. There's genuine fear in the community. My customers tell me they don't feel safe with a murderer on the loose in their town.' Mr Thaiday credits Bartlett with curing his diabetes.* There's more, wanna hear it?*

'That's enough for now. I'll read the rest later. Who wrote that trash?'

'Someone called Staff Reporter.'

'Bastards. Hiding behind anonymity.'

'It could be a good thing.' Taylor opened the wrapper of her Mars Bar. 'We might get a lead or two.'

'No.' Jack shook his head. 'I doubt it. All it does is make us look incompetent.'

Taylor tossed the chocolate bar and paper aside when her mobile bleeped. 'It's a text from Batista. Brisbane's agreed to send up a team of senior officers to help with inquiries, so that's something. Not for a couple of days, though.'

'Better late than never.'

'Is that professional jealousy, DS Lisbon? I thought you'd be glad. You yourself wanted them.'

He gave her a side-eye. 'I am glad. When this is all over maybe we'll get a staffing boost.'

Jack swung the car onto the highway.

'While we're obsessing with Harlow,' said Taylor at a set of lights. 'Don't forget there's a couple of other likely suspects. We can't be everywhere at once. Extra bodies on the ground means we can at least keep an eye on Masiker, Sharpe and Bartlett junior. Plus check out some of those potential jealous husbands we haven't had time to chase up.'

'True. I can't argue with that. These two cases are a massive strain on resources. I heard Batista was all set on recruiting a couple of lollipop ladies to help out.'

Taylor burst out laughing. 'I can imagine.'

'It's great to have the help, but I've got another idea I reckon we can implement all on our own. This press coverage is a disaster, we need to get this solved, fast.'

'What do you want to do?' Taylor gripped the handle above the door as Jack took a corner a touch too quickly.

'Set up a sting.'

* * *

Taylor wisely chose to sit in the car with the engine and aircon running, where she could do more research into Lou-Har Pty Ltd. Jack got the fun job of rigging up Zane in the junkie's house.

'I ain't doin' it. It's a suicide mission.'

'Come on, Evan. Need I remind you of your obligation to look after that little girl of yours.' Jack patted the tape holding the wire in place, securing it to Zane's bony chest. A couple of lonely black hairs surrounded flat nipples. 'I'll be listening, mate. This is your chance to impress.' Blue veins pulsated around the man's neck, rivulets of sweat trickled down his armpits. Jack pulled his hand away as quickly as possible to avoid touching the toxic perspiration.

'This is blackmail. Now I remember why I always hated the pigs.'

'It's not blackmail. It's called a trade-off. Look at it another way: you're helping us figure out whether Andy Harlow is a nice guy we're harassing for no good reason, or a bastard who needs locking up. In return for your co-operation, I don't punch your fucking lights out.'

'I already told you I sold gear to him, so he ain't no nice guy. Arrest Harlow for possession and distribution of drugs. Why waste time with this cloak and dagger shit?

'Two reasons. One, he'd end up fingering you as his supplier, which means I have to arrest you and then it's bye-bye kid, and two, to do that we'd need to find gear at his place which requires a search warrant, and I've been given the hint that an application for one would likely be rejected.'

'Don't you need a listening device warrant to secretly–'

Jack thrust a piece of paper in Zane's face. 'My, aren't you well schooled in procedure? You could be a lawyer if you weren't such a loser. As it happens, the same magistrate who has a reputation for being tough on search warrant requests saw fit to approve this one. So, it's fucking legit.'

Appropriately contrite, Zane dropped his head.

'You'll be fine, sunshine. Just do as I told you and everything will be all right.'

'Can I take a little something to calm my nerves? I'm shitting myself.'

Jack went to rest a hand on Zane's shoulder, remembered the man's abysmal hygiene and jerked it back. Instead, Jack flicked him under the chin. Zane looked up, more zombie than human, eyes dilated to their maximum extent. 'I can tell you're already coked up or on speed. I need you functional for this to work. More stimulation would be a dumb idea.'

'Please, just a line.'

'No, mate. But you can when the job's done. Plus a promise from me not to charge you for anything for the next year.'

'I appreciate that.'

Jack declined to tell Zane that, according to one of his favourite maxims, lying to crims wasn't really lying.

'Now, repeat it for me one more time. What's the plan?'

'In one hour I meet Harlow at the park two blocks from the Iron Horse. I tell him I can get him cheaper HGH on a regular basis if he agrees to buy bigger amounts. But if he wants a piece of the action he has to decide tonight. To show my good faith, I offer him a batch for a third of the price he's been paying.'

'Excellent, Evan. He can't say no to that.'

'What if he does, or smells a rat?'

Jack sniffed twice. 'The only thing he'll smell is your effing body odour. Man, you stink to high heaven. On second thoughts, it's probably for the best you're a soap dodger. He'll be less inclined to want to feel you up.'

'Is he gay? If he is, there's no way I'm–'

'To see if you've got a wire on, you idiot.'

Jack put his hands to his head. Zane spearheading the sting operation was enough to give anyone ulcers, but the risk had to be taken. The press weren't lying, the cops were getting nowhere. The one thing that gave Jack hope was the fact Louise Harlow's business was in trouble. There was something in the tender way Andy looked at his wife, held her hand, that gave life to that hope. He loved her; to see Louise lose what she's built up on the sweat of Vietnamese slaves would devastate him. And for that reason, he'd buy the gear from Zane.

Jack attacked the stubborn roll of Scotch tape with his teeth, attached the offending newspaper article to the heavy bag. At 8:20pm, he had the cupboard-sized gym in the apartment complex all to himself. It was too wet outside for a run after a voluminous rainstorm, the roads were slippery and the cane toads abundant, and he couldn't be arsed driving to his favourite McGrath's gym. This would have to do.

On with the strapping, the cracked black gloves. Then the stretching routine to protect his middle-aged body from strains and sprains. It was easy to confuse enthusiasm with ability; warm-ups were more important than ever. A disruption to routine caused by careless injury would piss him off, might make him abandon his training altogether. How easy it would be to take the lazy way, to slip back into the persona of the cynical, heavy drinking, chain smoking, fat cop who cared only about himself.

That must never happen, he'd come too far to revert to that pitiful caricature again.

And so stretching took on special importance. Each movement required full concentration and effort. Glutes, hamstrings, shoulders, ankles and wrists. No punching until the fifteen minute routine was complete and a fine layer of sweat coated his body. A full-length mirror by the door proved Jack's new way of life was paying off. Muscle definition like when he was a twenty year old, broad in the shoulders, biceps hard, slim in the waist.

Now, it was time.

He lined up the newspaper article and laid the first jab and cross combos, hammering into the bag, determined to smash the stuffing out of it. Worse than the newspaper article was Evan fucking Zane. The spineless junkie pulled the pin – and the wire from his chest – and failed to show at the meeting. The detectives had sat in a stifling unmarked van for an hour after the agreed rendezvous between Harlow and Zane. They even called in the techies to check the connection when no sound was coming through, gave their undercover man the benefit of the doubt. The equipment was working fine, Zane was the problem.

Jack punched on like a locomotive. He revelled in the fibres twitching in his arms and legs, stomach and chest. A series of thunderous body rips, left and right combinations high and low, got his heart pumping. Sharp, loud exhalations, screaming obscenities at those conspiring against him, accompanied every punch. Twenty minutes in, the hits began to slow and the impact soften, it was harder to hold his hands without shaking. Four more minutes, summoning every ounce of energy, and he could go no more. Exhausted, he bent to pick up the shredded remains of the newspaper article. Some slow warm-down stretches before he collapsed on the floor with his back to the wall, rehydrated with an electrolyte drink, rested for a few minutes. As he gathered his sports bag, his favourite punk band launched into their signature tune. Jack snatched at his mobile. Number withheld. If it was Zane calling to apologise, he'd drive over to his house right now and rip him a new one.

'Hello, wot?'

'You sound out of puff, Detective? Been running after bad guys?' The gruff voice was a bit slurry, but unmistakable. Carl Masiker.

'Training hard in case I have to.'

'Good to hear.'

'Why are you ringing me at this time of night?'

A pause.

'You there?'

'Yeah, sorry. Look, I saw the story in the *Times* today. Got me thinking.'

'You wanna cash in on the reward? Sorry, mate, but I'm afraid you'd be ineligible since you've already spoken to the police.'

Masiker muttered something incomprehensible.

'Say again?'

'I may've withheld some...information that...might help...yer 'vestigation.'

'What did you say?' *Please let this be the breakthrough.*

'I wanna help.'

'What is it?'

'Nah...not saying over the phone. I need to talk face to face with ya. An' don't bring that uptight sheila, she wasn't very nice to me last time we met.'

'Have you been drinking, Mr Masiker?' In the background, Jack could hear a lively crowd, muffled piano music. Billy Joel covers. The gym owner was out on the town drowning his sorrows.

'Yeah, ha ha. How can ya tell? No wonder you're a fucken de...de...detective.'

'It's pretty obvious. Where are you?'

'Pelican Bar, know where it is?'

It was Dave's Bar in Jack's mind. 'Yes. I'm on my way.'

Race upstairs as fast as his tired legs could carry him. Showered. Dressed. Car. Esplanade.

Masiker looked a mess. Shirt untucked, he could barely sit straight on the barstool. Reminded Jack of himself not too long ago.

'What is it you want to tell me?'

'Not tell, show. Here, you might find this in'erstin' viewing.' Masiker slid a green and white USB drive across the bar. 'Don't tell no one I gave you this. I just wanted to...protect my family.'

'You never struck me as the family type, Carl.'

'Well, I am. I live for me wife and kids. I pretend I'm this big, confident bloke, it's all a sham. I...' Jack thought the man would burst into tears, but it became a hysterical laugh. 'I couldn't have even bought the gym if not for a lucky inheritance. Aunty Beryl died and left me a squillion. She thought I was a legend 'cos I played a handful of games in the NRL. What a joke!'

'I'd heard about your good fortune. But you're wandering off track a bit there, Carl. Back to business.' Jack tapped on the flash drive. 'What's on it?'

Masiker stumbled to his feet, went to put his wallet in his pocket and dropped it. Jack picked it up and handed it back, suddenly struck by the look of anxiety twisting Masiker's features in shifting knots.

'Is someone threatening you?'

'Just leave me alone. I never asked for any of this. It's all on...the video. You're smart enough to figure it out.'

Masiker lurched across the foyer and stumbled out into the hot, balmy night.

Chapter 21

What the hell's this? I saw Masiker download all the CCTV footage. I don't get it.' Taylor craned forward in her seat on the couch as Jack inserted the flash drive into a socket on the side of his smart TV; much easier to watch the show on the big screen than crowded around his undersized laptop which was barely bigger than an iPad. He'd called her on his way home from the Pelican Bar; it was late, nearly 11:00pm, but this was this worst violent crime to hit Yorkville in years. She complained about the hour, but he needn't have worried; Taylor's car was already in Jack's driveway when he arrived.

Jack clicked on the remote and the MP4 video file opened. 'He must have pinhole cameras set up all around the gym.' Jack had a flash back to the Brisbane bank siege he'd foiled two years ago, remembered how these clandestine security devices had shown the police what was happening with the hostages trapped inside. 'He might have others set up for voyeuristic purposes. I trust him as far as I can throw him. I'll be recommending a sweep of the place. If Masiker's spying on people in the change rooms, look out.'

'You think that's likely?' Taylor helped herself to a handful of salted cashew nuts from a bowl on the coffee table.

Jack cracked a can of ice-cold beer, handed it to Taylor. He made do with a Diet Coke. 'Could be.' Jack told Taylor how he'd help bust a ring of fitness centre operators in London who took clandestine videos of women showering and shared the images online. One prominent Member of Parliament had her career ruined when she was caught getting intimate in a shower with another female member. 'Now do you understand why I don't trust blokes in this business?'

She agreed it was indeed despicable. 'But let's concentrate on the murder and missing person cases first, OK?'

The video file opened and Jack clicked the big white PLAY arrow in the middle of the screen. 'There's our vic. Strange to see him alive and well.' Jack pointed at the TV with the remote. The first scene showed Owen storming onto the gym floor. Sharpe and Bartlett were packing up training gear.

'Hang on, there's audio on this. Better than CCTV,' said Taylor. 'Can you turn it up?'

'Sure.'

The video and sound quality were excellent. Masiker hadn't spared money getting a top-of-the-range system to spy on his customers and staff. Time stamp: 21:47, Tuesday 27 October.

'I thought the pair of them never trained on the same night?' Taylor gestured at the TV with her beer can. 'I'm sure Masiker said that.'

'He did. Said they'd tear each other apart. But only Sharpe looks like he's been training.' Jack paused the video. 'See, Kennedy's in a pair of jeans and a t-shirt.'

'You're right. It's like he's popped in to stir up trouble. Hang on, I think there's about to be a confrontation.'

The video resumed. On the screen, Owen Kennedy and Danny Sharpe stood toe to toe, nose to nose, snarling at each other like pro fighters hamming it up before a televised weigh-in. Only there was no acting involved. Terry Bartlett was squatting by a bench two metres away, stuffing towels into a sports bag and wearing an anxious expression.

Kennedy: *Hey, I just heard the news. Sucked in for failing the drug test, dickhead. Looks like I'll be fighting Jeremy Clifford for the title. He's a more worthy opponent than you, you fucken weasel.*

Sharpe: *Piss off Kennedy. I was framed.*

Kennedy: *Bullshit. You're a liar as well as a cheat.*

The two men banged chests together like elephant seals. Bartlett leapt between them in a flash, straining to keep them apart.

Bartlett: *Enough! Owen, go home. I don't know what you think you're playing at. If Vince knew you were stirring up shit...*

Kennedy: *Leave him out of it.* The champ pulled back his fist, held it for a moment before dropping his arm to his side. Bartlett let out a sigh of relief.

Kennedy stormed off out of the camera range, his laughter echoing in the cavernous gymnasium.

Sharpe's complexion was beetroot red. Bartlett placed a hand on his charge's shoulder, looked upwards as if seeking divine help: *That was our last training session, son. I can't keep you on any longer.*

– *What the fuck!*

– *You know I've got no time for cheating fighters. My reputation is all I've got in this business.*

– *You can't drop me. I'll pay you double.*

– *Sorry, son. I don't need your money. It's a matter of principle. I won't change my mind.*

Sharpe buried his head in his hands before screaming at Bartlett.

– *You fucking arsehole! My career's ruined!*

– *No it isn't. I made sure you only copped a small fine. If not for me, you'd have been rubbed out for a year, maybe more. I've taught you all the skills you need. Jeremy Clifford gets by without a trainer, and you've got years more experience than him.*

– *Don't compare me to him. C'mon, man. Please! I'm begging you. I need you if I'm gonna have any chance of winning the title.*

– *Sorry, son. I've made my decision.*

– *You'll be sorry, Terry. I'll make you pay for this.*

Sharpe flexed his fingers like he wanted to hit something hard, strode out of camera-shot taking long, bouncy steps. Off camera he shouted indistinct obscenities that gradually faded.

The vision cut abruptly, shifting to another part of the gym. Time stamp showed 22:21, the same night. Andy Harlow and Terry stood among a forest of weight-lifting machines, engaged in a heated argument.

– *I just had a word to Danny in the carpark. Why the fuck did you drop him, Terry? The lad's just made a silly mistake.*

– You know my feelings on drugs, mate. Zero tolerance.

– He only got a fine, for fuck's sake! If it was serious, he woulda got banned. Musta been a tiny dose.

– Any amount is too much.

– Why are you even worried? The public will forgive him as time goes by.

– Listen, Andy. He got off because of ME, because of MY influence, you idiot. You're the one I should sack for supplying him the growth hormone!

Harlow's meaty right hand darted out, grabbed Bartlett by the collar of his shirt, wrapped his right leg around the front of Bartlett's thighs and flipped him over.

'Look at that, Claudia. A classic judo throw. Too quick for Bartlett even though Harlow's a fat slob.'

'Yeah. I wouldn't have picked Harlow for that one.'

Harlow used his superior weight advantage to muscle Bartlett to the ground. Bartlett resisted, to no avail. He screamed out. *Help!* Harlow adjusted his position, sprawled his big body across Bartlett's lighter frame, jammed his forearm into Bartlett's windpipe; Bartlett's eyes bulged and his face reddened, he wriggled underneath, looking for a way to get the heavier man off him. Harlow pushed off Bartlett, supported himself on the ground with one hand, wound up and slapped Bartlett viciously across the cheek. Harlow stood, barked at the vanquished opponent who cowered on the ground.

– You're pathetic. I expected you to support Danny, not abandon him.

Harlow walked off to the left of camera, Bartlett struggled to his feet, wiping blood from a small cut on his lip. Other gym members arrived. Bartlett started swinging randomly at anyone who approached him.

Vision ends.

'And then we have the official CCTV you got from Masiker the first time,' said Jack, slugging on his soft drink. 'An angry Bartlett being led out of the gym by two uniforms.'

'Do you reckon there's enough on there to bring in Andy and Danny?'

'More than enough. Actual violence by Harlow, accusations of drug supply, and a direct threat from Sharpe. Let's grab them first light tomorrow morning. Like the KGB used to do.'

'Sorry?'

'They always arrested people at 4:00am when the suspects were at their most vulnerable. Half asleep and unable to think properly.'

'You must be crazy if you think I'm getting up at that time. *I'll* be unable to think properly.'

'OK. 6 o'clock?'

'Still too early, but I grudgingly agree. Someone needs to keep an eye on you.'

'I'll pick you up at 5:30am.'

Taylor thanked Jack for the late-night entertainment, gathered her keys and was gone. Jack checked his watch. Just after midnight. He speed dialled a drowsy-voiced Batista with a request for boosted manpower for two early morning raids. Request granted.

Chapter 22

'I thought you couldn't handle service station sludge?' Taylor smiled through tired eyes as she accepted the steaming brew from Jack.

'I can't. This comes courtesy of the Golden Arches 24-hour drive-thru.'

'I beg your pardon? You're dropping your low standards even further.'

'Unbelievable as it sounds, their stuff isn't revolting. Go on, try it...'

'Hmm. I preferred the coffee we got at Harlow's.'

'Something tells me he ain't gonna be offering us any this morning.'

Jack nudged the Kia against the curb in the relatively quiet post-dawn. Constables Wilson and Smith sat parked across the street from Danny Sharpe's apartment complex, between two clumps of cane palms. A marked police car and the two of them in uniform. Jack assumed everyone would be in plain clothes and unmarked vehicles for the raids, but it didn't matter. The police regalia added an element of drama to the operation. The warming sun had been up for half an hour but hadn't had a chance to cook the town. Most people would still be asleep, delaying their appointment with harsh reality.

Jack spoke to Batista over the two-way radio. 'We've arrived, sir. Please confirm officers are in place at Harlow's residence.'

'Confirmed. Constables Trevarthen and Semmens have been watching the mansion since before sunrise. All quiet.'

'Roger that, sir. Have Wilson and Smith been here that long, too?'

'Affirmative. I didn't want the suspects sneaking off in the dark.'

'Indeed.' A though occurred to Jack. Maybe they'd already flown the coop.

Dammit, he should have hit the targets immediately after he'd seen the video. So what if it was late? The motives had been established and he ought to have acted.

Jack prayed he hadn't fucked up. 'OK, Claudia, let's get a wriggle on.'

Taylor waved at the officers across the street, pulled hair through a red scrunchie. The uniforms alighted from the vehicle, joined the detectives at the glass entrance to the main set of stairs. A light blanket of humidity promised to grow heavier as the day progressed. The only sounds came from unseen insects and birds. Radios turned down, the officers entered as quietly as possible and walked up to Sharpe's apartment. The time for stealth over, Jack banged hard on the door. Taylor stood close beside him, the other two a step below. The door swung open by itself. The lock had been busted, splinters of wood and plaster powder lay just beyond the threshold. All four cops entered, guns drawn and held at eye level.

'Danny!' Jack called. 'Police. Are you here?'

Silence.

'Stay where you are, sunshine. There are four armed officers here, it's best for all concerned you co-operate.'

'He's not here, Jack,' said Taylor.

'I'm not taking any chances. He could be in his bedroom with a fucking machine gun for all we know.'

'You two.' Taylor turned to the constables, eager determination etched on their young faces. They'd probably never seen action like this since graduating from the academy. 'Wait here and watch the front door while DS Lisbon and I check the bedrooms and bathroom. We'll yell out if we need you.'

Inside, the lounge and kitchen had been ransacked even more thoroughly than Bartlett's house had been. Two recliners and a sofa were upended, someone had attacked the furniture fabric with a knife and pulled the stuffing out. Looking for something, perhaps. Drugs or money. Smashed crockery and glasses littered the kitchen floor; it appeared someone had sunk a boot into the TV screen. Two dark green plants lay on the carpet surrounded by a couple of kilos of black potting mix.

A zig-zag crack ran from top to bottom of the bathroom mirror, the contents of drawers were tipped out. No Danny Sharpe.

In the bedroom, sheets were ripped off the bed and lay in a crumpled heap on the floor. Nothing was hanging in the wardrobe except a purple satin dressing gown. Jack edged closer to the wardrobe, pulled back a sliding door. Inside, a squashed down dark green garbage bag. 'Here, what's this?'

Taylor opened the yellow draw-tie and peered inside. 'A pair of boots covered in dried mud. Wasn't this place searched already?'

'Yes. And these definitely weren't here. Wilson!' Jack called. He appeared at the doorway in a flash, Constable Smith on his shoulder, both of them breathless.

'Yes?'

'Get this to the lab. NOW!'

* * *

Jack turned off the siren three streets from Inglis Avenue. The rest of the journey was made in silence, save for the purr of the car's engine. Rev this baby and it roars, but Jack was able to coax the Stinger along at a decent clip without looking and sounding like a hooligan.

Trevarthen and Semmens were guarding the property exactly as programmed. Both of these men had grown up in North Queensland, beefy ex-footballers who weren't afraid of a scrap. Perfect back-up in case Harlow got nasty. Jack remembered the video, how quickly Harlow had neutralised Terry Bartlett, himself a handy brawler.

Jack and Taylor stepped out of the car, the two uniforms followed to the gate as per previous radio communication. Jack pressed on the intercom button.

'Yes?' A timorous Louise Harlow answered within ten seconds, surprising Jack. He'd already been scanning the surrounds, looking for a way to breach Fortress Harlow and storm the joint.

'It's DS Jack Lisbon and DC Claudia Taylor again. We need to speak to your husband. Is he in there?' *In there*...it sounded a lot more sinister than "is he at home."

The gate swung open before she answered. 'No. Come in...I...' She burst into tears.

'Quickly now everyone. She shouldn't have answered so fast at this time of the morning. Something's severely fucked up.' Jack broke into a sprint, the others struggled to keep up. The glass-panelled double front door was wide open like a pair of welcoming arms.

Chapter 23

Louse Harlow sat staring into space, a crystal tumbler of clear liquid in hand. Jack guessed it was vodka. Panda eyed, reminiscent of Alice Cooper circa 1975. A couple of shiners the colour of squashed mulberries completed the picture of abuse. The lump developing on the right side of her forehead formed a fleshy canopy over the eye underneath.

'Send an ambulance to 3 Inglis Avenue,' Jack barked into his radio. 'One adult female assaulted. She requires urgent attention.'

Taylor took a seat next to Mrs Harlow on her unfeasibly large sofa, stroked the top of her hand in a comforting gesture.

'Who did this?' said Jack, tucking the radio back into its holster.

'Who do you think?' She retained a degree of haughtiness despite having been attacked. A woman not to be cowed into submission. 'That low-down mongrel of a husband, that's who.'

Jack glowered, felt his blood pressure rising. He might be old school, but beating a woman, one as small and frail as Louise Harlow, was sickening. Never mind she was an exploiter of foreign workers; her ultimate punishment for that would come in another form.

'Are the kids safe?'

Mrs Harlow spun her head around after Taylor had asked the question, their faces inches apart. 'What?'

Taylor recoiled slightly, screwed up her nose. Jack had guessed right. Vodka was the booze with the greatest repellent factor. 'Your children,' Taylor repeated. 'Are they safe?'

'Oh my god! Can someone go and check on them please?'

'Did he hurt the kids?' said Jack with a sharp edge to his voice. A wave of red passed before his eyes.

'I don't think so. They're in their bedrooms upstairs, I think. Jesus, I can't... remember...'

The two uniforms dashed up the staircase, calling out to the children. Two small voices replied and Jack breathed a sigh of relief.

'The ambulance will be here soon.' As he paced back and forth, Jack kept glancing at Mrs Harlow's battered face; a swelling above the other eye now, trying to catch up with the first one. How he'd love to give Andy a beating the bastard would never forget. That would only happen if he somehow managed to get the man alone, as remote a possibility now as a White Christmas in Yorkville. He forced himself to stop pacing. 'Tell us exactly what happened.'

Half the contents of the glass disappeared down the lady of the house's throat. 'I'm not sure. It all happened in a blur.'

'It's all right, Mrs Harlow,' said Taylor soothingly. 'In your own time.'

'Yes, but please, just the main details,' said Jack. 'I've got a feeling Danny Sharpe's in grave danger now.'

'Oh, Jesus. OK, then.' Mrs Harlow reached under the coffee table, a shaking hand pulled out a bottle of Stolichnaya. She poured a third of a glass and downed it. 'Andy woke up early this morning in a terrible fluster. I had a look at the time on my iPhone, it was 5:15am, still before sunrise but the sky was lightening. I followed him to the home office downstairs. He was mumbling to himself, incomprehensible words and grunts. I thought maybe he was sleepwalking. He used to do that when he was younger. I blame all the head knocks from Thai Boxing. Did you know–'

'Please, Mrs Harlow.' Jack had to stop her from rambling, not easy when she was in a state of shock.

'Sorry. I'm just...where was I? Oh, yes. He started packing papers, his laptop and whatnot. He told me to gather my things, too. I asked why and he screamed at me. *Just do it!* I said he'd lost his marbles and he let fly with his fists. I fell to the ground, hit my head on the edge of a table, must have passed out for a few minutes. When I came to, I ran to the garage but his Mercedes was gone. Please, you need to find him and lock him up.'

Jack knew the answer before he asked the question. 'This isn't an isolated incident is it?'

'No.'

'How long has he been hitting you? Years, right?'

A cloud of confusion descended on Mrs Harlow. 'Oh no, you have to understand, he's been a good husband, for the most part. It's only in the last couple of months that he's undergone this radical change. Violent mood swings, lashing out at the least provocation. I don't understand it.'

Jack understood it. Harlow wasn't only selling steroids, he'd started to consume them himself. Still, it was no excuse.

More vodka found its way into the tumbler, some spilled onto the table. 'It's a bit of a coincidence, you all landing on my doorstep like this. I never called you. What's happening?'

'I'm sorry to have to inform you,' said Taylor, edging the bottle out of the woman's reach as she spoke. 'Your husband is suspected of involvement in the murder of Owen Kennedy and the disappearance and possible homicide of Terry Bartlett.'

No histrionics, but a nod of capitulation. She knew, she'd always known.

Faint sirens grew louder until they were shrieking in the driveway.

'Before the ambulance officers assess you, can you please tell us if you have any idea where Andy could have gone?'

'No, I haven't a clue. If you want to search the house, be my guest.'

Constable Trevarthen sat with the two children, a boy about seven and his slightly older sister, in front of a television watching cartoons, while Jack and the others made a rapid inspection of the house. Paramedics advised Louise Harlow to go with them to the hospital but she refused point blank, so they treated her on the spot. The quick sweep came up empty, however a thorough search might turn up something valuable. Only they didn't have time for that with Andy Harlow on the loose and Danny Sharpe missing. Jack radioed the station, demanded all available officers be dispatched to the Harlows' house to hunt for clues. Batista promised to rouse every last cop in Yorkville from their slumber and send them over.

Jack pulled out his mobile. 7:13am. Perhaps Masiker knew where Harlow had gone. He dialled Masiker's number, no answer. He left a quick voicemail message, told him to expect a visit within the next twenty minutes. The gym owner was likely on deck at the Iron Horse; pre-work fitness fanatics would have already started their exercise routines.

'He's probably there,' said Taylor. 'Masiker boasted about how conscientious he was, gets into the office before any other staff to greet early-riser customers.'

'Let's hope he's been true to form this morning.' His reply was a whisper through gritted teeth.

In the car, Jack slammed his palms into the steering wheel. *Too late to act, once again. Idiot!* He reached across Taylor's body, popped the glove box and pulled out a silver hipflask.

'Oi! What the fuck, Jack?'

'I need this.'

'Like Mrs Harlow needs it? Don't be a fool.' She snatched the flask from his grip, hurled it out the window. It bounced on the paved driveway with a clank.

'Hey! That was full.'

'Shut up and drive.'

He stole a look at her profile, refusing to engage him face on. 'Who are you, my bloody mother? One sip, that's all I was going to have. One sip.'

She snapped her head around. 'If you think I'd believe you wouldn't drink the entire contents, you're a bigger fool than I thought you were. On second thoughts, let me drive. You need to calm the fuck down.'

Taylor was right. He wouldn't have stopped at one sip. This was his ultimate test. See this through, no alcohol, nail Harlow. Simple. He jammed a stick of nicotine gum in his dry mouth, unbuckled his seatbelt. 'OK, Claudia. Take the wheel.'

Approaching the entrance to the Iron Horse, Jack wished he'd retrieved the hipflask. The situation was getting even more out of hand. Two paramedics were loading Masiker into the back of a white-and-yellow Mercedes Sprinter van. A group of spectators in sports gear stood around, worried expressions through sweaty faces. Jack and Taylor raced to the closing rear doors. 'What's happened?'

A petite female paramedic said: 'Not sure. He was lying in a pool of his own blood at the entrance where a couple of young fellas found him.'

'Is he conscious?'

'Fading in and out,' said the male paramedic, whose pony tail was a perfect match for Taylor's. 'He hasn't been able to string a sentence together, mainly noises, which tells us he's in a lot of pain. If you don't mind, we have to get him to the hospital. He's lost a fair bit of blood from a serious head wound.'

As the door was about to close, Masiker's right arm shot out from under the blanket and he gave a loud groan.

'Stop!' said Jack. 'He's trying to say something.'

'I'm sorry, sir.' Pony tail wedged his forearm into Jack's side and tried to push him away. 'He's badly injured. No time for chat.'

'Listen, sunshine.' Jack shoved him back twice as hard, the man stumbled over his shoes. His colleague gasped. The police ID hovered an inch from the paramedic's nose. 'I'm a police officer. This man you're carting away could hold the key to solving a fucking murder. Let me speak to him or your mate there will be loading you in the van too, got it?'

The pony tail flapped up and down in acknowledgement. Its owner grabbed the silver handle, opened the door and gestured for Jack to jump in. Taylor offered the first responders a smile of apology on behalf of the detective's behaviour. She rapidly questioned the bystanders, all of whom had seen or heard nothing, and went back to the car to wait for Jack.

Inside the ambulance, squeezed in among a battery of medical equipment, Jack leaned close to Masiker. 'What happened, Carl?'

'He...barged in, demanded a copy of the video I gave you. And one from another night.'

'How did he know about your secret cameras?'

'No idea.'

'Did you give him the videos?'

'No. I told him I wiped everything from the hard drive.'

'Good thinking, Carl.'

'He said he didn't believe me and I told him to fuck off. He got so mad. Jesus, I saw a flash of his fist and then...nothing.'

'We know he can't control his temper. He attacked his own wife. Tell me–'

'Please, you have to catch him.' Masiker's fingers curled around Jack's wrist with surprising strength for someone who'd just had the shit beaten out of him. 'My...family.' Masiker turned his head away, coughed up blood that spattered on the sheet.

'Don't worry about them. Harlow's not likely to be hanging about.'

'He made threats. He's gonna kill my wife and son.'

'No he won't. He's on the run now. Help us find him.'

'Will you check on my family? He might have gone there first.'

'Yes, yes. Of course. Think hard, where could he have gone?'

'I wish I knew.'

A tap on the shoulder. 'Please, Detective, we have to go. Now.'

'What?' Jack spun around. 'Can't you wait one more second?'

Pony tail shook his head, took a step back as if fearing Jack would take a swing at him. 'If this man dies or has complications due to delayed treatment, I'm going to see you answer for it, not me.'

'Listen, mate.' *Was this guy just out of med school?* 'He's speaking coherently now, he's fine.'

'Are you a doctor as well as a cop?'

'Enough of your attitude, mate.' Out of the corner of his eye Jack saw the female paramedic take out her mobile to film the interaction. He felt his shoulders stiffen. Why was everyone so uncooperative?

'There could be bleeding on the brain,' insisted Pony tail. 'It's imperative we get him to the ER department.'

Jack stood, ready to disembark the ambulance, when Masiker yelled out. 'Wait! There's another...*cough*...USB drive in my...*cough*...safe. A master for the last three months.'

'What's the combination? Whisper it to me.'

'Every second digit of my mobile phone number...*cough*...in reverse order.'

'Gottcha.'

A leap to the tarmac. Thunk, thunk of ambulance doors. Wailing of sirens.

Back in the Stinger.

'What took you so long?' Taylor wore an expression of utter exasperation. 'I was watching that exchange. You're a real charmer, aren't you?'

'Listen.' The remark was ignored. 'Call Batista and get a squad car over to Masiker's house. He's worried Harlow's gonna fuck up his family. I highly doubt it, but I've been wrong before.'

'Can I get that in writing?'

'Just do it, then follow me inside into his office.'

Eight...six...zero... a turn of the handle and the heavy door swung open. Inside lay not only the promised flash drive, but something just as interesting. Box upon box – maybe fifty – of human growth hormone, steroids, wads of cash and, the biggest surprise, a Heckler and Koch USP pistol.

Taylor made a quick call, requested someone come and collect the goodies.

'Holy shit, Claudia. Quite a treasure trove.'

'Worth a fortune. But none of it as valuable as this.' She reached into the safe, took the flash drive from the top shelf and dropped it in her handbag.

Chapter 24

All available officers were gathered in the squad room, some sitting, most standing, to watch the video from The Iron Horse. Jack and Taylor stood either side of the TV monitor.

'OK,' said Batista from the back of the room. 'Let's see what we've got.'

The Inspector and his two senior detectives had already viewed the video when Jack and Taylor returned from the gym. Their job now: explain to the rest of the team how the footage they were about to see correlated with what they knew already.

'Thanks, boss.' Jack's smile lacked humour. 'This is a rarity in our business. A murder caught on camera. Pay attention.' The last bit was unnecessary, all eyes were glued to the screen.

He pressed the clicker.

Time stamp: 22:14, 28 October.

The video started: Masiker was working out in the gym alone, the rhythmic bass of a sound track thumping away quietly in the background. He exhaled sharply at the high point of his bench presses, three big black weights sat on each end of the barbell. The man groaned with effort, his arms quivering. He replaced the bar on the rack and sat up quickly, eyes wide. Andy Harlow and Danny Sharpe strode into view, stood close to Masiker, who had a confused look on his face. The camera, mounted at a height of about 2.5 metres on the opposite wall, showed the backs of the visitors' heads and Masiker front on.

Harlow – *You gotta help us, Carl. We need to lay low for a while.*

Masiker – *What's going on?*

Harlow – *Nothing you need to concern yourself with. We're desperate, mate. I know you've got a couple of properties.*

Masiker – *I've got three and they're all rented out to families. Long-term leases. I can't turf them out to accommodate you.*

Sharpe – *Come on, Carl. You've helped people out in a bind before. Especially us fighters.*

Masiker – *What can I say, boys. Nothing I can do. Especially if you won't tell me what it's about.*

Harlow – *Dammit, Carl! If you can't do that, at least put this in the safe for us, will ya?* (Harlow hoisted a hold-all into the air).

Masiker – *What is it?*

Harlow – *Best you don't know. Just stick it in there for a week or so and we'll collect when the time's right.*

Masiker (shook his head) – *Sorry, this is all too suss. I can't help you. Now, I'd like to finish my session, if you don't mind.*

Masiker swung his body around, lay on the bench and regripped the barbell. Harlow seized the gym owner by the shins, yanked him backwards and out from under the barbell, grabbed him by the throat.

Harlow – *You'll do as I say or Danny and I will be paying that little wife of yours a visit. And if you talk to the cops, you're both fucking dead, understand me?*

Sharpe's shoulders bounced up and down slightly; from the back it appeared as if he was laughing at Masiker's discomfiture, trapped on the weight bench with Harlow's grip around his neck tightening.

Masiker – *Let me go! All right I'll–*

At that moment Owen Kennedy entered the gymnasium, dressed in shorts and singlet, carry-bag by his side. He walks with a cocky gait befitting an MMA champion.

Kennedy – *What the hell's going on here? Let him go, you bastard! And where's Terry? He's never late for a training session.*

Harlow released his chokehold, turned to face Kennedy.

Sharpe (spun around, shoved Kennedy in the chest) – *Fuck off, Owen. This is none of your business.*

Kennedy – *Everything that happens in this gym is my business. I can guess what's in the bag you want Carl to hide, you bloody drug cheat.*

Sharpe snapped out a left jab at Kennedy, who ducked and let fly with a lightning elbow strike to Sharpe's chin, the sickening sound of bone on bone ringing out. Sharpe dropped like he'd been shot by a sniper, pulled himself into a foetal position. Kennedy stood legs shoulder width apart, glowering and yelling at Sharpe who lay motionless.

Jack stopped the video.

'This is where it gets exciting, so watch carefully.'

The video restarted: Harlow dashed out of shot, reappeared with a cast iron kettle bell, which he swung hard over the top of Kennedy's head while the latter was still taunting Sharpe. Kennedy fell flat on his face, arms by his sides, and didn't move.

Groans and gasps arose from the audience. Jack stopped the video.

'We can assume the blow was fatal and Owen Kennedy didn't suffer. That's the only comfort I can take out of this.'

Taylor added: 'Harlow's wife told us her husband had been a good man until recently. I guess that's a relative term, but even so, this is evidence of roid rage in its extreme form. Please roll the video again, Jack.'

Sharpe, recovered from the blow he received, leaped to his feet, put his hands to his head and started screaming and jumping about like he's on hot sand. Masiker stared open-mouthed, not at the man on the floor, but directly at the lens of the hidden camera. Harlow noticed this for an instant, but immediately switched his attention back to Kennedy's still form.

'You'll notice he's clocked Masiker behaving oddly.' Jack paused the video. 'I reckon Harlow's subconsciously filed this action of Masiker's away, put two and two together later and that's why he's fronted this morning and demanded a copy of what we're now watching. Let's continue.'

Sharpe – *Oh my God, not again!*

Harlow – *Danny, calm the fuck down!*

Sharpe was breathing like he's run a marathon, chest heaving. After about fifteen seconds he nods. – *I'm okay, I think.*

Masiker (stares at Sharpe) – *What did you mean "not again"? Jesus Christ, have you pair of idiots...*

Harlow – *He doesn't mean anything!*

Masiker – *We have to call the police. I'll say it was an accident.*

Harlow – *Like hell you will.*

Masiker sat motionless on the weight bench, colour drained from his face, while the others inspected the body, checking for signs of life. Harlow and Sharpe exchanged a look, shaking their heads. Harlow removed his polo shirt and wrapped it around Kennedy's head.

Harlow – *Carl, don't just sit there like a stunned mullet. Go and get something to put over his head. Something plastic. There's a deep gash, he's bleeding like a stuck pig.*

Masiker – *Are you sure he's dead? Maybe we should call an ambulance?*

Harlow – *Of course he's fucking dead. I can't detect any breathing or a pulse. Now, do as I say or Mrs Masiker's gonna end up like this interfering prick, you got me?*

Masiker disappeared, returning within 30 seconds with a blue garbage bag. He handed the bag to Harlow who secured it around Kennedy's head and pulled the drawstring tight.

Harlow – *You mention any of this to anyone, and you're fucken dead, understand?*

Harlow and Sharpe carried Kennedy's body out of shot. Masiker slumped, head between his knees, his sobs echoing in the empty gym to the accompaniment of the muffled workout tape. He stood, picked up the bag Harlow left behind, and moved out of shot, his entire body speaking defeat.

Jack stopped the video. 'And here comes the exclamation point to this whole clusterfuck.'

The action switched to the car park behind the gym, a spot out of reach of the "official" CCTV. Sharpe and Harlow took shuffling steps as they carry Kennedy's body to a lone vehicle parked under a light. Harlow eased the body's feet to the ground, popped the boot.

Jack stopped the video, zoomed in. 'Look here.' He pointed with the remote. 'There's another body already in there.'

'Holy shit!' cried Constable Wilson. 'It's Terry Bartlett's car.'

'It sure is,' said Taylor. 'With the owner's dead body inside.'

157

Jack switched off the video. 'That's the end of the show, folks. Now, let's hunt down this pair of motherfuckers before they do any more damage.'

Chapter 25

'Where to now?' Batista opened a new box of paperclips. 'It's a big country. This could be needle in a haystack stuff.'

'They've only got a small jump on us,' Jack said. 'They ain't getting away.'

'Come on, Lisbon. They could be anywhere by now.' The Inspector twisted a paperclip until it snapped clean in half. The rate at which he destroyed paperclips made Jack think it might be smart to invest in the company that made them. 'You can put a lot of miles behind you in, what is it now, five hours since Harlow clobbered Masiker.'

'No, we'll get 'em.' Constable Wilson announced in a loud voice then coughed into his fist.

Taylor jumped in her seat, swung her head around. 'Ben, you're supposed to cough before you speak if that was meant to be a warning.'

'Sorry.' Wilson smiled an apology. 'A quick heads up. Every police station in Australia has been alerted and supplied with copies of the videos, all airports, ferry terminals, major train stations. The media department has sent updates to all the press outlets, social media's buzzing with the news of our two fugitives. Harlow's and Sharpe's faces are everywhere. I'd give them no hope of getting away.'

'I'm not putting my faith in anyone but us finding them, especially since the Brisbane officers haven't arrived yet.' Jack was on his feet, jacket slinking over his shoulders. 'Harlow's a loose cannon and Sharpe, well, his name doesn't correspond with his judgement. Come on, Claudia. Let's go pay Carl

Masiker a visit.'

'Why?'

'I think there's more he could be telling us.'

Dr Walter Chesson, head of the Emergency Department, was one of those doctors Jack hated at first sight: a boorish white-coated dilettante who relished his authority a little too much.

'What are your names again?' asked the doctor. 'Are you relatives?'

Jack stiffened at the medico's attitude. 'Detective Sergeant Jack Lisbon and Detective Constable Claudia Taylor. We're investigating two homicides. It's imperative we talk to Carl Masiker.'

'I'm afraid that's out of the question.'

'Why?'

'He slipped into a coma an hour ago. I'm unable to say if he'll recover. The blow to the skull he sustained was almost fatal.'

'What do you mean he's in a coma? I was talking to him at 7:00am.'

'Were you now?'

'Yeah. He was perfectly lucid, spoke like a Shakespearean actor.'

The doctor licked his finger, flicked pages attached to a clipboard, read the notes over the top of his glasses. 'There was a delay in getting him to the hospital which proved to be critical. In fact...let me see...one of our orderlies mentioned that it was you, Detective Lisbon, who interfered with him carrying out his duties.'

The paramedic had been right. Jack prayed Masiker would recover, otherwise there'd be an inquiry, his job on the line. Again. He forced himself to be calm. 'With respect, I did *not* interfere. I needed to get crucial information out of him. We're hunting a pair of killers.'

'That's no concern of mine, Detective. I wouldn't want to be in your shoes if the patient dies.'

'Dies? What the hell...'

'C'mon, Jack.' Taylor grabbed Jack by the wrist. 'He's just winding you up.'

'How dare you!' Chesson roared, spittle spraying. 'Do you think I'd make light of a patient in a coma?'

The question hung in the air like smoke from an explosion as Jack and Taylor darted for the exit. Patients and hospital staff gawked in their wake.

Back in the Stinger, Jack's hands shook as they lightly gripped the steering wheel. 'What if he does die, Claudia? I'm gonna be royally screwed.'

'That won't happen. I'd say it's a shock-induced coma. He'll come out of it sooner rather than later.'

'What makes you say that?'

She shrugged. 'A guess?'

'Cheers. That makes me feel much better.'

'Stop acting sorry for yourself, Jack. How about we swing by Masiker's house, maybe his wife's at home. She might be able to shed some light on those properties Harlow mentioned in the video. He and Sharpe could be holed up in one of them.'

'Masiker said there were no vacancies.'

'He could've been lying.'

'If Harlow suspected Masiker wasn't telling the truth, what's to say he didn't pay the wife a visit? He was specific with his threat to her on the video.'

'Quite possible,' Jack agreed. 'We need to have a word with her. I don't think she's gonna be home, though. The paramedics would've called her en route to the hospital.'

'You're right. She's probably sitting by his bed in the ER ward as we speak.'

'Should we go back? I don't think that doctor's going to be keen to let us in after his little tantrum.'

'Let's ring her.' Jack snatched the receiver, radioed the station to see if Mrs Masiker's mobile number was on file. They were in luck. Gail Maree Masiker was on the frequent caller list. Two weeks ago she complained about a loud party in her street. The duty sergeant revealed she often called in about barking dogs, noisy neighbours, hooligans burning rubber, pretty much anything that ticked her off.

Taylor called the number, turned on loudspeaker. Mrs Masiker was indeed sitting by Carl's side in the emergency ward. A quick intro by Taylor and sympathies extended for her husband's plight.

'Thank you.' The woman spoke in a nasally voice indicative of recent crying.

'Oh dear, this whole thing is a tragedy. Who would've thought Andy Harlow could do such a thing?' Mrs Masiker choked off a sob. 'Kill two men and... nearly Carl, too!'

'Has Harlow or Sharpe approached you, threatened you or your family in any way?'

'No, thank God. The kids are at school and I'm here. I don't feel in any danger.'

Jack paused for a second. 'We understand you own a number of rental properties. Are they all tenanted?'

'What a strange question? But yes, as it happens, they are. Same tenants for years. Why do you need to know that?'

'Just routine.' Hope was fading faster than the curtains in Jack's lounge-room. 'Have you any idea at all where Harlow and Sharpe might have gone?'

Bleeps from medical equipment echoed down the line.

'What?'

'Do you know where they could be hiding out?'

'There's only one place I can think of. Last August, Carl and I separated for a while. He went to stay at his uncle's property, a mango farm out at Kilroy. Set up an outdoor gym and a boxing ring. He created a kind of retreat for some of the fighters to go to for some down-time. I know Bartlett and his crew went there. Carl reckons they loved it and he wishes he'd kept running it as a separate business. Now...*sob*...'

'Where's Kilroy?' Jack whispered to Taylor.

'Three hours' drive inland,' Taylor whispered back.

Hope was returning. 'Can you give us the exact address?' Jack's question was more a demand.

'Oh dear,' ...*sob*... 'I can't remember. I'm sure you'll find it on the Internet. His uncle's name's Steven. The farm's called Masiker's Mangoes.'

'Thanks so much for your time, you've been most helpful. Best wishes to your husband and family.' Taylor ended the call.

The business's phone number was on the homepage of its website; Jack dialled while Taylor jotted down the address. *Optus advises that the number you have dialled has been disconnected.*

'Holy shit, Claudia. Maybe someone's yanked the phone out of the socket.'

'Not a good sign. Is there a mobile number?'

There was. Straight to voicemail. Jack left a message for Steven Masiker to call back urgently.

'Harlow's there, I can feel it.' Jack felt his pulse quicken.

'It's a long, bumpy drive out to Kilroy.'

'Shit.'

Jack radioed Batista. 'Inspector. I think I know where they are? We need a helicopter.'

'You've got evidence, I take it?'

'It's a logical conclusion.'

'That sounds like a euphemism for a hunch. I'm going to need more than that to request a helicopter, Jack.'

'I think Jack's right, sir.' Taylor relayed that Carl Masiker was in a coma, the exchange with Gail Masiker, the fact the phone numbers didn't connect. 'It's all pointing to Kilroy. Harlow and Sharpe could have taken the uncle prisoner. Or worse.'

'I'll see what I can do, but don't hold your breath. I can't recall a police helicopter ever being sent up to Yorkville.'

'Sir,' said Jack. 'We−'

'Get your arses back to the station. I want a full report on your conversation with Mrs Masiker. In the meantime I'll call the local cop shop out at Kilroy, ask the Sergeant to pop over to the farm and check it out.'

'Tell him to be careful,' said Jack. 'Harlow's off his rocker and Sharpe's no better.'

Two blocks from the station Batista called on the radio.

'As I predicted, no dice on the helicopter. All available aircraft are busy looking for a lost bushwalker on the Gold Coast.'

'Are you kidding me? This is a possible siege situation.'

'Wouldn't matter, mate. You know how long it takes a chopper to fly up here from the Gold Coast?'

'No.'

'Too fucking long. You and Taylor are going to have to drive out to Kilroy.

I'll put Wilson, Trevarthen and Semmens on stand-by. All spare officers are attending a bad traffic accident, so you'll have to manage on your own for now. I suggest you swap the Stinger for a Hilux. The roads out that way are shit.'

Chapter 26

The telephone reception was almost as bad out bush as the roads. The two cops stopped at a roadside café with half-decent Wi-Fi. They connected to Skype and called the local cop who answered on the second ring. Jack had found a picture of him online while Taylor bought soft drinks. Sergeant Robert Gupta had a neat, clipped beard, tended to overweight. A brief bio revealed he'd infiltrated a criminal gang five years ago. Risked his life to foil a multi-million dollar cattle stealing operation and got a commendation for his efforts. Indian extraction judging by the surname and complexion.

'Bob Gupta speaking.' The accent was Australian as the outback; warm and slack with drowsy vowels.

'DS Lisbon. What's happening there, Sergeant?' said Jack.

'I'm just pulling into the drive. It's a long, winding one; I won't see the house for another couple of minutes.'

'Do you know the property?'

'Sure do. Been there plenty of times.'

'To sort out trouble?'

Gupta laughed. 'No, not at all. Steve's a great bloke, a legend in Kilroy. The population's only 301, so I guess that's not hard.'

'Why is he a legend?'

'He sponsors the football team, works hard for the community. He throws regular barbecues, invites everyone along. We all love him out here.'

'Family?'

'His wife died of cancer a while back and his three kids have left the nest. I guess he gets lonely once the farm labourers go home at the end of the day.'

Jack rubbed his forehead. A popular resident of the town getting killed by a couple of desperadoes would be extra bad news. 'Let's hope he remains a local legend and doesn't become a national celebrity for all the wrong reasons.'

'You think he's in danger?'

'I'm sure of it.' Jack opened the Hilux door, he and Taylor climbed inside. The engine started with a sweet hum and jets of cool air filled the stifling interior. 'You're on loud speaker by the way.'

'No dramas.'

'Do you remember when Steve's nephew Carl stayed with him last year?'

'Yeah, I met him. Nice bloke. Everyone was excited a rugby league superstar had come to town. It's hard to comprehend the mess he might be caught up in.'

'Carl played half a dozen games in the NRL, hardly a star.'

'I beg to differ. Hang on...Holy shit!'

'What's wrong?' Jack's heart skipped a beat. He and Taylor exchanged a look of alarm.

'A huge 'roo leapt in front of me, nearly wiped me out.' Gupta gave a throaty chuckle. 'They're a menace in these parts.'

'Please be careful,' said Taylor. 'We don't need another casualty.'

'Can you find a place where you can spy on Masiker's property without being seen?' said Jack.

'I think so. There's a ridge about 300 metres from the house, plenty of trees about. I can stop just below it, watch the front door through binoculars.'

'I suggest you do that until we arrive. If you see or hear anything out of the ordinary, let me know sharpish.'

'Roger that.'

The isolated rocky formations grew more numerous the further west they drove. The landscape changed gradually, dense rainforest giving way to sparse grasslands and ghost gums, pinnacled limestone outcrops, rising high above the plains. The fat storm clouds they left behind in Yorkville became fluffier, less ominous. One constant didn't change, though. It was still bloody hot, 37 degrees according to the car's digital thermometer. Jack wasn't keen to abandon the refreshing air conditioning pouring out of the vents in the Hilux. He chewed hard on nicotine gum, stared out the window and tried to imagine how the rest of this crazy day was going to pan out.

'Hey.' Taylor tapped Jack on the shoulder. 'Are your eyes painted on? You missed the sign.'

'Shit.' He pulled the SUV into a tight U-turn, sprayed a fan of gravel behind the vehicle. 'Sorry.'

A rusty tin sign swung in the light afternoon breeze. *Masiker's Mangoes.*

Within five minutes Jack and Taylor had traversed most of the deeply rutted driveway; like Gupta they had a close encounter with a big red denizen of the bush. Bounded over the bonnet of the Hilux, leaving the detectives open-mouthed and breathless. As they crested the penultimate rise, Taylor spotted the rear end of Gupta's Land Cruiser, covered in more dust than the inside of a vacuum cleaner bag. 'There he is.'

After tucking the Hilux in behind Gupta's vehicle, quick introductions and hand shakes, the local cop revealed he'd observed three men moving about hurriedly in the house through a bay window. Then they disappeared from view and he hadn't seen them since.

'Were they armed?'

'Not that I could see. But I can tell you Steve's got a gun closet with two kick-arse rifles in it. He culls 'roos when they get out of control. The odd wild dog. Those weapons are kept under lock and key. Every random check I've done on him, he's been in full compliance.'

'A model citizen as well as a local legend,' said Taylor

'As for the other two blokes,' continued Gupta. 'I can't tell you.'

'But you didn't see them waving pistols about?' said Jack.

'No. Doesn't mean they don't have 'em stuffed down their pants, though, does it?'

Jack nodded. 'True. We should assume they *are* armed.' He flashed Taylor a worried look. 'Remember the HK pistol in Masiker's safe?'

'Uh huh. But it's unregistered. We don't know who it belongs to. Could be Carl Masiker's just as easily as it could be Harlow's.'

Jack shook his head. 'Nah, it's Harlow's. Even if it's not, they might've forced Steven to open his gun safe and give them his rifles. Let's take another look.'

The copse of stringy barks offered excellent screening, practically impossible for anyone down in the farmhouse to see them. The three officers lay flat on their stomachs, each scanning the front of the house with a pair of high-powered binoculars. From the high vantage point, all of them could clearly make out Harlow's gold Mercedes SUV parked next to a utility pick-up. A hundred metres to the right, two red tractors inside a structure the size of a small aircraft hangar. To the rear of the building stood another large shed; Gupta explained it was the cool room for storing fruit from the mango trees which sprawled in neat green rows at least a kilometre towards the horizon. In the distance, the abandoned remains of an old zinc mine glistened in the bright afternoon sunlight.

'You guys seeing any sign of human life anywhere?' said Jack, wiping a trickle of sweat from his eye. The heat was almost stultifying; if not for the shade the gum trees provided he was sure his blood would literally boil.

'Nothing.' Taylor blew a buzzing insect off her top lip. 'Piss off, fly!'

'Hang on a second.' Gupta wriggled, propped himself up on his elbows. 'I can see movement through that big window. That's Steve's lounge room. Look.'

Jack and Taylor focused on the window, about 300 metres distant. Harlow and Sharpe were dragging a man under the armpits, hands tied behind his back. Steven Masiker resisted, dug his heels in, wriggled like a feisty bull trout on a ten-pound line. The intruders sat him on a wooden kitchen chair. Harlow yelled at the captive, who yelled back in equal measure. Sharpe paced erratically, his body language conveying panic and uncertainty. Jack noted the resemblance of Steven Masiker to his nephew. The same fleshy features, although the older man, probably in his late sixties, sported a bushy moustache and a shaved head with a shadow of short black hair around the sides. Like Carl, he was tall and rangy. Harlow reached into a pocket and produced a roll of electrical tape, roughly wound it around the farmer's mouth. Jack thought of the pain ripping it off was going to cause. Hopefully, Steve would get to feel that pain later, because it would mean he was alive.

'Why the hell are they doing that to him?' Gupta's voice was filled with alarm. He scrambled to his feet. 'This is bullshit, we have to get down there.'

'Not so hasty,' said Jack. 'They're both desperate, there's no logic to their behaviour. Who knows what drugs they've ingested, either.'

'We can't just leave Steve there with those two crazies.'

'If we storm in, I can't guarantee he's going to come out alive. There's no cover between us and the house, just a vast empty space. They'll spot us for sure. I can't see a way to gain access from the back unnoticed either.'

'What do you suggest then?' Gupta couldn't hide his frustration. 'Dig a tunnel and pop up in the fucking lounge room?'

Jack let the sarcasm slide. 'When's sunset?'

'About 6:30pm. Why?'

'That gives us,' Jack glanced at his watch, 'just over two hours. I'd love to get this over and done with before nightfall. I just can't think how.'

'I've got a pair of night vision binoculars if we have to keep watch after dark.' Gupta said hopefully. He lay back down on his stomach, almost instantaneously rolled onto his side to brush away a jagged rock.

'Let's hope it doesn't come to that. I'm gonna hit up the boss for some inspiration.'

Jack returned to the Hilux, radioed Batista. 'Sir, we've got a situation here. The suspects are holed up in Steven Masiker's farm, possibly armed.'

'Christ, that's not good. Have you got visuals on the suspects?'

'Only when they're in the lounge room.'

'Are they aware of your presence?'

'Negative, sir.'

'What else can you see?'

'Nothing inside the house. The curtains are drawn in all other rooms. If they decide to pull the blinds in the lounge, we'll have no idea what's happening. As we speak, they've got Steven Masiker gagged with tape and hogtied to a chair, they're roughing him up a bit. It's frustrating the hell out of me to watch it.'

'Try to stay calm.'

'I'm doing my best sir. It's not easy in this heat.'

'I understand, Jack. Can you sneak up on the house?'

'There's too much open ground surrounding the property. We'd be sitting ducks if they've got hold of Masiker's rifles.'

'Wait till nightfall. Have you got night vision goggles?'

'No sir. I wasn't expecting to be playing ninjas out here. But Gupta does have a pair of infrared binoculars. Problem is, we can't all use them at once. We'll have to use the flashlights on our mobile phones if we decide to advance on the house.'

'I'll leave you to monitor the situation. Don't do anything without obtaining my approval first, you got me?'

'Yes, sir.'

'I'll request a unit from the Special Emergency Response Team head over there.'

'What's the ETA?'

'Fifteen minutes for them to scramble, approximately three hours travel time.'

'That's too fucking long! Why don't we have our own aircraft up here?'

'Write a letter to the Police Minister. I'm sure he'll give it his fullest attention.'

'Hilarious.'

'Listen, I've got an idea. I'll contact the Air Force. There're some Black Hawk and Chinook helicopters at Garbutt Base, if I recall.'

Jack scratched his head. Perhaps sending in the cavalry wasn't such a smart idea. 'Might be best if you don't call them, sir. Special ops goons crawling all over the place and hulking great choppers flying overhead aren't likely to instil calm in Harlow and Sharpe. Could send them right over the edge.'

'Not sure I'm liking where you're going with this, DS Lisbon. Are you proposing...'

'I'll keep you posted, sir.' Jack ended the call. Batista called straight back, Jack hit the "end call" button. He'd blame poor reception.

Jack, Taylor and Gupta would have to get the job done themselves.

Back at the top of the ridge, Jack briefed the others on his chat with Batista.

'He's requesting help from SERT and the military.'

'What? I'm not sure that's proportionate to the threat here.' Taylor screwed up her eyes.

'Me either,' said Jack. 'I more or less hinted we'd get the job done ourselves.'

'You what?' Gupta's eyes widened. 'Your boss is right. Why not let the professionals handle it? They'll have trained negotiators, the lot.'

'Because I know deep in my gut the noise and spectacle of a Francis Ford Coppola movie descending on this farm will only lead to disaster. And negotiations won't work with these guys.'

'I agree with Jack,' said Taylor, slugging water from a canister. 'We're going to have a better chance of ending this ourselves.'

'Holy shit.' Gupta wiped his brow with his sleeve. 'I hope you know what you're doing.'

'Me too.' Jack pulled out his Glock and made sure he had a full clip.

Just after sunset the three police officers checked they had sufficient charge on their mobile phones to operate the inbuilt flashlight apps. Each guesstimated they had enough battery power for them to run on low for a couple of hours.

'Even at the dullest setting, won't they still see the lights?' Taylor's initial enthusiasm seemed to be waning the closer it got to show time. 'What if they suddenly decide to stare out the window while we're crossing the open ground.'

'We might be OK,' said Gupta. 'Fireflies are active this time of year, trying to attract mates. The phone lights will blend in with them. Our dark shadows could be 'roos grazing.'

'Yeah, and what do lots of people do to kangaroo in paddocks?' said Taylor. 'Shoot them, that's what.'

Neither Gupta nor Jack could offer a reply to that entirely logical conclusion.

As the natural light faded and darkness descended, the luminous insects began to twinkle in the trees around them and across the fields. Soon, the sky was bedecked with starry-jewels, meteorites flashed through the atmosphere, extended tails glowing red. Jack gaped at the crystal clarity of the stars out here in the bush. He'd seen nothing like it in his life.

'We're lucky there's no moon tonight,' said Gupta. 'Otherwise...'

'Indeed,' said Jack. 'Now, are we all ready?'

At precisely 6:40pm, the three officers carefully made their way down the short incline, in a half crouch, stepping around rocks and clumps of vegetation. They spread out in a line, two metres apart. Their mobile phone lights were pointed straight down: to minimize the chance Harlow and Sharpe actually could tell the difference between glowing fireflies and artificial light from cell phones, and to prevent a nasty fall. Wombat holes dotted the terrain, camouflaged traps that could twist ankles. Halfway across the paddock, someone inside the farmhouse pulled the loungeroom curtains closed. Now they had no way of keeping an eye on Steven Masiker.

'Oi,' Taylor cried out in a whisper-shout. 'I can barely see. There's a swarm of moths in my face. They're...ugh...'

'Shhh, said Jack.

'Pull your shirt over you face and hold the phone out to the side,' said Gupta. 'They're attracted to the light.'

'Gottcha.'

With about 150 metres to go before they reached the house, a naked light globe switched on above the front door, instantly drawing a swarm of bugs. Jack dropped to the warm dirt, face down. He heard rustling sounds to his left and right as Taylor and Gupta did the same. He thrust his chin forward, tilted his head back to see what was happening. The two wanted men each carried a long-neck beer bottle in one hand, a scoped rifle in the other. The guns looked like they could penetrate the Great Wall of China. The men headed for a chair and a framed swing seat on the front veranda. They were laughing and joking, the sounds of their conversation reaching the cops in the still, clear night. Harlow was full of swagger, anxiety made Sharpe's voice quiver.

'You don't really plan to kill him, do you, Andy?' The fighter took a huge slug from the bottle, spat on the wooden decking.

''Fraid so, mate.'

'But why? He's done nothing wrong.'

'Being related to that dickhead Carl is reason enough. Guilt by fucken association.'

'If you say so.'

'I do. Now I'm your exclusive full-time trainer, you gotta learn to do exactly as I say.'

Sharpe nodded as he rocked back and forth in the swing chair.

The two sat in silence for a while. Harlow reached into his pocket, pulled out a pouch and started rolling a cigarette. A while after he lit up the aroma pierced the air and it was clear he wasn't smoking tobacco. The two men shared the joint, not a word was spoken between them for at least two minutes.

'Psst, you two, sneak around the back,' Jack whispered. 'Go in a wide arc and don't make any unnecessary noise. Once you're inside, liberate the hostage. I trust you can break into the place without making a racket. Once you've got Steven, get the fuck out of there and run for the mango plantation.'

'The house is miles away,' protested Taylor.

'It's only about 150 metres. Listen, they're going to kill the man. Both of you, crawl on your damn stomachs. I'll slowly make my way as close to them as I dare.'

'Why don't we just take a pot shot at 'em from here?' said Taylor.

'We're still out of effective range. If we gamble and miss, they race inside and Steve's fucked. Maybe they'll start firing back at us and then we're fucked. Those powerful rifles trump what we've got for distance.'

'Jesus, Jack. Why do I wish I'd never met you?' Taylor hissed.

'Shut up and go!'

'C'mon,' said Gupta with gentle encouragement. 'You've got this.'

Taylor's and Gupta's backsides began wriggling away from Jack, in opposite directions at 45 degree angles; the adrenalin coursing through their bodies ensured they covered ground fast. Harlow and Sharpe lowered their voices, words now a low rumble.

Have they realised they're being watched?

They reached down for their beers, clicked a toast to something.

No, they have no clue we're here.

Soon they'd finish the bottles; in their frame of mind they'd be wanting to get drunk. Jack knew he would if he was in their shoes. Which meant they'd need to go back inside.

Hurry up, you two...

Once past the western side of the house, Taylor and Gupta stood, quickly stretched to get proper feeling back into their extremities. They trotted with light steps to the corner, made a left and headed for the back door. Gupta twisted the handle. Not locked.

'Follow me, Claudia.'

She didn't argue, the local cop knew they layout of the house. Through the open-plan kitchen and into the lounge. Gupta put a finger to his lips. 'Be quiet, Steve. Not a word'. He and Taylor loosened Masiker's bonds, escorted the shaking man to the back door.

'Those cunts were going to kill me after they'd drunk those beers. Oh, sorry for the language.' A look of shocked embarrassment passed across Masiker's face. 'Didn't know there were ladies present.'

A loud bang. 'Shit, that's the front fly screen slamming. We have to hurry.'

By the back door, Steve grabbed a big Dolphin flashlight from a steel wire rack. He moved with a limping gait.

'Can you run, Steven?' said Taylor, arm around the older man's waist.

'Run? I can barely fucken hobble. Pardon my French.'

'Where are the keys to your ute out the front?'

'In the ignition, mate. This is Kilroy. No crime out here.'

Loud footsteps came from the lounge room.

'Where's the bastard gone?' thundered Harlow.

'I dunno, we both checked the rope. He must be Houdini!'

'Or someone's untied him. Quick, you check out the front, I'll have a look round the back.'

Jack crawled another 50 metres over jagged stones, gritted his teeth as prickly weeds bit into his skin. Finally he was close enough. He stood slowly, planted his feet firmly into the dusty ground, raised his gun to eye level. Out of the corner of his eye he saw a white 4-door Nissan Navara cough to life; its rear tyres spun in a blur until the vehicle took off like a rocket. Gupta sat at the wheel, the others, Jack hoped, were crouched down in the back seat. The two fugitives burst through the front door, shotguns slung over their shoulders, searching for the source of the noise. They stood as statues, hands on hips, as Gupta put ever more distance between the pickup and the house.

'Fuck!' Harlow stamped his feet. He felt in his pocket, extracted a set of car keys. 'Come on. We have to catch him.'

'Why?' said Sharpe. 'What's the point? Let him go.'

'He heard us admitting to wasting Bartlett and Kennedy, that's why.'

'Come on, Andy! We need to get the hell away from here. He'll raise the alarm with the local cops and−'

'Too late!' Jack shouted from the relative safety of the eastern corner of the house. He'd managed to slink away from the line of fire in all the chaos. 'Get on the ground before I blow your fucking heads off your shoulders!'

A firefly dove directly at Jack's eye, made him drop his gaze for a couple of seconds. A glance up again, and Harlow had grasped Sharpe in a fearsome headlock. Both rifles lay on the deck, a pistol pressed to Sharpe's temple.

Fuck.

'Don't do it Andy. Let him go.'

'No. You let *us* go, or this punk gets a bullet.'

'Punk? He's your boy, your full-time fighter.'

'Please...' Sharpe blubbered.

The kid's pathetic, lost his edge, Jack thought. Or the weed's made him slow and vulnerable. Putty in the hands of a manipulator like Harlow.

'Shut up, you muppet.' Harlow tightened the headlock.

Images of the siege in the Brisbane bank came flooding back to Jack. He'd overcome two gunmen, today he only had to bring down one. The difference between this standoff and the bank siege boiled down to one crucial element. The man holding the gun here was a hundred times craftier than the meth-addicted bank robbers. Jack would have to handle Harlow with kid gloves for now, otherwise Sharpe's brains would be blown out of his thick skull.

'Listen, Andy. You've done enough damage already. Go easy on Danny and I'll see it's taken into account when you're dealt with.'

The headlock around Sharpe's neck tightened, the fighter now a pathetic specimen, eyes bulging like a terrified frog. 'Dealt with!' Harlow bellowed.

'Fuck that. No, that's not what's going to happen. You're going to escort me and the young bloke out of here.'

'Where do you want to go?'

'Cairns airport.'

Chapter 27

'OK. I'll help you.'

Harlow's forehead wrinkled in distrust. 'Why?'

'I'm concerned about Danny. You've dragged him into this mess. He's got his whole life ahead of him.'

'He's a big boy, he's made all his own decisions.'

'Andy, I'm gonna be honest with you.' *Like hell.* 'I'm sick of breathing in insects and dust. Do the right thing and it won't turn out so bad for you. Let's head back up the hill, hop in the squad car and drive back to Yorkville.'

'I said the airport.'

Jack shook his head. 'You're dreaming if you think you can get away, sunshine. There's nowhere for you to go. If you co-operate I'll see if I can cut you a deal.'

Harlow's head stretched backwards at a crazy angle. He let out a blood-curdling cry that carried across the landscape. 'Cut a deal?' His raspy voice was a scraping violin. 'You've got to be joking, mate. No way I'm surrendering to a pig like you.'

Jack's heart hammered in his ribcage. He could only wonder what was flooding through Sharpe's mind as his Harlow maintained his savage grip and jammed the gun harder and harder into the man's temple.

'We've got enough evidence to convict both you and Danny, put you away for years. By the time you got out it'd be straight into a nursing home. But I don't want to see lives wasted. You don't want that. I'm sure Louise ands the kids don't want that.'

A flicker in the corner of Harlow's eye as he sighed deeply. 'Don't bring my family into this!'

'Why not? Louise is facing all kinds of trouble with her business. Now you, making one mistake after the other. She's going to fall apart unless you man up and start doing the right thing for once in your life.'

Silence.

'What about your two young kids, Andy? Sweet, innocent little—'

'Enough!' Jack could hear the man wheezing as he struggled to maintain the headlock on his partner. 'What do you want from me?'

'First, you let go of Danny and put the gun away. Then we talk.'

Jack imagined cogs whirring inside Harlow's head. The trainer retracted his arm from Danny's neck, swapped it for an avuncular embrace. He slid the pistol into the back of his shorts. Bizarrely, instead of stepping away, the young man snuggled into Harlow's side, like a whipped dog loyal to a cruel master. The surreal scene unfolded as if in slow motion.

'That's better.'

'What's the deal?'

'Admit to your crimes, tell us what you did to Terry Bartlett, and I'll push for a big reduction in your sentence.'

'Why would you do that?'

'Like I said, I'm worried about your wife and children. As for Danny, he's still got a life ahead of him. Spending the rest of it in prison would be just another tragedy.' Jack sheathed his own weapon, detached a pair of handcuffs from his belt and held them in the air. He couldn't believe the bullshit he was prepared to spin to get Harlow and Sharpe to co-operate. 'Turn around and let me put these on you.'

Harlow must have had an epiphany. He complied without further protest, turned around, his hands held close together behind his back.

As Jack got closer, Harlow growled: 'Why no restraints for him? He's as guilty as I am.'

'I've only got the one pair. I'm gonna have to hope he doesn't try anything stupid. You're not going to try anything stupid are you, Danny?'

'No.' It was barely a mumble. No fight left in him now.

'How about immunity if I give you information on the source of all the HGH and steroids?' said Harlow, shoulders twitching.

Jack gave an involuntary laugh. 'It was Zane who fingered you! You can forget about immunity.' He smiled as he went to attach the first cuff. Click. The second one never made it to Harlow's wrist.

An almighty swing of the elbow caught Jack unawares. A rookie mistake, he'd been confident the big man had fully surrendered. Before Jack could react, Harlow spun around, his right fist slammed into Jack's cheek, sent him sprawling to the ground. With his ears ringing and pain arcing through his skull, Jack commando rolled as far away as he could in the semi-darkness, eating dirt as he tumbled. He reached for his back pocket, snapped to a crouch position and took aim at where he thought Harlow's midsection would be. He squinted, blinked grit from his eyes. Harlow had somehow managed to wrestle Sharpe to the ground, stand back up and place a foot in the middle of his back.

You fucking idiot, Lisbon!

'Stay still, pig! Move and I'll blow the kid's brains out. No more mucking around. Toss your weapon over here. NOW!'

'Jesus mothering Christ, Andy!' Jack entreated. 'Are you completely mad?'

'Yeah, maybe I am.'

'It was all an accident...' Finally, Danny had summoned the courage to speak.

'What happened, Danny? You can tell me,' said Jack.

'SHUT UP!' Harlow shrieked.

'Stop him, for God's sake!' Danny pleaded. 'I'll tell you everything. It's all Andy's fault. Terry...he never deserved to die...'

'You traitorous fuck.' Harlow pulled his leg back; a ferocious kick in the kidneys drew an agonised yelp from Sharpe. Jack saw the lad try to push himself up, but Harlow stamped his foot in the small of Sharpe's back like he was trying to extinguish a grassfire.

The click of the trigger. A flash. A bang.

And just like that, a bullet to the back of Danny Sharpe's skull ended a life of promise unfulfilled.

'Stay still and drop the weapon!' Taylor's shaky voice boomed in the night air. 'I won't hesitate to finish you off if you don't comply.'

What the hell? Where did she come from?

Jack looked up. She'd appeared like a phantom. The barrel of Taylor's pistol pressed firmly into Harlow's cheek. A small cloud of dust rose as Harlow tossed his gun to ground. He'd run out of aces.

'Game over, mate,' she said.

As Taylor secured the second handcuff dangling from Harlow's right wrist, Jack leapt to his feet, sprinted the couple of metres separating him from Harlow and smashed him in the mouth with the hardest right hook he could produce. 'Damn right it's game over!' The smack of fist on bone rang out as loud as the sound of the gunshot had. Harlow was unconscious before he hit the ground. Jack leaned over to inspect his handiwork.

'Nice punch, cowboy.' Taylor's body trembled, her fake bravado masked the terror she must have felt.

'Thanks. He's going to wish you'd killed him by the time I'm done with him.'

She shook her head. 'For fuck's sake, Jack. You've broken his jaw. Don't hit him again or I'll have to write it up as unnecessary brutality.'

Jack ignored the remark, rumbled around in Harlow's shorts pocket and extruded the roll of electrical tape. He wound some around the man's mouth and used it to bind his arms tight to his side. 'Hoist by his own effing petard.'

'I've no idea what that means. Aren't the handcuffs enough?

'The quote's from Shakespeare. It means karma's a bitch. And yes, the cuffs *are* enough but I don't like to take chances with vermin like him. Now he can get to experience what he though was acceptable for another human being. An innocent one.'

Taylor turned her attention to Sharpe's body, Jack's mobile phone torch showing a growing pool of blood around the man's head. He felt for a pulse knowing it was a futile gesture, looked up at Taylor and shook his head. 'What are we going to do with him?' she asked.

'Wait here. I'll get the Hilux. We'll stash him in the cool room until forensics gets here to go over the scene.'

A quick call to Batista as Jack returned to the car confirmed his suspicions. The military had denied use of any of their aircraft. 'Doesn't matter, sir. The siege is over.'

'Why do I get the feeling you're understating what happened?'

A cough into the fist as the hot night breeze stirred up dust. 'Send forensics and a couple of uniforms to secure the place. Taylor and I have Harlow under arrest.'

'Sharpe?'

'Dead sir.'

'What the fuck!'

'Harlow shot him. Claudia and I witnessed it, there's no getting out of this one for Harlow.'

'But why?'

'Young Danny was about to let us know what had happened to Terry Bartlett and Harlow shot him point blank.'

'What a mess.'

'I would have been dead, too, if Claudia hadn't shown up in the nick of time.'

'Are you and Claudia OK?' Batista's voice wavered. 'I'll get Cairns hospital to send their chopper if it's available.'

'No need, sir. We're unharmed.' Jack rubbed his aching face where Harlow had struck him. 'We'll keep an eye on the body until the troops arrive. As for the perpetrator, I wanna bring him in myself.'

'What state is Harlow in? I imagine he's putting up a fight.'

'Not exactly, sir. I'll keep you posted.' Jack hung up the phone before Batista could press for details about Harlow's health. He likely needed urgent hospitalisation, but when the smashed jaw was detected Jack would say the man fell hard trying to escape. At least the electrical tape would spare him and Taylor from verbal abuse when Harlow regained consciousness.

He popped a nicotine gum into his parched mouth and jumped into the SUV. One piece of gum left. He may have to search Uncle Steven's house for a pouch of tobacco, perhaps a stiff drink. Taking care to avoid animal burrows and boulders, he nursed the car down the rutted hill to the middle of the paddock.

His high beam floodlit two bodies on the ground. Next to them, hand on hips and tottering like a loose fence post, stood DC Taylor, all colour drained from her face.

Jack gripped the interior grab handle, hoisted himself into the passenger side. He waved at Wilson and Smith as they drew up level in the driveway. The constables stopped, Wilson wound down the driver's window. 'Where's the body?'

'In the cool room,' Jack replied. 'Dr. Proctor's already there with a couple of her colleagues. You'll see the vehicles parked out front.'

'Anything we need to be aware of?'

'Just insects the size of sheep,' said Taylor. 'Apart from that, the danger's over. Just turn up and look as enthusiastic as you can. They'll do a quick examination of the scene where Sharpe was killed, then inside the house to look for evidence they tortured Masiker.'

'You think it'll take long?' said Wilson.

'Shouldn't do. There's nothing to investigate.' Jack turned as he heard Harlow give a groan in the back of the Hilux. 'Claudia and I saw the lot.'

'Good, only I've got a date with—'

The window was back up before Wilson could finish. Jack didn't give a monkey's about the man's love life.

Two minutes along the main highway Jack asked: 'What happened to Gupta and Uncle Steven after you escaped?'

'Masiker was in deep shock. He had injuries. Bruises, lacerations. Harlow knocked him about after he and Sharpe lobbed on the doorstep uninvited.'

'What an arsehole.'

'Yeah. Gupta dropped me at the car and raced Masiker to a GP in Kilroy township.'

'I'm so glad you didn't go with them, Claudia.'

'Believe me, I was tempted. Somehow my sense of duty took over from self-preservation. Gupta loaned me his infrared binoculars before he left. I watched your standoff with the bad guys unfold from the top of the ridge. When it was clear things were getting out of hand I knew I had to move.'

'I'm forever in your debt for saving me, Claudia.'

'I've never been so scared in my life.' She turned on the water to wash a film of squashed insects from the windscreen. 'You owe me big time, DS Lisbon.'

'I hope you're not planning on constantly reminding me about it.' Jack turned his head but she kept focused on the road.

'Do you really think I could be such a bitch? It's part of the job description to save colleagues. You learn it on day one.' Something in her voice told Jack she wouldn't hesitate to rub his nose in it down the track. He'd be looking out for any opportunity to save her arse and square the ledger. There was nothing worse than being indebted to someone.

Taylor held the vehicle's speed at a steady 90kph, eyes constantly scanning ahead for kangaroos and other suicidal wildlife. It was almost a pointless exercise, critters jumped out of the shadows from every direction. They collided with a few animals and hundreds of insects, but no serious damage was done to the car; Jack thought they must've killed half a dozen 'roos and wallabies within the first 100 kms. Taylor winced every time there was a bump against the chassis.

'Listen, Claudia. How about we just put a couple of bullets in Harlow's brain and chuck him in the bush? No one's going to miss him. His life's worth less than any of the dead beasties on the side of the highway.' Jack glanced in the rear vision mirror. Harlow, trussed up like a Christmas turkey, groaned pathetically.

'No. We need Harlow to tell us where Terry Bartlett is. Have you forgotten about him?'

'To tell you the truth, in the middle of this train wreck, I almost had.'

'Lots of people still want closure on this, Jack. With Sharpe dead, the only one who can give us any answers is that piece of human garbage on the back seat.'

The rest of the journey took place with the radio turned up to drown out the sound of Harlow's pitiful moaning.

At five minutes before midnight, Taylor turned into the entry of Yorkville General Hospital. In the underground carpark, Jack pulled Harlow to a sitting position and set about removing the tape from his mouth. The scent of the joint he'd smoked wafted from Harlow's mouth, made Jack want to gag. The last centimetre of tape clung grimly to the stubbly skin around the prisoner's bloody lips. Claudia gasped as the last bit of tape came away and the end of Harlow's bottom jaw flopped down. Harlow tried to speak but the broken bone turned his efforts into garbled nonsense.

'Stop whining or the tape goes back on.' Jack gave the man's face a gentle slap, drawing an expression of disgust from Taylor. 'Will you keep quiet?'

Harlow winced and nodded.

'Good. And don't even think about making a complaint against me, or I swear you'll regret the day God put breath into you.'

Harlow whimpered as the officers escorted him to the elevator. 'Yes, I know it hurts.' If it wasn't for the sarcasm, Jack's tone could be described as compassionate. 'You'll be all patched up in no time. Then you're going to answer our questions. Then you're going to jail. Got it?'

As they walked, Taylor tugged at a loose piece of the tape securing Harlow's arms to his side. 'Leave that on,' said Jack.

'Come on. It's not very dignified, is it?'

'I don't give a toss. His dignity is the least of my concerns after what he's done.' He put an arm around Harlow's shoulder. 'You don't mind do you, old son?'

The hatred burning in Harlow's eyes could have melted a candle. As the two men stared at each other, The Clash erupted on Jack's phone. 'Yes?'

'Just a heads up, Sarge. There's a gurney on its way down to the carpark to collect the precious cargo.' As soon as the words were out of Constable Trevarthen's mouth, the elevator doors opened. Standing with a male and female nurse was the charming Dr. Walter Chesson.

Harlow was placed in a ward on the top floor offering a commanding view of Yorkville's botanical gardens. The scene of serene natural beauty below was a perfect match for Chesson's newfound friendly attitude. The head doctor had done a 180 degree turn once the police made clear the seriousness of his new patient's alleged crimes against humanity. The fact Batista had spoken to him personally and two grim-faced uniformed constables stood guard outside the ward seemed to have added a frisson of excitement to the situation for

Chesson. The clincher, though, was Carl Masiker coming out of his coma and showing signs he'd make a full recovery and be discharged in a day or two. Jack had skilfully batted away questions about how Harlow's horrific jaw injury occurred, ably assisted by Taylor nodding agreement each time he answered one of Chesson's questions.

'He's been given powerful pain killers that've made him a bit woozy, so he shouldn't give you too much trouble.' Chesson smiled broadly. 'Be sure to let me know if there's anything you need. Please be as quick as you can. That jaw of his needs treatment within the next half hour.'

Jack tipped him a salute. 'Will do, Doc. Basically, I'd appreciate it if you could turn all visitors away, especially the press.'

'Understood. You needn't worry, though. Unless there's been a leak, no one is even aware he's here.'

Just before Chesson closed the door, Jack ventured with all the seriousness he could muster: 'I don't suppose you've got any of that sodium thiopental lying about, do you?'

'Pardon?'

'Truth serum. Mr Harlow has a pathological aversion to telling the truth, so I thought, you know...'

'Um, no we don't stock that drug.' Chesson fiddled with his stethoscope and blushed. 'My shift ends in an hour. You'll need to speak with my replacement after that. Good evening.'

With the medico out of the room, Taylor burst out laughing. 'Jesus, Jack. What was that all about?'

'The man's a complete tosser.' Jack shrugged.

Taylor sat one side of the bed with a notepad; her phone rested against a jug of water on a mobile table and recorded the scene. Jack sat on the other side of Harlow, squeezed up next to an IV pole. Harlow's jaw was smashed so badly he couldn't eat; he was able to speak, but with difficulty. To assist in the interview, Constable Trevarthen had obtained a mini white board and a marker pen.

'There'll be no legal representation for you unless you co-operate in full and don't get violent. Nod if you understand.'

Harlow nodded.

Jack readjusted his sitting position. 'Importantly, an operation to rewire your jaw won't be sanctioned until we're satisfied you've told us all you know. Got it?'

Another slow nod.

'If you're honest with me, I might even let your wife and kids come see you. I wouldn't hold my breath though, sunshine. I hear they want you to rot in hell. Ready to begin?'

'Yesh.' When he spoke, Jack noticed the all bottom the teeth on the left hand side of Harlow's face sat a centimetre or so higher than the ones on the right. Harlow scrawled on the whiteboard, held it up. *Fuck you!!! This is against the law!!!*

Taylor whispered in Jack's ear. 'I'm not sure I'm comfortable with this, Jack. The man needs urgent medical treatment. Anyone can see it.'

'Thank you, DC Taylor. Your comment is duly noted.' He turned back to Harlow. 'This here is a good, decent woman. Unfortunately for you, I outrank her, and she's going to do as I say.'

Jack leaned forward and took the white board and pen from Harlow. 'You're speaking well enough to dispense with these.' As he leaned back in his seat, he dropped the pen and immediately bent down to recover it. As he returned to an upright position, he saw Harlow grab the IV pole with two hands and yank it so hard it popped out of its base. The patient wielded the steel pole above his head and went to take a swing at Taylor. Jack instinctively launched himself at Harlow, smothered the pole and Harlow's arms with his body before his opponent could get up any momentum with the improvised weapon. The men's faces were pressed close together; Harlow's skin was clammy and his breath smelled like stale blood. The temptation to land a head butt on Harlow's nose was almost too much to resist. Somehow, Jack did. 'Do that again, and I'll finish you off here with my bare hands!'

He regained his seat as Harlow, exhausted by the effort expended, collapsed back onto his pillow. Taylors eyes bulged. 'You OK, Claudia?'

'Yeah. I think we should call it a day.'

'Like hell.' Jack produced a pair of handcuffs, snapped one around Harlow's right left wrist, the other to the metal rail running around the bed.

'One more chance to get it off your chest, Andy. Where's Terry?'

'I dunno what you're talkin' about.' The voice was weak.

'Yes you do. You shot Danny when he was about to tell us what you'd done.'

'Kid was delusional.'

'Then why'd you kill him, huh?'

Harlow closed his eyes, kept them shut, began to breathe deeply.

'Don't play possum with me! I know you're faking it.'

'Come on, Jack.' Taylor gathered her handbag and phone and stood. 'He's clearly not interested in a deal.'

Harlow's eyes sprang open. 'I *am* interested in a deal. I want immunity in return for information. I can tell you about the entire HGH and steroid network in North Queensland. It's huge.'

'Tell us where Bartlett is, goddam it!' Jack roared.

'Get me the deal – immunity – and I'll tell you everything.'

'You're going to need a lawyer to negotiate with us and the DPP. Do you have one?'

'Get me that woman Danny used.'

'Denise Hutchinson?' Jack blew a puff of air through tight lips. 'I'm not sure she'll want to represent the killer of her former client.'

'Alleged.'

'Are you fucking serious? I saw you pull the trigger. DC Taylor saw you pull the trigger. Ballistics will determine the bullet in Sharpe's head matches your gun exactly. What fantasy land are you living in?'

'Alleged until the final verdict.'

Jack sucked in a deep breath and pressed the buzzer to summon a nurse. A chubby redheaded in her forties appeared at the door. 'Organise proper care and treatment for this man. I'm appalled that so-called Dr Chesson hasn't patched him up properly yet.'

'Yes, sir.'

In the car, Taylor said: 'Are you serious about that offer?'

'Like you said, people want closure. Harlow's the toughest nut I've ever tried to crack. No threats I make are going to make him tell the truth. Only a deal of freedom or a massively reduced sentence will work.'

'No way the DPP's going to agree, Jack. Surely you know that.'

He nodded. 'We've at least got to try, hey?'

Chapter 28

The media liaison unit alerted the press at 8:00am. *Andrew Harlow has been arrested and charged with the murders of Owen Kennedy, Daniel Sharpe and Terrence Bartlett, and a string of other offences.* News websites were updated, morning TV bulletins hammered the story for all it was worth and social media, as they say, went into melt down. Jack's phone ran hot with messages and texts from all media outlets. Holly Maguire was the most insistent: three phone calls and five texts. As instructed, Jack let them all go. The time for answering questions would be at the press conference called for 2:00pm.

A representative of the prosecutor's office called the Inspector at 11:32am. A minute later Batista forwarded the DPP's email elaborating the decision to the investigation team's respective inboxes. *No plea deal.*

'I reckon there's only one way Harlow'll cough to where he put Bartlett's body,' said Jack as he clicked the email closed. 'A prosecuting lawyer from a Grisham novel appears and tricks the bastard into spilling his guts.'

'So that was a no, I take it?'

'You've been cc'd the message, but I'll summarise it for you. Harlow's appeal to the DPP was rejected out of hand.'

'So, my bold prediction has come true.'

'Blind Freddy could have picked that one.'

'Was there an official reason given?'

'Turns out murdering three fellow human beings doesn't predispose the DPP towards offering deals. Especially when two of the bodies were recorded on camera and one killing was carried out in the presence of two police officers. Plus there's no public interest served in a plea deal.'

Wilson appeared with take-away coffees for Jack and Taylor. 'Wanna know what Harlow just admitted to me from his hospital bed?'

Jack sat bolt upright in his chair. 'What?'

'Bugger all.' The constable flashed a "gotcha" grin as he set the styrofoam cups down. 'He's clammed up tighter than a...'

'A clam?' said Taylor.

Wilson nodded. 'I was thinking of a fish's whatsit.'

The three sipped their coffees in silence, Jack reclining in his swivel chair while the others stood. They watched Batista finish a phone call in his office and stride across the squad room. 'Let's not drop our heads over this,' said the Inspector. 'Even if we never find Terry Bartlett, there are air-tight cases against Andrew Harlow for three homicides. Not to mention drug dealing, kidnapping, deprivation of liberty and threatening a police officer. Not even a John Grisham lawyer could get him acquitted.'

Jack gently lobbed a pen across his desk. 'Have you planted listening devices around my desk, sir?'

'No, why?'

'Never mind.'

Batista straightened his back like a father about to give a speech at his daughter's wedding. 'Claudia, type up a press release to go out an hour before the press conference. Make sure you accentuate all the positive work our team has done to bring the suspect to justice, to allay fears in the community, all that warm fuzzy stuff. Your own efforts haven't gone unnoticed, by the way. Jack's recommended you for special acknowledgment.'

'Come on, sir. It's my job.'

'Rubbish. You showed exemplary courage under extreme circumstances. You saved DS Lisbon's life.'

'Am I supposed to put that in the press release? I don't think I can write about myself as some kind of hero.'

'Fine. Get the constable here to write that bit.'

'Consider it done,' said Wilson. 'I can sing her praises without going overboard.'

'Jack,' continued Batista. 'Get around to Charlie Bartlett's barbershop, stress to him we haven't given up on finding his father.'

Jack nodded. 'Yes, sir.'

'Have either of you contacted Carl Masiker or Louise Harlow?'

'I rang Carl's home number first thing this morning,' Jack tore open a packet of nicotine gum, flicked a pellet into his mouth. 'His missus told me he's arranged for someone to run the gym for him while he recuperates. They're going to be OK.'

'Louise Harlow feigned calm when I rang her,' said Taylor. 'Her business is teetering on the brink, and now Harlow's not bringing in income, she reckons she'll have to sell the mansion, all their assets.'

'Poor lovey,' said Jack.

'On the plus side, she's prepared to testify against her husband in terms of the illicit substances.'

'That's damn hypocritical of her when it was his dirty money keeping her dirty business afloat.'

'I get the feeling the shame of having a mass murderer for a husband is a motivating factor for her to turn on him. She built her company up on her own without his input. She definitely made mistakes with the labour hiring side of things.'

'That's an understatement,' Jack observed. 'My experience with exploiters like her is they don't change. If she's clever enough to survive, she'll move her operations to another third-world country, whatever it takes to turn a dollar.'

'Maybe. My feeling is she won't chuck the towel in.'

Batista turned to Jack. 'Will Masiker testify, do you think?'

'Does it matter? Even if no one was prepared to speak against Harlow except me and Claudia, the prick's gonna be wearing prison-issue clothes till the day he dies. There's enough physical evidence to convict with zero witnesses. My guess, a quick trial with a unanimous guilty verdict.'

'Would you stake your life on it?' said Batista.

'Absolutely.'

At 2:00pm the station's dedicated press room was a squall of noise. Local reporters were joined by big stars of the small screen for the special event. The major TV stations in Brisbane chartered flights to get their top performers to Yorkville. This was the biggest crime story in Queensland since the Baden-Clay case in 2012 and no one wanted to miss out.

Batista spoke for ten minutes, outlined the status of the case. 'We're asking for an expeditious trial and the swift delivery of justice. It's what our community wants and what it needs. Hopefully, our court system can accommodate that desire.'

'There's still a body missing.' An angular-faced woman waved a microphone like she was shooing flies. Jack recognised her from advertising signs around town. Viktoria Mellor, seasoned journalist from a nationally syndicated current affairs show. It covered stories in more detail than regular news. She'd somehow gotten hold of Jack's mobile number and texted him with a request for an interview. He'd ignored the text but seeing her in the flesh, he had second thoughts. She was confident and forceful with a husky bedroom voice. If Batista sanctioned it, maybe... 'Detective Lisbon, you're the lead investigator. How close are you to finding Terry Bartlett?'

He leaned in, took his time. 'Ms Mellor, is it? I've seen you around town.'

'I've only just arrived.'

'On the billboards, I mean.'

The crowd of journalists and camera operators laughed.

'Yes,' she replied unfazed by Jack's sideshow. 'Why don't we know where Mr Bartlett is? His family must be at their wits end.'

'Our suspect is co-operating and we hope to...'

Batista's phone lit up on the desk beside Jack. The Inspector picked it up, put a hand over his mouth to speak into the receiver.

'Detective Lisbon?' Mellor repeated.

'Yes, sorry,' said Jack. 'As I was saying, we have faith our suspect will reveal the whereabouts of Mr Bartlett after more targeted questioning.'

'But so far your questioning has been unsuccessful, am I right?'

Turn it around Jack. She'll embarrass you.

'To be fair,' Taylor took up the gauntlet. 'The suspect has sustained head injuries in a botched escape bid and his mind has been, ah, affected by substance abuse. Give it another few days, and I'm sure Andrew Harlow will tell us what we are all desperate to find out.'

'A few days? Is that good enough?' Holly Maguire called from the back of the throng.

'OK ladies and gentlemen,' Batista pocketed his mobile. 'I think that will be enough for today. Once the court appoints a trial date, I'm sure we'll all meet again.'

As they hustled out the back door, Batista whispered to Jack. 'Get your skates on, Detective.'

'What is it?'

'A body's been found at Jensen's Creek. It could be Terry Bartlett.'

'I'm sure it's him, sir.' A warm feeling surged through Jack's bloodstream. Not of joy, but of relief. Time to put a lid on this thing.

The Yorkville court system wasn't like those in the capital cities. Unburdened by a backlog of unprocessed cases, it was able to operate quickly and efficiently. Jack had seen nothing like it. In London, justice moved at a glacial pace, sometimes over 100 days between the completion of the offence and the start of the trial. Occasionally, that amount of time or more could pass between a crime being committed and someone even being charged. Brisbane was similar. Up here in the tropics, though, the system ticked along like a production line. Terry's body was found on the afternoon of Tuesday, 10 November. Today was Friday, 20 November, and, Jack hoped, the last day of the trial's evidentiary phase.

At 1:17 on day three of proceedings, Jack smiled as Dr Proctor answered the prosecution's technical questions with aplomb. The old dear had been testifying as a forensics scientist longer than Jack had been alive. Proctor was robotlike in the witness box. Unflinching and stern, it would be a brave or stupid person to call her expertise into question. On days one and two, she provided a battery of solid testimony to send Harlow to jail for the abduction and murder of Owen Kennedy. Now it was time to close the lid on the Sharpe case.

'So you have no doubt the bullet came from the same gun found at the scene?' said the DPP's wunderkind, slick, black-suited Quentin Coen, conveniently nicknamed "The QC".

'None.' Proctor held up an enlarged photograph showing the markings to prove her assertion. 'The 9×19mm parabellum cartridge definitely came from the accused's gun, a Heckler and Koch USP.'

Coen shuffled papers, looked up at the judge. 'That's all in relation to the murder of Daniel Sharpe, Your Honour.'

'Thank you, Mr Coen.' The judge addressed defense counsel, Jared Farnsworth. 'Does the defense wish to question the expert witness in relation to this matter?'

Jared Farnsworth shook his head. Three years out of university, he was the only lawyer in town willing to defend Andy Harlow. The fact Harlow had no money was no deterrent for Farnsworth, who was rumoured to have taken the case pro bono for the exposure. He began with unbridled enthusiasm. At the start of the trial he stunned the court when he questioned the fact his client was being tried for so many crimes at the same time. He claimed a combined hearing would be a denial of justice for his client and requested it be split into separate trials. The judge, His Honour Geoffrey Byrne, slammed Farnsworth mercilessly.

'I cannot believe the audacity of such a request. Have you any idea of the resources required were I to acquiesce to your proposal, Mr Farnsworth? The cost? Not to mention the time wasted empanelling separate juries. Your request is denied.'

When all the prosecution's evidence had been presented for the Owen Kennedy murder, Farnsworth made a huge mistake. He placed Harlow on the stand.

'Mr Harlow, what is your explanation for the victim's blood being in your car?'

'Not my car, you moron.'

'What?'

'It was Terry Bartlett's car. Fuck me, Your Honour, is it too late to get another lawyer?'

'Yes it is too late!' The judge roared. 'Any more use of language like that and I'll add contempt of court to your already long list of charges.'

Harlow shrugged and stared daggers at his mouthpiece.

'I'm sorry,' Farnsworth stammered. 'Why was the victim's blood in the boot of the car?'

'He was an MMA fighter. They bleed a lot. Could be a hundred reasons why. Nothing to say it was me.'

'That's all for now.' Farnsworth resumed his seat.

'What? You were going to ask me more stuff, remember?' said Harlow, gripping the edge of the witness box.

'I think that's enough for now.' The defense lawyer collapsed back into his chair.

'Would you like to question the accused while he's on the stand, Mr Coen?' The beak peered over his spectacles.

'No, Your Honour. The physical evidence will be more than enough to secure a conviction.'

Judge Byrne nodded sagely while Farnsworth cradled his head in his hands.

Now it was day three and Farnsworth's eyes twitched and his hands fidgeted as each of his objections was overturned and each successive witness delivered their evidence. At least he'll have the notoriety to dine out on when the trial's over, Jack thought to himself.

'Mr Coen, anything further for Doctor Proctor before we adjourn?' Judge Byrne asked.

'Yes, Your Honour. I'd like to question the expert witness about the last crime, the murder of Terrence Bartlett. It won't take long.'

'Proceed.'

'Thank you, Your Honour.'

During a rapid fire question and answer session, the pathologist confirmed that, like Owen Kennedy, Terry Bartlett was killed by blunt force trauma to the head. His body was disposed of in a tributary of Jensen's Creek rarely frequented by freshwater crocodiles and never by salties. Which meant the body was more intact than Kennedy's had been. Decomposition was well advanced by the time of discovery, however tissue and entomological analyses showed the murder occurred at the roughly the same time as that of Owen Kennedy.

'But the bag around the head?' said Coen.

'I'd say it was to prevent blood flow rather than to suffocate the victim.'

'Speaking of blood, did you find Mr Bartlett's blood in the boot of his abandoned car?'

'No.'

'I'm sorry?' Coen was flustered for the first time in the trial. He consulted his notes. 'But I thought...'

'The detectives found it. I analysed it.' Proctor smiled smugly as the gallery chuckled. 'And yes, Mr Bartlett's blood was detected in the vehicle.'

'My mistake. Much obliged to you, Doctor. You may step down.' QC fiddled with his glasses for a moment. 'That about wraps it up for us, Your Honour. The prosecution rests for all three homicides.'

Once the murders were dealt with, the judge directed the hearing towards the lesser counts of deprivation of liberty and other crimes perpetrated at the mango farm in Kilroy. A half-hour of Steven Masiker on the stand, weeping as he detailed being tortured by Harlow and Sharpe, was enough on its own for any jury in the world to convict. In reality, it was icing on the cake.

The sentence handed to Harlow was a record for Yorkville. Sixty-five years with no eligibility for parole. Twenty years for each of the murders and a bonus five for the other offences. Andrew Harlow would die in jail. The accused remained impassive throughout the Judge's summation.

At 5:26pm Judge Byrne dismissed all present and ordered the now convicted triple murderer be taken to the high-security Copperhead Correctional Facility. Jack sighed and stood. It was time to reacquaint himself with a long lost friend, cold lager in a tall glass. One would pull him up, no more. Then home and a sleeping pill. But not straight away. Opening his car door, he spotted Charlie Bartlett with his arms around his weeping mother, boyfriend Jeremy Clifford standing off to one side, hands in pockets.

'Mind if I have a word?' said Jack. 'Not interrupting anything am I?'

'Where's your partner?' said Charlie. 'I thought you and her were always together.' Charlie released his mum from the embrace but held onto her hand.

The gesture touched Jack in a way he didn't expect. That kind of love between a parent and child was something he'd never experienced. At least he couldn't remember it.

'No. Not always. She's out there protecting society. Only one copper was required to see this thing through to the end. Muggins here drew the short straw.' Jack affected a goofy smile.

'What can I do for you, Detective?' All emotion had been drained from Bartlett Junior.

'I'm not sure really. I guess I just wanted to know you're...OK.'

A blank stare was Charlie's reply. Jack switched his gaze to Mrs Bartlett, but she quickly looked away and buried her face in a lace handkerchief. Amazing how a woman could feel such grief for the ex-husband who deceived her. She and Terry must have shared some good times. They'd produced Charlie, a good man, someone his parents could be proud of. And he would be a constant reminder of Terry having been in her life. Out of the corner of his eye Jack saw Jeremy kicking stones, probably keen for the annoying detective to leave them in peace. None of them wanted him there.

'Stupid of me to impose.' Jack turned to go. He could already taste the beer. Perhaps it would wash away the foul bitterness in his mouth.

'No, wait.'

'Yes?'

'We're grateful for what you've done. I only wish Harlow had the balls to admit to what he did to my father.'

'Me too. Perhaps he will one day.'

'You think so?'

'No. He pleaded not guilty to everything. Even the drug dealing. I can't figure him out. Best for all he's headed for jail and will rot away inside it.'

'Or someone inside gets to him,' said Jeremy Clifford.

'I'll pretend I didn't hear that,' said Jack.

'He's fucked, and I don't care if you heard me or not. I know blokes inside who'd shiv the bastard for a packet of smokes.'

'Let it rest, Jeremy,' Jack urged. 'The man will suffer more by being locked away for the rest of his life. Killing him would be the merciful way out.'

'Nah. Not only did he murder Charlie's dad, it's because of him I've got no one to fight for the title.'

'Won't it be declared vacant now? From what I hear you'd wipe the floor with any contender.'

'Yeah, I probably could. But I was ready prove myself by beating the best, you know? Not taking on some chump. There's no one else in my division I can't beat with my eyes shut.'

'I don't know what to say, sunshine.'

Clifford dropped his head. 'There's nothing you can say, Detective Lisbon. Whatever will be will be.'

Jack nodded, shook everyone's hand and walked away, for some reason thinking of Doris Day. He shoved two pieces of gum in his mouth and had a rethink. Taylor was on a date with some bozo she met online and he couldn't think of any colleagues he'd like to get drunk with. And he'd never stop at one. *Don't delude yourself.* A job well done and justice served would be rewarded another way. Maybe a gruelling gym session with lots of bag work. Then he had another thought. He flicked through his phone contacts and found the number he'd added "just in case". He'd done some Internet stalking in between breaks during the trial and found out she was single. He got in the car, turned on the AC and dialled the number.

'Yes?'

'Is that Denise Hutchinson from Chapman, Kinberg and Associates?'

'Who's calling?'

'DS Jack Lisbon.'

'What on earth do you want?'

Not promising. 'I was wondering if you'd ah...'

'Yes?'

'I'm interested in some of the legal aspects of the trial I've been involved in. Things I don't understand, stuff that might be useful in future cases.'

'Like what?'

'Oh, like ah...' *Jesus, Lisbon, think.* 'Like rules of evidence in a murder trial, what's admissible and what's not when there's no body.'

'But there was a body. Three of them. I've been following the trial, you know.'

'Yeah, of course. But Terry Bartlett was only found at the last minute.'

'Mmm. These things can be rather complicated.' *Was that a hint of interest?*

'Not subject matter for a short phone call.'

Be bold, Lisbon. 'How about we meet up for a drink and discuss it further. My shout.'

'I'd be delighted, Detective Lisbon.'

'Call me Jack. Meet you at the Pelican Bar at 8:00 o'clock?'

'You're on.'

The TV news was nothing but doom and gloom. Alarmism and sensationalism. But it's what the people want, apparently. What they're led to think they want, more like it. That bloody Holly Maguire, exaggerating again. A tourist was mugged outside a nightclub on The Esplanade at 3:00am last night, and now people sleeping in their homes are in grave danger. What utter crap. Jack felt like throwing his Diet Coke at the screen. Instead, he pulled out his phone to make the call he'd been planning for a week.

'Hello?'

'It's me.'

'I know it's you, Jack.' His ex, Sarah, spoke without the usual venom. Maybe absence did make the heart grow fonder. 'Your number's come up on the screen, you muppet.'

'What time is it there?'

'Quarter after ten in the morning. You do know what day it is, doncha?'

'I do indeed. Care to put her on?'

Rustling sounds and static while Sarah handed the phone to Skye. 'Hello, Daddy!'

'Happy birthday, sweetheart.'

'Thanks. I'm eight now!'

'No way!' He heard the signal of an incoming call. Ignore for now.

'Yes, I am.'

'Did you get the present I sent?'

'Yes, it's awesome. I showed it to all the kids at school.' A stuffed kangaroo.

Made in China but he cut the label off. Let her think it was a genuine item. 'When are you coming to visit me and Mummy?'

'Not for a while, darling. But I'm saving hard. Maybe you can come visit me one day. Would you like that?'

Skye squealed with delight. 'Yes, please. I want to see a real kangaroo. Have you seen any?'

'Sure have.' Mainly flying over the car and squashed by the side of the road. 'They're really cute. Just like you.'

'OK, that's enough.' Sarah's voice in the background. 'Say good-bye to Daddy now.'

'Bye Daddy!'

'Happy birthday again! Talk to you soon, love.'

'She's got to be off to school now, Jack.'

'I understand.' The incoming call signal buzzed again. Hopefully it was Denise, wanting to thank him for the great night they had discussing legal matters. And a few other things.

'Sounds like you're getting on all right over there. The move must've been good for you. I seen you put that killer away. It's been all over the news here.'

'Really?'

'Yeah. Quite the big time detective. I can only say I'm pleased how you've pulled your socks up.'

'Thanks. That means a lot.' And it did. She'd always been sparing with praise. Mainly because he'd been an arsehole ninety percent of the time. 'Can I call the kid more often?'

'Sure, Jack. I don't see why not.'

'I appreciate that...Hang on, there's something breaking on the news here. I'll talk to you later, OK?'

'Sure.'

The newsreader spoke against the backdrop of an image of Copperhead Jail, the razor-wired entrance. 'We understand a prisoner has been stabbed multiple times in a frenzied attack. We've received an anonymous call the victim is Andrew Harlow, last month himself convicted for the murder of three men. We'll keep you updated as we learn more. Meanwhile...'

Jack called Batista. 'What the fuck? How does the press know this before us?'

'Because they got a tip off from inside and we didn't. Get your arse over there and see what's going on.'

'Yes, boss.'

DC Taylor was already on her way and promised to wait for him at the front gate. The prison's own response team had dealt with the incident and determined there was no threat to anyone other inmates or guards. Jack put on the Buzzcocks' *Love Bites* CD to accompany him on the one hour drive to the prison. The legendary punks were belting out "Ever Fallen in Love", a classic Jack knew off by heart. But he heard none of it. In his mind all he could picture was a fuming Jeremy Clifford punching and kicking seven bells out of Andy Harlow and singing "Que Sera Sera".

About the Author

BLAIR DENHOLM is an Australian fiction writer and translator who has lived and worked in New York, Moscow, Munich, Abu Dhabi and Australia. He once voted in a foreign election despite having no eligibility to do so, was almost lost at sea on a Russian fishing boat, and was detained by machine-gun toting soldiers in the Middle East.

When not writing novels, he works as a Russian language specialist for an international conservation organisation.

He currently resides in the wilds of Tasmania with his partner, Sandra, and two crazy canines Max and Bruno.

You can connect with me on:
- https://blairdenholm.com
- https://twitter.com/blairdenholm
- https://www.facebook.com/blairdenholm

Printed in Great Britain
by Amazon